A PERFECT SENTENCE

07976
968195
or
01300
320007

A PERFECT SENTENCE

PATRICK STARNES

All Rights Reserved

Copyright © Patrick Starnes 2017

This first edition published in 2017 by:

Thistle Publishing
36 Great Smith Street
London
SW1P 3BU

www.thistlepublishing.co.uk

"Revenge is a kind of wild justice."
-Francis Bacon, *Of Revenge*

CHAPTER ONE

Airports, I hate them.

To be fair this wasn't always the case, but I've rather gone off airports now that any Tom, Dick and Ali with a mail-order AK-47, hate in their hearts, and right on their side, can and do make shooting galleries out of arrival and departure lounges. Which isn't to say that I don't use them because I do, but not without considerable trepidation that I'll end up one of those stunned saps clutching a bleeding head on tomorrow's newscast or front page or, come to think of it, in a body-bag.

So, picture Gatwick's North Terminal on a brain-meltingly hot and humid Friday in August 2013. The Buchan family is going on holiday to the Italian Lakes, Riva del Garda to be precise. As with many of our holidays the planning per se is cursory and consequently we'll be paying far too much at the chichi Hotel du Lac et du Parc (why the French name in an Italian resort some two hundred kilometres from the border?) in Riva. Actually, this time there are mitigating circumstances for the frantic last minuteness of the whole operation. Sixteen-year-old Catherine was supposed to go camping in the Auvergne with a school group but got sick and had to cancel, which was fine by her as camping is not apparently her thing. And twenty-one-year-old Charlie, who has fallen like a ton of cosmically humourless bricks for an American girl improbably named Cassandra Laporte, wasn't going to take any

PATRICK STARNES

time away from wrapping up at Imperial College before going off to MIT on a full scholarship. Nevertheless, we prevailed upon him to come with us with the bribe of asking the girl along for the ride. Riva is chosen because Fran - my long-suffering family-counsellor wife of some twenty-five years - and I have vaguely pleasant memories of a holiday spent there when we were at university.

Long before my fear of impending death or dismemberment, I've never been able to sit still in airports. I'm forever dashing off to change money, buy books, newspapers, iPods, duty free booze, lozenges, have a pee, down a sharpener, or simply wander around gawking at the passing cavalcade. Fran, who is congenitally incapable of wasting time, takes the opposite approach and has probably got through more work waiting in check-in queues, sitting in airport lounges, or dentists waiting rooms than I have in my entire lifetime.

Coming back from one such sortie I stop and observe my family - still a long way from the check-in counter - from across the crowded concourse. Fran is of course reading a report, wielding a yellow fluorescent Stabilo Boss like a lancet. At forty-six Fran is in very good nick. Pretty and petite, she has short brown hair and is encased in her habitual airspace of quiet, thoughtful reserve. She's wearing a linen jacket, a bottle-green blouse, oatmeal slacks, expensive looking sling backs, and she looks what she is: an attractive, successful professional and *mère de famille* for whom life so far has held few unpleasant surprises. This is not a criticism, simply a fact. For the record the quiet, thoughtful reserve does not extend to the sack where she's an enthusiastic and inventive partner.

Perhaps one of Fran's few surprises to date is standing next to her in the person of Catherine, our bolshie anarcho-nihilist daughter. Slouched in an attitude of ineffable boredom, Cat is staring sullenly at nothing in particular. She's plugged into her phone and from time to time her head bobs up and down like a turkey's. Her hair is brutally avant-garde, vanilla coloured and gelled. The ring in her nostril glitters malevolently. She's wearing Doc Martens, tight black jeans and a creased black T-shirt short enough to show off the paste diamond in her bellybutton and her ghostly white, slightly puffy midriff. Can this be the forever smiling child of recent memory? Wistfully I fantasise that the dapper Manager of the Hotel du Lac etc. will refuse our daughter entry into his elegant establishment unless she dresses and acts like a human being.

Behind, the lovers are as ever entwined around each other in a deeply irritating embrace. Charlie is fairly standard issue: wraith thin, a tad under six feet, long blondish hair forever falling over his tortoiseshell bespectacled blue eyes, regular features, the odd pimple, engaging, slightly loopy laugh. He's wearing tan chinos, brass buckled rep belt, pink Ralph Lauren button-down, and sockless Sebago Docksides. In fact he looks more like what he's shortly to become, a graduate student in America, than what he is, the product of the grossly over-priced private English educational system.

The girl (who in their right mind would call a child Cassandra?) is far from standard issue, at least not to look at she isn't. Since April when he met her, Charlie's kept her pretty much to himself - or rather she has kept him to herself as she has a lair somewhere down by Covent Garden - so I've little idea what she's like as a person, other than that she's direct to the point of rudeness and like many of her generation (not, thank God, our children) peppers her conversation with the word 'like'. She seems to be fond enough of Charlie but both Fran and I fear for our emotionally and sexually immature (we're pretty sure he was a virgin until April) son. Gold medal and scholarship winning biochemist

Charlie Buchan may be, but doughty womaniser he isn't, or at least wasn't.

Cassie has what can only be described as a truly astonishing head of shoulder length, Irish setter-coloured hair. Even if she were unattractive (which she's far from being) this extravagant, almost meretricious mane, would attract plenty. Not surprisingly, Charlie can't keep his paws off this gift of colour and texture and is constantly running his hands through it like some Klondike pan handler.

She's a few years older than Charlie and is a divorcée who works as a bartender in the student union at Imperial College. Charlie says her father, who's dead, was in charge of security at various nuclear installations around the States, so she was brought up at a bewildering succession of places like Diablo Canyon California, and Scriba New York. Apparently the mother ran off with a truck driver when Cassie was fourteen and hasn't been heard from since. She was a sophomore at SUNY, Albany, when her father died of asbestosis, and as there was a handsome insurance pay off, she dropped out of college to travel and ended up marrying an Old Etonian con artist she met on some Greek island, only he turned out to be an abusive alcoholic. Apparently she dumped him after six months or so, but not before he'd absconded with a fair portion of her patrimony. She hasn't had an easy life, as Charlie remarked owlishly one morning when he appeared at breakfast after sleeping in his own bed for the first time in a more than a week.

Cassie's got the slightly freckled complexion you'd imagine would accompany her burnished hair. She's about the same height as Charlie and is slim (virtually anorexic according to Cat, living up to her moniker) but with surprisingly large breasts and legs that don't give up. I haven't the faintest idea what colour her eyes are.

A PERFECT SENTENCE

I don't think I much like Ms. Laporte. Right now she's in a deep clinch with my son with one hand pulling his head onto hers and the other flirting with his crotch. I'll have to have a word with young Charles. Fran looks up from her report, sees me and smiles. The queue accordions forward and the lovers disengage reluctantly.

In the departure lounge, Fran settles down with Amis *fils'* latest. I think about this for a while and conclude that as far as she's concerned, once through passport control and the laughable security precautions, she must see herself as officially on hols and therefore permitted to read something other than the soul numbing, work-related crap she devours like a garburator.

Cat picks at a scab on her chin to the accompaniment of whatever brain damaged group is the flavour of the week, but - and this is a big and profoundly consoling but - she's reading *The Return of the Native*. Christ alone knows how she can attend to Hardy's darkly fraught novel with the depressing caterwauling that I can just hear leaking from her ear buds barnstorming through her head, but what do I know? She's always been a reader and even at her sullen anti-social worst (right now) good books have been an integral part of her life. Also, unlike most of the pack she runs with, her marks are consistently excellent although I suspect that's more because she's quick and the work comes easily to her than because she gives a brass farthing about where she's headed.

Our flight to Milan is delayed.

I flick through the newspaper with scant interest. But then it's some time since I've paid much attention to the political, social, or commercial lurchings of our tired planet. Mercifully, I still find people interesting. Non-people also, it seems, as I always read the obits and for some mysterious reason also the royal court things even though I'm a not-so-crypto-republican.

Charlie and his moll have wandered off, she with a hand in his back pocket, he with one of his cupped around a tight buttock. The tiny black (what's with all this black?) skirt she's wearing simply can't be classified as such. It's really little more than a cummerbund. Still, at least she's got the figure for it; I've seen many who shouldn't be out in public in full length Barbours let alone the micro skirts they affect.

I'm showing my age (fifty last month) with all this red-necked tut-tutting and head shaking. Oh, well. Fran snickers at one of Martin's sallies. The faint crackling from Cat's phone grates. Bored, I cruise the shops.

Harrods. Bally. Louis Vuitton. The House of Caviar. Timberland. Swatch. I confess to a curious weakness for Swatches. I must have three or four of them in my bureau drawer, and Fran has made me promise not to buy her another one until she gives me the all-clear. There's something about the bold colours and designs, the innards exposed like miniature Richard Rogers structures that I find reassuring. Oddly, I don't wear a watch. I spot a swarthy man wearing dark glasses and assume the worst: imminent mayhem.

I order a lager at a bar which I don't think was in existence the last time I was in the North Terminal. That was in May when Fran and I went to Villefranche-sur-mer to gaze at the sea and think about my having been made redundant by the Open University, my employers of the last ten years. "Last in, first out," as the Head of the Department of English quipped bleakly when he broke the news to me. Well, I haven't been having a great deal of fun recently, at the OU or anywhere else for that matter, but being remaindered at fifty certainly makes you think.

Next to me an Irishman who was born to haunt airport bars the world over, orders a Caffrey's and fiddles with an unlit cigarette. The hands are huge and mottled; the poor cigarette looks innocent, unfairly done by, and for some reason I think of Fay Wray in King Kong's leathery grasp. Paddy clears his throat, and, sensing a well-oiled Irish overture than which there can be nothing remotely more tedious, I skedaddle leaving half my beer softly burping on the counter.

BA 566 to Milan is still delayed. Take your time guys, take all the time you need to check every moving part on the 737 ... 57 ... or whatever it is. No rush, just get it right.

THE ST. ALOYIUS ECUMENICAL CHAPEL
ALL ARE WELCOME
OPEN 7:30 A.M. TO 10:00 P.M. SEVEN DAYS A WEEK

I've seen such chapels in many airports and have often wondered if anyone ever uses them. Feeling like an ecclesiastical voyeur (curiosity not reverence being my fuel) I gently push open the blond wood door and step into a dimly lit room with rows of officey looking chairs facing an altar spotlit from above. There's a simple wooden cross on the alter, and piped organ music, doubtless ecumenically correct, drones mournfully reminding me, with the swift directness of such instants, of my love (hopeless because of her sixteen to my fourteen) for Becky Ritchie who used to sit with her parents in the pew ahead of us in church.

Then, above the sound of the organ I identify another sound, unmistakably that of love making. In the deeper gloom to my left I can make out the back of a pink shirt and tan trousers and long pale legs locked at the ankles around the shirt's waist.

Charlie's fucking his doxy in church.

Transfixed, I dare not move. My son is humping Cassie with short little thrusts like interconnected electrical jolts. He's sob-moaning. The girl's riding over Charlie's blond mop, her head caught in the edge of the arc of light pinioning the altar and her opulent hair is spread like a teepee around his shoulders. She is silent but her mouth is open in a rictus of happening pleasure. Her eyes too are open, and she stares straight through me and keeps on riding him, and I see now that her eyes are colleen green, which would be right. I mean, given the hair and the freckles and all.

I turn and flee.

Later, staring at the Alps miles below, snow topped and peaked like whipped egg whites, I see again the scene in the chapel in my mind's eye and am assailed by yet another wave of pure, lava-hot anger. I haven't told Fran yet and I'm not sure I shall. God, the silly little bastard probably thinks he was doing something savage and free. And the girl. What a nasty bit of goods Cassandra Laporte turns out to be. Cool though, cool as a mint julep. She just went on riding her wave for all the world as though she hadn't been caught OTJ by her boyfriend's father in a chapel in one of the world's busiest airports, for Christ's sake. Well, we must have done something wrong old Frances Ann and I, we must have screwed up somewhere around the toilet training stage. Our son's got the judgement of a microchip and the morals of an alley cat. His sister walks around looking and acting like some kind of superannuated Druid. No wonder I feel down.

Fran takes my hot hand in her cool dry one.

"You okay?"

"So, so."

She's immediately attentive, concerned. The Amis is filed with the High Life and the other useless information on offer.

"What's wrong?"

"Dunno, really," I say, "just a bout of the wobblies."

Fran presses close to me. She puts a slim hand (I sometimes think I married her to ensure that those beautifully shaped, precise hands would remain in my life) on my thigh, high up and inside her thumbnail brushing my parts. To her right, I can see

Cat's not-so-dainty hand smothered in African trinkets thrumming out some tribal beat.

"Did you remember to take your pill?" Fran queries.

"I did."

Long before I was made redundant by the Open University I'd been experiencing debilitating bouts of depression, some lengthy, others shorter-lived but no less alarming. For the longest time, like the unimaginative stone-age great-grandson of the manse that I am, I did nothing. But the jags of the blues didn't go away - in fact they got worse and some days simply getting out of bed was a titanic effort - and finally Fran convinced me to get help. So I've been in therapy with one Harvey Grosz for eighteen months with so-so results, and on friend Prozac with better ones although there are still times when a melancholy as thick as a Grand Banks fog rolls in and I flirt with the all too imaginable thought of simply deleting myself from the scene. In short, I'm in the throes of what appears to be a barely manageable mid-life crisis. Turning fifty and losing my job within a few months of each other didn't help, but not having immediate financial worries has certainly made it easier to try to sort out the way forward. Fran's practice is healthy, there was a reasonably generous Open University golden handshake and the pseudonymous Chester Dillon line of detective books I've been churning out for more than a decade still sells surprisingly well. So we'll manage, but I'll have to find something if we're going to continue frequenting the Hotels du Lac etc. of this world.

Fran kisses me. Her mouth tastes of peanuts and the New Zealand Chardonnay she's drinking. Cat mutters "Oh, for God's sake" and turns away to distance herself from her vulgar parents. She's on record as saying that sex between people over-twenty-five is gross.

"A stretch of sun-'n-fun' is what the doctor ordered, just what you need." Fran declares brightly.

Maybe, but surely what I really need is the sense - gone missing these last few years - that my life might amount to something more than a series of more or less knee-jerk reactions to situations I seem increasingly unable to decode. Oh, I've no illusions (I'm not looking for Meaning, just the reverse of the unease I mostly feel), not a single delusion of grandeur, and anyway I'm aware that your Mozarts and Shakespeares are every bit as prey to the blahs as are we humble spear-carriers. No, what I crave is the feeling of magic as the Hydra bound ferry noses out into the dark night leaving the twinkling lights of Piraeus behind, or the quickening of pulse as gloaming settles over a large autumnal city and men and women hurry toward dark trysts.

I can pinpoint the moment when all that and more, much more, seemed to fall away from me leaving me small and unquiet and, above all, unuseful. A Department of English coven. I have just lost a silly argument over marking (my A is her B-plus and so yawningly on and on) with Ruth Evans the woman with whom over the years I've had a sporadic affair which has never threatened to become anything else. We cheerfully use each other; on long winter afternoons when the rain is coming down stair rods and the sub-committee on dog turds has come to no useful conclusion, Ruth and I drive to a no-surprises travel lodge on the M1 and bonk ourselves to a standstill. It's fun and nobody gets hurt. Ruth lives alone in Milton Keynes with a disabled mother, and Fran never asks questions.

The meeting breaks up. I catch up with a scurrying Ruth in the hall.

"Ruth?"

She stops and looks at me as if I was a visitor from Laputa, not the person with whom over the years she's indulged in some pretty frank sex.

"Fuck off."

Just like that. Final and complete schism. I remember feeling that it wasn't even worth finding out what I'd done or hadn't done to have been struck off the civil list so dramatically, so arbitrarily. But a light did go out, not because I'd lost a friend but because, ultimate alienation, I was helpless to do anything about it. Returning home down the motorway, I find myself crying like a baby.

"I'm looking forward to the next two weeks. Maybe I'll learn to windsurf. I read somewhere that Garda's a mecca for the *cognoscenti*," I remark to Fran with zero conviction.

Fran nods and strains past me to get a look out of the porthole. We're losing height now. The brown and gold Po Valley shimmers off in the distance beneath a heat and pollution haze. The great river runs like a snail slick through the scorched land. I squeeze by Fran and Cat and wait my turn by the toilet. Cassie emerges from it and it is I, the fifty-year-old father of two and author of more than half a dozen of Pete Lenski (my daffy, bumbling, detective) thrillers, who averts his gaze.

"Nearly there," I comment moronically as I slither past her and into the john. Returning down the aisle, I see that she and Charlie are joshing about something, and it suddenly occurs to me that I'm envious of their youth and the sheer good fun they're so evidently having. Charlie waves, I give him a sickly thumbs-up sign, and the girl smiles an open, unselfconscious smile.

Later, after the inevitable hassles at the airport, we're bowling along the *autostrada* in our rented Renault Espace, and I'm beginning to feel better. Cat's asleep in the back seat, Charlie and his girl are snuggled together in the middle one, and Fran, who has hiked her trousers above her knees and propped bare feet on the dashboard, is humming 'Everything's Up To Date in Kansas City'.

"Better?" she asks.

"Much. Sorry to be such a drag."

"Don't be daft. Everyone has the right to bursts of devastating self-doubt, near lethal spasms of existential angst. My God, look at that, will you."

We've left the *autostrada* and are now heading north along the western side of Lake Garda on a narrow road carved into and often through the mountain, seemingly miles above the intense blue of the lake. Ahead, in the narrow cleft formed by soaring cliffs, the sky is black. Nervy lightning cracks the smoky diorama of the sky, there is the far-off belly rumble of thunder and white caps are chasing each other across the lake.

"Weather," Fran comments.

"I'll say. Where the hell are the lights on this buggy?"

The heavens open. The rain comes down straight and hard. I squint through the windscreen which now resembles a dissolve-to-twenty-years-ago gimmick in a fifties movie.

At the last instant I see a greyish blur right in front of us and slam on the breaks. The thud is sickening. Me languishing in an *oubliette* in a gloomy Italian keep flashes before my eyes. In the event I've winged a totally arseholed shepherd. There's lots of blood and the man is clearly in shock, but he doesn't seem to have broken anything and keeps hollering lustily in a language which doesn't sound much like Italian. I've always dreaded having to cope with such a situation and more or less freeze (mostly more), the kids stand gawking and useless and Fran, who doesn't do blood, hasn't even left the van. In other words, the Buchans fail to rise to the occasion.

Cassie Laporte does.

Deftly she staunches the blood gushing out of a cut over the guy's eye and gets Cat to press a sock to it. She asks Charlie to find a stick and soon has a tourniquet in place to slow the flow of blood from a gash in the man's forearm. Then she orders me to help her move him (he smells like a mouldy Yak) to the van where she coaxes him to lie down with his legs above his head and covers him with mounds of the trendy sportswear folks like us waste our money on. And all through this, she has been cooing and clucking sympathetically at the wild-eyed goatherd (I've downgraded him on account of the pong) who finally calms down and then passes out.

At the *ospedale* in Riva a doctor assures us that the fellow will be fine once he sobers up and pooh-poohs the suggestion that we should report ourselves to the police. Ah, *Italia*.

The Hotel du Lac etc. turns out to be a nice enough place full of Germans and Swedes with terrific tans and large cars. Cat has a single somewhere up in the attic, our room is next to Charlie and Cassie's, and I hope and pray the builders haven't skimped on the insulation. Nothing in life has prepared me for overhearing my son and his missus making love or, for that matter, their tapping into our own sweet intimacies.

Feeling the need to be alone after a somewhat strained dinner at which I drink too much wine, I say goodnight all around and wander off through the hotel's obsessively groomed and extensive grounds. The storm has long since passed although the wind is still up and is combing through the trees like a dream in search of its maker. I feel okay if still vaguely unnerved by the events of the day. I suspect the stomach-churning sound of the man bouncing off the side of the Espace will stay with me for some time.

I pause at the edge of the lake. Water is slapping against the breakwater and off to the right the lights of Riva burn bright and friendly. The bare rigging on nearby but unseen boats whines and tinkles faintly. White caps gleam and somewhere out on the lake a motorboat chugs through the heaving water. The sky is clear and star filled, and in the dark the mountains rising sheer and breathtaking on either side of the lake are almost too dramatic, too much of a good thing.

It's hard to believe that it's more than twenty years since Fran and I camped (in a rip-off joint just down the road) with Mary Bakewell, a Newnham friend of hers, and Tom Prendergast, Mary's Australian zoologist boyfriend. Apart from the generic sun-and-wateriness of it all and the exhilarating sex, all I can remember of that holiday is getting legless on *grappa* at a disco in town and Tom's car breaking down every hundred kilometres or so on the way back to England.

Twenty-six years ago, to be exact. Requiem for a more or less wasted life. One achingly boring doctorate on the eighteenth century Poets Laureate, two half careers (which somehow don't add up to a whole one) at McGill and the OU, some unremarkable and barely remarked upon publications, two children who are fine really, one marriage (ditto, I think), a clutch of Chester Dillons, and some infidelities which were more about ageing than sex, Ruth excepted. Ruth was about flying the outer edge of the erotic envelope, and I lost her to an unknown slight.

Once, Ruth and I went to Cambridge. I guess the idea was to take a stroll down memory lane, show Ruth - an Aberystwyth graduate - my old stomping grounds, take a room at the Garden House, roger the afternoon away with the Cam and swans and the back of Darwin in view. But it was all wrong. The undergraduates strolling through the courts of my college made me feel limitlessly old. Those in the pub we went to were loud show-offs unaware that the best was already behind them. Ruth must have felt the chill on me for it was she who suggested we return to our motel on the M1 and leave Cambridge to those for whom such places are meant: initiates, not clowns looking in through the bars.

"Mr. Buchan?"

So engrossed in my thoughts am I that I haven't heard Cassie coming up on me. She's standing with her arms wrapped around her shoulders and her hair blowing wildly in the wind. Her face is wanly lit by the far off lights of Riva.

"Hello Cassie. Beautiful night."

Dammit, I'm supposed to be pissed off with her.

"Gorgeous."

"Why not try Keir?"

"Sure, whatever."

"Where's Charlie?" I ask irrelevantly.

An almost imperceptible shrug (which seems to be one of her trademarks) precedes, "Reading. I've never met a guy who reads as much as he does, even if most of it is crap."

"I guess you'd have to say we're a reading family," I say as smug as a bug in a rug and add, "but we're certainly not a first aid one. You were great back there ... uh, with the guy I hit. Just great."

She brushes hair away from her eyes and holds it in place with a palm on her temple. "Oh, that was a snap. There was a time when I thought I wanted to be a paramedic. Like I was up to burn treatment before I dropped out."

"And now you're a bartender," I say unable to keep the condescension out of my voice.

"And now I'm a bartendress," she replies evenly, somehow suggesting a pride in her calling and her gender that is the perfect rejoinder to my snobbery.

"Time to head back, I guess."

"Sure. Mr ... ah ... Keir, I just wanted to say how sorry I am about ... well about what you saw in the airport ..."

It's my turn to shrug to demonstrate what a fine liberal sort of a fellow I am.

"You're just lucky it was me, not some fire breathing Islamic fundamentalist with a scimitar."

Cassie emits a murky chortle and comments, "Don't I know it. For the record, it was my brilliant idea. Suddenly got the hots. Pretty clueless really."

"It takes two to … you know … screw," I remark pleased as a peacock with both my worldliness and the racy alliteration although also annoyed with myself for seeming to collude.

We're approaching the hotel. There are lights in both our rooms which are on the ground floor and have little verandas giving directly onto the gardens. Somewhere a TV is spewing canned laughter into the defenceless night. Cassie stops to light a cigarette (she's virtually the only person I know who still smokes) and shaking her head says, "Of course, but let's just say that it wouldn't have occurred to Charlie. Like unfortunately he'll do just about anything to please me."

"Unfortunately? Sounds like what most gals would give their canines for."

She looks at me curiously as if trying to ascertain whether I'm serious or not, then obviously deciding that I'm neither, says matter-of-factly "Don't be silly", opens the door to their room (I glimpse a naked Charlie on the bed, reading as billed) and goes in without looking back.

Fran is in the shower. She's singing. I pause by the door and listen to her thin clear voice and am suddenly struck by a sense of loss so real, so palpable that I can taste it like sick rising in my gorge.

"… and love grows old and waxes cold and fades away like the morning dew."

I sit on the bed and wait for the squall to pass. I'm just about through the worst of it when Fran emerges from the bathroom, naked and pinkly glowing.

"Nice walk?"

"Fine."

"Hello, are you all right?"

"Sure. Why d'you ask?"

"Don't know, you look rather, I don't know ... zonked."

"No I'm fine. Really. I had a chat out there with Cassie."

"And?"

Fran is sitting sideways at the vanity brushing her hair. I love the faint, suggestive bounce of her smallish, firm breasts as she does that.

"And I was not very politely but very definitely put in my place by the lady."

She stops brushing and swivels around to face me. "Really, about what?"

"Oh, she implied, no, she *said* that Charlie's too keen to please her, too emollient. I made a rather stupid remark and she picked me up on it, is all. It was just an odd experience being smacked on the botty by someone young enough to be your daughter."

"And old enough to be your mother too, if you ask me. She's a hard one to figure out is our Cassie. There's quite a bit of hard, savvy, street broad in there, some wide eyed ingenue - although I'm not sure that isn't a bit of a con - and more than a dash of common-or-garden temptress thrown in for luck."

I wonder, briefly, if I'll reveal how much very common and not-so-garden vamp goes into Cassie's psychological profile, but decide Fran can live a perfectly viable life without knowing about that particular can of worms.

Instead I say, "My guess is that she'll have forgotten about him before his plane has reached its cruising height next month. The bad news is that the reverse is unlikely to be true."

Fran sighs. She takes our children's failures and successes more to heart than I do. She stands up and stretches voluptuously, like a cat. Although English to the core of her being, Fran is delightfully unburdened by any prudery, any lingering Victorian notions that bodies should be neither seen nor heard.

"What's a girl have to do to get laid around here?"

CHAPTER TWO

The pattern of the holiday is swiftly established. During the day Fran and I have each other to ourselves because Youth never arises much before three in the afternoon, often later. When it does, palpably hung over (a father-to-daughter about the iniquities of under-age drinking elicits rolling eyeballs and pained sighs), the three of them struggle to the beach where they sleep some more. Dinner *en famille* (we quell a mutiny involving age-specific sittings) is rarely without incident, but the pleasant surprise is that Cassie turns out to be a witty companion full of funny, often poignant stories from her peripatetic youth. Our children carp endlessly about the food, which is actually pretty good, and generally make it clear that they would be having a far better time of it if Fran and I could see our way to disappearing.

Then one day in the middle of week two Fran loses it, snaps: "I don't give a fearsome fuck what they want to do, today they're coming with you and me on a bloody boat trip around this bloody lake. In other words, they're going to see something other than the inside of a bedroom or some fur-lined disco."

"Fran, they're grown up ..."

"Keir Buchan!"

"Right."

I draw the lovers. Fran disappears upstairs to root out her hibernating daughter. I stand in a splash of honeyed sunlight by

Room 23's veranda wishing I were somewhere, anywhere, else. On the little white plastic table there's an ashtray full of the butts of the Marlboros Cassie smokes. A wasp is expiring like some Roman orgy victim in the sticky heel of a beer glass. Cassie's Donna Tartt sits next to Charlie's Robert Heinlen. A pair of gold sandals winks at me from under the table. Flash freeze the whole shebang and enter it for the Turner Prize, I muse, recalling some of the horse shit whey-faced Art College drop-outs foist upon a public gullible enough not to tell them to run along and get honest jobs schlepping Big Macs. I pause, crooked index finger inches from the door in a parody of the-bailiff-pays-a-call. Not a sound. I wonder if they sleep naked. Of course they do. And they make love three or four times a night, or day because they always roll home in the soft Italian dawn. I knock, Beethoven's Fifth style, presumably to add levity to an otherwise doleful task. The silence which follows is of the boundless variety. I knock again, serious no-nonsense raps that are intended to command respect. More silence. Christ almighty, maybe they're still out on the tiles. Or murdered in their bed by a passing psychopath.

"Wakey, wakey, folks. The tour director's on the warpath. Charlie?"

Finally I hear a muffled "Fucking-A", then whispering and a door slamming.

Charlie, clothed only in a Hotel du Lac etc. towel, opens the door and peers out like the village snoop in a Mauriac novel. He blinks, young and defenceless as a fawn in the bright sunlight. His eyes are bloodshot and his uneven reddish stubble (which looks as though sheep graze on it) and tousled hair irritate me though I'm at a loss to know why. After all he's simply a young man who has been rooted out of bed too early after a hard night on the town. He gives off a fugitive whiff of something I can't quite identify and then do. Sex.

"Hi, Dad. Christ, what time is it?"

"Nine o'clock and your mother's doing her nut."

"Oh, yeah, about what?"

Charlie stretches and yawns prodigiously. The ribs on his hairless, asthenic chest stand out in bold relief. His nipples are small and carrot coloured.

"She's taking exception to your current lifestyle. Apparently we're all in for a jolly toot around the lake. Kick-off's at ten so you'd better get cracking …"

Charlie groans and mutters, "Jesus wept, what *for*?"

I shrug and reply, "Possibly to provide you with a sense of place, a feeling that you've been somewhere different. I don't know, but I do know that her dander's up and if you know what's good for you you'll tag sweetly along. Oh, hi there, Cassie, morning."

Cassie's appeared behind Charlie. She's wearing one of his T-shirts ('It Ain't Easy Bein' Sleazy'*)* which barely comes to the top of her long, tanned thighs. She's brushed her hair into a sort of top notch and it explodes in the sunlight like a Roman candle.

"G'morning. What a neat idea. I love boat trips. Come on, Chuck, we can sleep like when we're dead."

She sometimes calls him Chuck which I'm not sure I much like. Chucks are big, loose-limbed *hombres* with slitty eyes and crows' feet who talk about Rick Perry as if he were the reincarnation of a long-dead saint instead of the profoundly ill-informed creep that he is.

It's a day for the gods. By the time the tour boat fusses away from the pier the sun's blazing out of a mythic blue sky. A breeze is blowing and the lake, a flintier blue than the sky, swoops south between the steep cliffs rising on either side.

Cat flounces down to the cabin ear buds firmly in place. Fran and I have a wager as to whether she'll stay below decks for the duration. Me yes, Fran no. The lovers wander off to a bench by the bow where Charlie promptly falls asleep with his head on Cassie's lap.

"You can take a horse etcetera, etcetera," I can't help saying.

Fran is not amused. "Honestly, darling, don't you think we have some responsibility to ... oh, I don't know ... aerate them."

I laugh. Sometimes Fran comes out with real lulus. I have a mental image of our children hung out with the Monday morning wash to be aerated. Gently fluttering.

"Come on Bird (a nickname the provenance of which neither of us now remembers), they're not that bad."

She shrugs and says they may not be but suggests that a good slug of fresh air and some information intake won't do them any harm. The PA system's already in action successively in Italian, German and English. Fran wanders off towards the stern and I observe some of our fellow day trippers on the upper deck.

An elderly German couple both cruelly warped by osteoporosis - he to the left, she to the right - so that when they stand together they form a sort of human arch - listen to the commentary with rapt attention as if some eternal and useful verity might be forthcoming. An English family - Brummie? Scouse? Geordie? I'm not much good on accents, French Canadian aside which is cheating - scoff chocolate bars (all English so doubtless brought in the Ford Sierra just in case the Eyeties don't know about Mars, Bounty, Aero) non-stop and gaze solemnly, masticating slowly, at the mountain road Mussolini had built along the west side of the lake at the cost, according to our guide, of the lives of hundreds of workers. Mum and Dad in their mid-thirties, both overweight, he tattooed like a shaman, she sweating like a racehorse, are as red as boiled lobsters while their children are as pallid as rock cod. Both boys (eleven and thirteen?) wear ski-boot-sized multi-coloured Nikes, laces undone, baggy grey sweats to well below their knees, Wayne Rooney strips (Brummies then) and haircuts from some inner circle of barbering hell.

Seeing them like that I'm visited by an intense wave of sadness for our fucked over world. But the evil moment passes as do they all and then I think, "Hold on pal, they're here aren't they? They've scorched down thousands of kilometres of *autobahn/strada* where they've eaten chewy wiener schnitzel and lumpy lasagne in antiseptic, deeply unfamiliar surroundings. They've set their tents up next to rowdy Germans and played ping pong with a Dutch family all of whom speak better English than they do. They're here now learning about Mussolini's spin on full employment, lemons and Tennyson's 'olive-silvery Sirmio', not down at The Red Lion getting legless by midday, or cruising the project looking for trouble. They're here, not there."

A gaggle of Swedish teenagers is hupta-schlupting around a slatted wooden bench on which they've spread their picnic. All save one (who is black and doubtless the son of a 70's draft dodger's contribution to a multi-racial Sweden) are blond, clean limbed, expensively dressed in bright casuals and look as though they come from a different galaxy than the Brummies.

A handsome smooth-faced man of about my age who I take to be Italian (chemise Lacoste, elegant beige summer slacks, pricey looking loafers, Jean Vuarnet sunglasses) saunters by. I do a literal double-take. He's no more Italian than I am. He is in fact Vernon Scott, fellow pledgee of the AD's Class of '81, intercollegiate squash champion three years running, brother of Delia Scott into whose pants I vainly strove to get all one long winter term. A buddy without being a friend, he went on to medical school and we saw him and his wife Jane from time to time when we were living in Montreal, until he abandoned the prestigious Neuro for more the lucrative hunting grounds of Connecticut.

"Vernon! Vernon Scott."

Already past me, he stops in his tracks and without turning around hunches his shoulders and cocks his head (the hair painstakingly arranged in a vain attempt to disguise a baseball sized bald spot) as if awaiting further messages from outer space.

Still without turning around he says, "I'll be damned if it isn't ole' Keir Buchan."

It's a seriously impressive feat of memory.

And then we're shaking hands and talking at the same time: Conference in Brescia family up the lake at Riva where's Fran how's Jane sorry to hear that a nurse you say.

"Yeah, Jane and I just sort of ran out of gas. Sharon's great though. Terrific Mom for my second team, loves opera too. How are your kids? Jim and Sally wasn't it?"

"Charlie and Catherine. They're fine. Jesus, Vernon, you look great, just great." (He does: daily jogging with the Wolf Pack, seniors squash, sensible diet).

The edges of Vernon Scott's mouth quiver with self-satisfaction. He takes off his shades (I'd forgotten about the eyes, which are grey and as flat as a fen) and says, "Thanks. You're looking pretty chipper yourself."

He's lying. Despite a natural tendency not to put on weight and the spurious glow of a tan, I'm aware that I look like a man who has lost the plot. That's what shaving's really about, our daily reality check.

Vernon didn't much like my taking his sister out. Fraternity brothers we may have been, but the Scotts were Old Montrealers with all that that entailed while the Buchans were hicks (my father a dipsomaniac small town GP, my antecedents undistinguished) with all that didn't entail. Once at a TGIF party during the winter of my doomed assault on his sister's virtue, a very drunk Vernon cornered me in the billiard room and announced that if he found out that I'd been screwing his sister he, Vernon S. Scott, would personally cut my balls off and throw them into the St. Lawrence. All said with fraternal joshiness, but you just knew he hated the thought of anyone, let alone a non-private school yokel, sticking it to the lovely Delia. Once I stopped seeing (read, was dumped by) Delia and she'd picked up with the dynastically sound asshole she was eventually to marry, Vernon warmed to me again, and in our last year we saw quite a lot of each other sharing as we did a passion for the Montreal *Canadiens* and he having access to ancestral Scott season tickets at The Forum.

"You know, Keir, I was really surprised to hear you'd moved to London. Not get tenure or something?"

"No, I got it all right, but I was getting stale and Fran wanted to be nearer her parents and mine were dead or thereabouts ... so. I don't regret moving although I may."

"How's that?"

Vernon is losing interest. The Aztec eyes are on the move seeking, I suspect, Fran who once told me he'd made a pass at her.

"Lost my job. I'm on the shelf, for the moment only, I hope."

"I'm sorry to hear that," he says although he plainly couldn't give a shit.

"Where's my old doubles partner?"

He's not the only one losing interest. Fran and he may have played tennis together two or three times in the ten odd years we overlapped in Montreal. How many more hours is this trip supposed to take?

"She's around somewhere. She'll be thrilled to see you."

Vernon nods unsurprised that anyone would be anything but tickled pink to see him again. "Well, she'll have to step on it 'cause I'm getting off at Limone which this looks like being. Got on at

Riva but I've got to give a paper this afternoon. Shitty job but someone's gotta do it."

I'm greatly relieved. We are in fact approaching a pastel shaded village clinging limpet like to the side of the mountain. The boat reverses its engines and the water boils green and blue as we crab towards the dock.

"Come on, I'll see you off," I enthuse gaily now that I'm soon to be a free man.

We wait by the gangway as the sailors expertly make the boat fast. All around us villagers with large wicker baskets full of market produce chatter and laugh with the raucous energy of people unconcerned by what other people think of them.

"Well it's been great, Keir. Who'd have guessed? I play truant for twelve hours and meet my old pal Keir Buchan. Makes you think."

"It certainly is a small old world."

"Give my regards to Fran ... and Jim and ... Sally. Look after yourself."

We shake hands: his the dry sinewy grip of the overpaid (until you need one) neurosurgeon, mine the dampish squeeze of the redundant English Prof on Prozac. He strides nimbly down the gangway, turns and waves and then plunges into the maw of a waiting Mercedes half the size of the village.

I go in search of Fran.

"Was that who I think it was?"

"Yep. I'd forgotten what a smug jerk is he. Why didn't you come and say hello?"

"Because I remembered what a smug jerk he is. I don't know if I told you at the time but when he took a run at me at the Cruickshanks' and I told him to go play in the traffic he got all huffy and puffy and said he'd never been so insulted in his life. Claimed I'd been giving him the come-on."

"Were you?" I ask knowing full well that the Vernon Scotts of the world aren't her type. The needy, the dispossessed, the vulnerable are. Which, presumably, is why I'm still in the picture.

"That I'll ignore. What on earth's he doing here?"

"Playing hooky from some neuro-boffin conference in Brescia. My God, all that seems ages ago now."

"All what?" she asks.

"Montreal. McGill. Weekends at the lake. The kids still kids. You still in grad school. Me still me."

Fran's face registers a brief filofax of emotions: annoyance, concern, pity, unease. Then she says in her clear precise way that I am still me, only more so, and that she loves me and that I should stop being an ass. She kisses me and I'm filled with a surge of gratitude for this fine, lucid woman who can bring me back from the brink so unerringly.

At Sirmione we disembark and join approximately one million fellow tourists in the narrow streets of what fifty years ago (or possibly at 9 a.m. one New Year's Day) might have been a pretty little town. The heat is overpowering and the hype worse. Lunch, however, turns out to be an unqualified success. We luck into a pleasant vine-bowered restaurant by the side of the lake. Our waiter worked in Cardiff for ten years and spoke good English, the wine a local white was excellent as was the food. A general conversation even broke out, and Cat managed to get through nearly two courses unconnected to her mobile entertainment unit.

On the return trip I pace the decks of the boat and mull over some twists in the plot of my Chester Dillon work-in-progress.

"Dad?"

"Hi, Charlie. How's the fellow?"

"Copacetic, I guess."

In spite of having lived in England for more than ten years now and having gone to schools and university there, Charlie's retained many of the North Americanisms of his youth.

"Where's Cassie?"

"Sunning up front, she can't get enough of it. And it's no good my giving her the old scientific anti-sun-bathing spiel. Beneficial rays are sacrosanct full stop. Great lunch, thanks."

"It was good, wasn't it? The best ones are always those you least expect, or so it seems to me."

Charlie's got something on his mind. Since he went to university he and I have drifted apart. We used to do quite a few things together: Wasps' games and from a precociously early age galleries and exhibitions. The rift (if that is what it is) has not in any way been acrimonious. At a certain point he simply ceased needing me which is, I suppose, normal. It is also hurtful. I know he and Fran sometimes have heart-to-hearts because she gives me a précis of them.

"Dad ... er ... um ... what d'you think of Cassie? I mean really, not your generic 'your mother and I think she's a very nice young lady' bullshit."

I should have known. I should have guessed that he'd want a report card, an impartial assessment, but only mind you if it's not the least bit impartial, only if it's a glowing endorsement of the lady's remarkable qualities.

"Think of her?" I ask fuzzily as if he'd just asked me to explain the chaos theory in two sentences or less.

"Yeah. Think of her"

What do I think of her? Well, I'm still not very impressed with The Great Ecumenical Fuck, but that apart it seems she's not nearly as bad as I'd originally thought. Oh, she'll still take Charlie to the cleaners and back, but I'm not so sure it'll be a malicious thing just a-time-to-move-on one. Time to relocate the tent, change the scenery and the *dramatis personae*.

"I think she's a very interesting person. Your mother put her finger on it when she said that she seems to be ... ah ... contradictory ..."

Charlie shoots me a surprised, hurt look. I seem to have got it wrong.

"What's contradictory about her?" he asks, plainly annoyed.

"Complex then," I try anxious to limit the damage. "To be honest I guess at first I thought she was just a good looker, now I think she's quite a few other things as well ..."

"Like?"

Charlie's playing hard ball. "Like funny and honest and ... well, you know ... plain old interesting."

He's got his hands in his pockets and is staring grimly at the lake frothing away from the side of the boat. He seems to be thinking hard. Finally he turns to me and says evasively, "I'm seriously thinking of passing on the MIT thing."

Unable to suppress my astonishment I goggle at him and repeat idiotically, "Pass on the MIT thing?"

"Yeah. I've tried to get Cassie to agree to come to the States, but she won't hear of it. Says she likes London, likes her job and doesn't want to live in Beantown or any other town over there. I think I can get MIT to let me defer the scholarship ... extend at Imperial ..."

It's time to take the gloves off. Carefully though, carefully does it. "Listen Charlie, I know how you feel, believe me I do ..."

He looks at me hard, his eyes have gone smoky which always happens when he gets mad, and he says flatly, 'No, you do not. And please spare me the if-she's-worth-it-she's-worth-the-wait line."

As that was precisely the angle I was about to adopt, I'm left sucking wind.

"I can't bear the thought of leaving her. I'm in love Dad, crazy, drop-dead, big-time, over the bloody moon in love, and I don't want to lose her to some ten-foot varsity oarsman with a monster dick and toe jam for brains."

The anguish in Charlie's voice is heartbreaking. The vulgarity is a small boy's valiant effort to suppress the tears, which I can see are very close to the surface. The problem is that he's almost certainly right. No woman half as attractive as Cassandra Laporte is likely to be ignored by the sniffing classes nor, more to the point, is she likely to want to be treated as though she were in purdah. For the first time since turning fifty I see some value in it: I'm mercifully on the far side of all that my son's going through now, never again will I have to experience the agony he's currently experiencing. Or the ecstasy, come to think of it.

"Mum and I were planning to offer you the flight home as a Christmas present ..."

Charlie's voice drips sarcasm, "Oh great. By which time Cassie'll be engaged or married to the above mentioned oaf and I'll be a disappearing, or disappeared, blip on her emotional radar screen."

"You're entirely welcome," I flash.

He looks at me as if to say 'Christ, the old fart's not brain-dead yet' and actually says, "Sorry, I didn't mean to sound ungrateful. Listen, Dad, d'you think you could have a word with her, see if you can get her to change her mind about the States? I mean, I know I should take the scholarship, get stuck into my Ph.D. and all that good shit. It's just that ..."

I say, "Sure, I'll have a go, for what it'll be worth," knowing that I won't try very hard.

"Meaning?"

"That I've a feeling Ms Laporte's not an easy one for turning."

He sighs a big theatrical sigh laden with all the pathos and self-indulgence of the closed circuit roller coaster he's presently riding.

"Don't I know it. By the way, d'you think Cat's ever going to come out of her blue period or whatever phase it is we're currently being treated to? I'm getting right royally pissed off with the rings in the nose and the diamonds in the belly-button and the existential flapping about like a seal out of water."

So engrossed has Charlie been in his own lubricious learning curve that I'm surprised he's even noticed his sister's existence let alone the clothes and accessories she wears.

"All the more reason for leaving perfidious Albion," I remark facetiously

"Very funny."

Then apropos of nothing, I blurt out, "D'you guys do dope?"

"Us guys?" he stonewalls and I know the answer.

"You and Cassie and your friends. I don't care one way or another. I'm just curious."

Charlie looks at me intently, the eyes teal slits, then he shrugs and says, "Light recreational. Not being a smoker it mostly makes me feel more sick than high, but sometimes it works. Ah ... Cassie's a bit more experienced but there's nothing to worry about, promise."

Cassie would be a good deal more experienced, wouldn't she? The husband fellow was probably a dope fiend on top of all his other failings. I'm not particularly surprised or even fussed to learn that Charlie dabbles in drugs. Actually, what's really surprising is that more people don't turn to drugs and alcohol as counter valents to lives lived in a world that has become so crammed - so incredibly cluttered with information and the endless deluge of decisions to be made, options to be weighed - that it's hard to fathom why we don't all end up juddering cataleptics, incurably stalled between door A and door B, act X and act Y.

Charlie clears his throat and it comes to me with an unexpected solar plexal jolt that I miss the easy intimacy, the jokey mateyness that used to characterise our relationship.

"I'm sorry about the OU business."

"So am I," I reply truthfully.

"What'll you do?"

I shrug with unfelt insouciance and say, "Something'll turn up. I think I've got some City Lit courses lined up for the fall. You know the form: the role of the food processor in the Modern Gaelic Novel, that sort of thing."

Charlie's not fooled, he rarely is. "That'll be a bit of a comedown after the OU, won't it?"

It's my turn to sigh. "It will."

Actually comedown is a massive understatement. For the last ten years the Open University has provided me with a community, a culture, a cause even, which has been a fine antidote to the frustration of trying to teach literature to bored undergraduates in a North American university in the eighties and nineties. We're approaching Riva and my quality time with my son is nearly over.

"Your mother and I are going to miss you, Charlie. We can't complain though as your going to Imperial gave us three years of your being at home which we hadn't expected."

"Until I met Cassie," he points out and then adds almost as an afterthought in a fake southern drawl, "Ahm gonna miss y'all too."

I doubt it somehow. Lately Charlie's been on the fringes of the family, and - if the truth be known- so effortlessly, so casually has he drifted away from us that I sometimes find him a little scary.

"Tell me to mind my own business if I'm out of line, but ... well ... does Cassie feel the same way about you ... I mean, as you do about her, if that isn't too convoluted a sentence to make any sense at all?"

Charlie measures me coolly and asks, "D'you mean is she in love with me?"

"I guess I must mean that." I respond awkwardly.

To my surprise he shakes his head and says thoughtfully but without apparent rancour, "Probably not, or at least not as I do her. But that's okay because no one could love me as I do her."

I wish I hadn't asked.

Charlie shakes his head and wanders off, and I find Fran. We notice that Cat is standing alone by the taffrail with the eternal ear buds in place, clearly out of it. So leaving our daughter to her misnamed music, we make our way forward for a coffee.

I tell Fran about my little conversation with Charlie. Fran is unperturbed, "Oh he'll go, he's not *that* dumb."

"Maybe not, but he *is* that in love, believe me."

Fran blows a rhubarb and says, "fiddely-diddely I …"

Just then there's an almighty caterwauling coming from somewhere near the stern of the boat. Shouts and cries fill the air. An alarm bell clangs stridently, and the boat shudders and creaks as the helmsman puts it into reverse and then swings forward and to starboard in a tight lurching arc.

"*Uomo in mare! Uomo in mare!*"

Along with most of the others on board, we push and shove our way to the back of the boat arriving there just in time to see our spluttering daughter (ear buds still in place) being dragged from the water, jack-knifed into a red and white lifebuoy with Charlie and a member of the crew helping to push her up into the boat.

Fran loses it, "Oh my God! She could have been … the propellers … Oh my God!"

She wades frantically through the throng with me in loose support.

In the event, Cat's fine. Frightened as hell and confused as to what exactly happened although very sure that whatever happened, it did so to the tune of Justin Bieber's 'As Long As You Love Me'.

"It was weird, one second I was grooving to Justin and the next I was thrashing about in the water. Don't look at me like that Dad, I mean, do I look like one of your natural jumpers, honest? Jeez, creepy."

The crowd dissipates and we sit in a puddle by the taffrail, a small chastened family mercifully on the right side of a personal tragedy and anxious to get back on terra firma. Cassie tactfully leaves us to ourselves, but I can't help noticing the perplexed look in her eyes and put it down to her thinking that the Buchans are a rum lot. Well, we are and we aren't.

Later that evening after dinner I go for a solitary walk during which I conclude that when all's said and done falling off the stern of a moving boat is probably much less dangerous than falling over the side. But still, it makes you think.

The following afternoon I manage to contrive a few minutes alone with Cassie.

"What'll it be?"

We're at the beach bar. Cassie, tanned to a rich mahogany, looks at me over the tops of the sunglasses she's nudged down her nose. The green eyes seem all the greener for the tan. She's wearing a black bikini.

"Diet Pepsi, please."

She unties the scarf holding her hair in place at the nape of her neck and rearranges it. I notice a hint of copper furze in her armpits. A milky way of freckles is scattered across her breastbone and strays down her cleavage. She has a slightly protuberant navel and near it a tiny tattoo, which being short-sighted I can't identify.

The bartender brings Cassie's Pepsi and a beer for me. We sit at the bar, and over her shoulder I can see Charlie carving his way through the blue mirror of the lake, and I'm put in mind of

Brueghel's painting of tiny Icarus plopping unnoticed into the sea while all around the world is getting on with it.

"Hell-o. Anybody home?"

"I'm sorry. I was miles away," I reply sheepishly.

"And here I was thinking I'd turned the enigmatic Dr Keir Buchan's head. Silly me."

Horrified, I stare at her like a village idiot, but she laughs and mouths 'j-o-k-e' and takes a slurpy drag on her straw.

"For the record I'd like to point out that I'm about as enigmatic as a fire hydrant."

She laughs again (a throaty, cigarettey sound) and says, "Wrong. Oh, you imagine you're just a plain ole' English Prof and part-time cynic, but the eyes tell a different story."

"What's wrong with my eyes?" I ask warily.

But she seems to have exhausted her interest in the subject and simply shrugs and says, "A lot. My guess is that this little coincidence has to do with Chuck asking you to 'have a word' with me. Right?"

I can feel my face reddening and ducking under her amused gaze I mumble, "Sort of. He's worried ... well ... concerned that once he's gone to the States you'll ... sort of forget about him ... perhaps you could ..." I trail off, aware how ludicrous I sound.

Cassie lets out a cross between a sigh and a groan and taking my wrist in a firm grip says with astonishing intensity, "Nobody, but nobody, tells me how to live my life. If Charlie thinks he loves me - and I don't doubt that he does - that's his business but that doesn't mean he *owns* me. Like I go out with whom I please. I go to bed with whom I please. If he thinks I'm going to toddle along behind him to Cambridge and wait for him outside the lab like some brainless bimbette, work in a stinking hash house or whatever, he's got another think coming. Right now we're having a great time, he's fun to be with and believe it or not - no parent can – he's dynamite in the sack and I'll miss him when he goes, but I'm not about to climb into my widow's weeds. If he comes back at Christmas and we're still an item, fine, we'll have a look see then. If not, so be it. Got it?"

Oh, yes, I've got it all right. I've grasped the point. Cassie Laporte is nobody's pushover. She's a free agent, and in all likelihood Charlie Buchan will be history before the leaves have begun to turn in New England. I am seized by compassion for my son who'll surely be sorely damaged by this worldly girl's betrayal (which it won't be one because she's never made any promises, but he won't see it that way). Still, the non-partisan part of me is filled with admiration for her tough credo, and I can't help thinking that if more people were as up-front about their feelings as she is, the world might be a less terminally screwed up place.

"I've got it, but has Charlie?"

She snorts twin jets of smoke and says, "I've told him pretty much what I've just told you. Like, he doesn't want to know."

"No, he wouldn't, would he? He's threatening to see if he can get his scholarship deferred, sort of hang around Imperial for another year."

Cassie clucks her tongue and shakes her head. "Oh, he'll go. At least you can trust me on that."

"At least?"

"You think I'm some kind of Ur-vamp who's messing your son around. Right?"

"No,' I answer untruthfully, 'I don't think anything of the sort. But you can't blame me for wanting to protect my son even from non-existent dangers."

She nods and says surprisingly gently, "Of course not, but there are some things that we can't do for the ones we love. Living their emotional lives is one of them. Thanks for the Pepsi. Oh, by the way, he pushed her."

Thoroughly confused I ask, "Who pushed whom?"

"Charlie pushed his little sister off that boat."

Utterly gob-smacked, I manage a vacuous, "Don't ... don't be absurd Cassie ... why would he ..."

"I've no earthly idea, but believe me, he did. I went for a pee, but the loo was occupied so I cancelled the event and went on back to the rear of the boat, just in time to see Chuck sort of nudge Cat, who was tuned into the trash she listens to all the time, over the rail thing. To his credit, if that's the right word, Charlie did dive in pretty much right after her."

I come up with an unconvincing, "I don't believe you," knowing deep down that I do.

She shrugs and replies evenly, "That's your affair. I'm just telling you what happened."

Grasping irrelevantly at straws, I say, "If you're right, which you aren't, shouldn't you be a little ... I don't know ... afraid for yourself ... I mean you two being an item and all ..."

Again the irritating little shrug, "Oh, don't you worry about me, I can look after myself just fine. Thanks again for the Pepsi."

And then she's gone and sashaying out in the shimmering heat towards the beach where Charlie is towelling himself down. One side of her bikini has ridden up a firm buttock and the sliver of untanned cheek exposed is a dazzling white. Right then and there I make an executive decision to keep Cassie's revelation from Fran and wonder what, if anything, I'm going to say to Charlie. Since he dived into the lake and helped rescue her, he must have instantly realized what a stupid, not to mention cruel thing he'd just done. Let him stew, I think, let him stew and then I'll have it out with him. In other words, the coward's way out.

I nurse my beer and can't help wondering why contact with Cassie invariably makes me feel as though I'm the younger party by some twenty-five years. She's wrong about one thing though, I have absolutely no trouble imagining her and Charlie having sex. It's not my fault as their airport exhibition has provided me with a template upon which I can with great ease construct a home movie of an encounter between the two of them ending with the dreamy far-off look in the girl's eyes as she draws out her pleasure and Charlie's yapping towards his release.

Time for a swim.

The day before we're due to leave, Fran and I get the hotel to make us a picnic and we head up the mountain road winding along the side of the lake. It's another Windex clear day and already the lake is alive with the skitterings of windsurfers and the more sedate movements of tour boats and other small craft.

The narrow road climbs steeply and soon it's as if we're literally on the top of the world. I park the van in a lay-by and we walk across a sun-seared meadow seemingly straight towards the far horizon. We settle in the shade of a lone olive tree. We drink ice cold beer that makes our temples throb, and while Fran goes through her picnic-preparing-shtick I lie on my back and squint up through the tracery of the leaves and think about nothing.

But nothing doesn't last nearly long enough. I realise with a little gag of nausea that I'm dreading going back to London. Dreading the long empty prelude to the sodden-leaf dog days of November (let alone all the endless winter months to follow) with the scantiest of structures to sustain me. Serious job gone. Charlie gone. Cat with one foot in the exit. Fran increasingly busy at work (she and her partner are 'restructuring' and business plans are the talk of our expensively redecorated kitchen) and with the bewildering array of activities she somehow seems to be able to have time to do without ever appearing to be in a hurry. I suppose I should have seen the writing on the wall, joined a bridge class, filled in applications for jobs that no one would (or will) dream of giving to a fifty-year-old, signed up for the Spanish lessons I've been meaning to take since coming to London, reactivated the membership in the tennis club I'd let lapse when I started getting thrashed by one-legged grandmothers and being a bad sport about it. But I did nothing. At some strata of my psyche I don't think I actually believed - or could process, which comes to the same thing - that the OU had let me go For Good. I think I believed that old Morton Last-In-First-Out Bradstream's fruity over-the-top voice would come zinging down the line explaining that at an Extraordinary Plenary Meeting the Department had unanimously agreed the re-hire me and promote me to Senior Lecturer retroactive to …

"A subway token for them?" Fran asks.

"I was thinking about Cat," I lie gratuitously.

"And?"

"And nothing."

"Oh for God's sake what was it you were thinking about our daughter?"

That's the trouble with knee jerk fibbing (something I've done since I was a child), you've often got to come up with the goods when the goods are absent on account of their non-existence. I nearly tell Fran about our son's moment of madness but don't.

"I was thinking that … that Charlie's going away just may be a good thing for her. You know, let her come out of her shell, be *Numero* Uno, or rather *Unico*, for a change."

That' the other thing about we little grey liars, we learn to think on our feet.

"Her shell!" Fran announces theatrically, holding up some hard-boiled egg shell. "This is a shell, what Cat's in is a self-constructed infantile cocoon. Although, come to think of it, she may do some growing up after that psychodrama back there on that boat."

"Whatever. I'm serious, I really think that a bit of being the only show in town will do her the world of good."

Fran shrugs and popping a cherry tomato into her mouth says, "If she even notices. Listen Keir, if Charlie really does go through with his bone-headed idea of giving up - there's no way anybody's going to let him defer the thing - one of the planet's most prestigious scholarships, are we agreed that he's on his own?"

"How so, on his own?" I ask, knowing precisely what she means.

"Out of the house on his own, for starters."

"I suppose, but I think you can take it as read that he's going to go. Cassie seemed pretty confident he would. In fact I rather got the impression during our little chat that she would drop him if he didn't."

Fran raises her sunglasses above her cool eyes and looks at me speculatively as though trying to appraise whether my judgement in this matter can be trusted or not.

"Really?"

"Yes."

She replaces the sunglasses with a long sad exhalation of breath. "Oh Lord, how glad I am to be beyond all that. Poor Charlie can't win: he goes to the States and runs the very real risk of losing his *ragazza*, he stays put and she leaves him anyway."

"A rock and a hard place if ever there was one. I don't reckon the next few months are going to be pleasant for any of us. I just hope he won't take it too hard."

Fran snorts, "Charlie? You know perfectly well that ever since he was a little boy he's taken everything hard. He's a barely house-trained nut case, is our son. By the way, you seem to have been mightily impressed by the lady."

"That's just it, she was impressive, very. It was a wholly convincing declaration of independence, a refusal to be anyone's property. It was ... oh, I don't know, touching."

"Bully for her."

Later after we've finished off the thermos of wine, we lie on our backs looking up through the leaves to a sky now a chickweed blue. It's hot but way up there on the roof of the world a light breeze is blowing causing the olive leaves to gossip and the grasses to whisper secrets to each other and cicadas are in full throat.

"Keir?"

"Yes?"

"You okay?"

"Mmm, just sleepy ..."

The combination of beer, wine, food and the heat have made me drowsy. Fran touches my face with the back of her hand and whispers, "Sleep then, we're not in a hurry."

"Mmm."

I dream a complicated dream involving lying to my father about a fire Jamie and I have lit at the bottom of our garden, my mother trashing our Ford Fairlane with a packing case opener (this in fact happened but it was my father, barking drunk, who ran expensively amok, not my gentle church mouse of a mother). And then Vernon Scott dressed in a toga is coming at me with a straight razor in the billiard room of the AD house on Peel Street. My crotch burns in anticipation of agony foretold as a flint-eyed Vernon stalks me around the green baize island separating me from emasculation.

"Oh, my."

Fran's lips are like liquid velvet. She has taken her blouse off and I admire the clean Brancusi curve of her slim brown back, the delicate tracery of her backbone and her glossy head as it rises and falls over my groin. Fran has never made any bones about enjoying oral sex. According to her it keeps both parties honest although if the truth be known I'm not absolutely certain what she means by that. What I *do* know is there's nothing like a good blow-job to cheer a chap up unless it be a good blow-job administered by the woman you love, on the top of an Italian mountain on a perfect summer's day with an incomparable view spread out like a gift below you.

"Careful."

But it's too late and I come extravagantly. Fran swallows and emits a wanton gurgle of pleasure. She claims this is the best part and delights in watching the surges of semen and never displays the slightest embarrassment as jism spurts and dribbles and drapes itself everywhere, 'like an interactive Jackson Pollack,' as she once memorably put it.

"Phew."

Again she chortles and says, "Well, that's certainly one way to take in the Italian Lakes."

Later after I've responded in kind (she tastes hauntingly of malt whiskey) we lie sated beneath our olive tree. Far off to the left two hang-gliders are poised on the crest of the cliff. Suddenly they are launched and the bright birds bounce up, obviously caught in an updraught, and then soar out over the lake thousands of feet below.

"Keir?"

Immediately on the *qui vive* because of her tone. I prop myself up on an elbow and try to adopt an attitude of interested attention although in truth I'm in no mood for a serious chin-wag about anything.

"Yes."

"I know about Ruth Evans."

I feel as though a trap door has opened beneath me and I'm hurtling uncontrollably down a chute towards an all-enveloping void.

"Ruth who?"

"Don't." She pleads.

There is real anguish in her voice. Fran clearly can't bear to have me go through a degrading pantomime of denial. She's right.

"Okay, okay. When? How? Why?" I ask

She has sat up and is gazing at the view, her elbows on her knees and her chin buried in her clasped hands.

"A: Just before Christmas two years ago; B: She wrote to me; C: She loathes your guts."

"I see. Why ... why didn't you tell me about it ... before now?"

"I rather assumed you knew."

"Very funny. Why now?"

She sniffs as if to say 'what an asinine question' and says nothing.

"Fran?"

"Oh, because I sense that right now you and I are at a critical stage, a watershed, a point of no return if you will, and if we're going to have a future I'd like it to be on the basis of shared truths even about lies."

"Which has been lacking so far?"

"Some of which has been lacking so far on both sides of the fence," she replies.

"How so?"

She bunches her shoulders and takes a deep breath. "After your girlfriend wrote I actually didn't think I minded that much."

"But you did."

She nods. "Apparently you promised to ditch me and marry her. Hence the intense hatred when you failed to deliver."

I'm aghast. Truly astounded. Never, ever had the subject of ditching, let alone marriage, come up between Ruth and me. Never. I experience a weird *ex post facto* shiver of relief that the woman hadn't murdered me in cold blood in one of our motel rooms, so obvious is it to me now that Ruth Evans is many, many sandwiches short of a full picnic.

"She's barking mad!" I blurt out.

"Well she certainly didn't come across as being particularly ... ah, balanced. Wait, there's more."

Of course there's more. There's always more.

"Fran, you don't have to ..."

"Just shut up and listen."

So, not looking at me, Fran explains that at first she really didn't mind that much. Apparently she'd always assumed I hadn't been faithful, but as long as I didn't contract Aids, was discreet and so on, she wasn't particularly bothered. According to her she'd never felt the least inclination to go to bed with anybody but me but appreciated that I might have a different spin on fidelity without it necessarily being fatal to our relationship. And then quite suddenly and unexpectedly she found herself furious with me. At the time we were spending New Year's on the Suffolk coast with David and Sarah Finch, friends from university days. So on New Year's Day she practically forced David to go to bed with her while everyone else was out having a jolly hockey sticks walk on the beach.

I remember the day in question perfectly. After lunch the first walk on the beach of the year loomed, but David said he had to some work to do and pottered off to his study. Fran begged off with a headache, and the rest of us bundled up in foul weather gear and tramped for miles along the beach with the sea high and pounding and clouds rolling across a low sky.

"I don't get it. You shag David, or rather you get him to shag you, to get back at me but fail to tell me about it until nearly two years after the event."

"I know, it's pretty daft, isn't it? The thing was that once the deed was done - by the way neither of us had anything close to a good time - I found I wasn't angry any more, guilty as hell, but no longer angry. I knew David felt pretty grim about it too, and he wasn't about to spill the beans, so I just decided to let the whole thing die a death. But now I want to level the field, start the next leg, if there is one, with a clean slate."

Dear Fran. She's almost pathologically honest, and as she sits there, still turned away from me, I understand just how much I owe her and how constant she has been. When I tell her so, she demurs, "Phooey to that. Anyway, I'm not very proud of the way I've handled this …"

"You've done just fine. Mine after all was the initial betrayal."

She shrugs and turning to me and smiling almost shyly, says softly, "What say we work on the future and let the past take care of itself?"

"Fine by me," I reply meaning it while out over the lake the two hang-gliders, now tiny bright icons, wheel and turn effortlessly in the huge sky.

CHAPTER THREE

Cassie comes to the airport with us. Even at ten in the morning the traffic is horrendous. In my considered opinion there are few situations better calculated to underscore the vacuity of modern urban living than sitting in a motionless lake of vehicles on the Cromwell Road staring at a VISIT THE LIONS OF LONGLEAT sticker and trying to ignore the two brats in the back seat of the car ahead who are sniggering and making faces at you.

Uncharacteristically, Fran keeps up a non-stop, one-way conversation with the lovers in the back seat. I fume at the wheel, surf radio stations and take peeks in the rear view mirror. Looking like a sick cow, Charlie has his arm around Cassie, and I can see a thumb gently stroking the underside of what is evidently an unsupported breast in a tight-fitting sweater.

At the airport I go into my usual wandering routine while Charlie checks in.

"I told you he'd go."

I'm ogling Swatches and haven't seen Cassie come up behind me.

"So you did, but he sure as hell doesn't look too happy about it."

She makes a wry face. "I didn't say he'd be *happy* to go, just that he *would*. He's pretty cut up. So am I for that matter."

The green eyes reflect the bright display case behind my back. Swatches dance in her pupils. I search for irony and find none. "You sound surprised."

She shrugs and replies, "Perhaps I am a little. I just hope he doesn't go and do something stupid."

"Like what?"

"Dunno. Like sometimes he can be pretty off the walls, do strange things ..."

"I *have* known the boy for a while."

Cassie looks at me with a funny little smile playing around the edges of her mouth. "He still wants me to go out there."

"And you don't?"

"Not really, but I may change my mind. How many shopping days are there until Christmas?"

"Too many for all of us, it seems."

"Too many whats?"

Fran and Charlie have come up behind us. He has his arm through his mother's, and their resemblance to each other is striking. Physically there's little of me in him although I know I've passed on to him a certain Gaelic melancholy, a tiresome propensity to see the dark side of things.

"Days until Christmas, including the shopping ones."

Charlie rolls his eyes and groans, "Ninety-eight not counting today."

Although it's only eleven-thirty I buy a round and we stand around making desultory un-conversation. Does Charlie have my new e-mail address? Good luck with the City Lit stuff. Tell Cat to drop the jerk first class with oak leaf clusters she's currently going out with. I agree but say it's her funeral. Don't forget to inquire about medical insurance first thing. All we need is a zillion dollar bill for an ingrown toenail or whatever. And so on.

Charlie nods distractedly. He and Cassie down their drinks and drift off to say their goodbyes.

Fran, who is fighting back tears, looks after them. "Poor dears, they must be feeling dreadful."

"I guess, but quite frankly I've got enough on my plate with how *I'm* feeling."

She nods, wipes her eyes with a knuckle and says huskily, "I know that."

Over Fran's shoulder I can see the lovers in a hopeless hip-grinding clinch. They break and each sways back at the waist the better to fix the other in the fickle archives of their minds. *Parting is such sweet sorrow*, my ass. And then we're all at International Departures and Charlie and Cassie kiss almost chastely and turn away from each other, obviously in agony. I embrace him and can feel his thin ribcage against mine and smell the girl's musky perfume.

"Bye-bye, old fellow. Look after yourself."

"You too, Dad. Christ, this is awful."

"Isn't it just."

Fran hugs him almost desperately. Briefly, mother and son's hair meld like different coloured sands whorled together.

"Bye, Mum. I'll be back before I leave."

Charlie has been a Marx Brothers fan ever since I took him to *Duck Soup* when he was still a schoolboy in Montreal.

"Good-bye, darling child. Be good."

With a strangled sob he disentangles himself from his mother and brushing rudely past a Muslim lady in burqa, strides down the ramp. After showing his boarding card, he turns and waves (sideways like Nixon saying goodbye on the White House lawn) and then disappears into the innards of the airport.

Fran blows her nose, and I swallow the nugget-sized lump in my throat. As we move off towards the exit, Cassie does a totally unexpected and affecting thing: she puts her arm around Fran's shoulders and falls into step with her as they thread their way through the crowd.

We don't talk much on the way back. Alfa Laval, Bell Honeywell, Lucozade, the cars streaming like mechanised lemmings towards the city, the terraced houses and ramshackle high streets glimpsed from the elevated motorway, all add to my confusion, my vague nagging sense of foreboding. But of what? The future presumably, the future without a purpose, or at least not one that I can readily discern. And then I have a sudden devastating vision of a milky eyed me velcroed into my Depens playing croquet against myself on the lawn of an old folks home in East Sussex. Some purpose, some prospect to gladden the heart.

"Darling, Cassie asked if we'd like to go around to her flat for dinner sometime."

"Sorry, I was yonks away. Sure, that would be great."

"Pasta?"

"Love it," I say untruthfully.

"Good. I'll be in touch. Right here's fine."

I pull over by the Natural History Museum and Cassie gets out. She leans her head in Fran's window. "Thanks for letting me come along."

Fran puts a comforting hand on hers and says kindly, "We're glad you could. Spread the misery as it were."

The girl sighs deeply, mutters "sometimes I wonder, I really do" and turning abruptly, strides long-leggedly up Exhibition Road without looking back.

Fran turns to me. "What was that supposed to mean?"

"That she sometimes wonders what it's all about, I imagine. She has a point."

"It?" Fran queries.

Fran's not being obtuse. She thinks clearly and pragmatically in units of problem solving. In fact she's the least theoretical, the least existentially haunted person I know which makes her both sublimely easy and sometimes curiously unsettling (what does she know that we don't?) to live with.

"Would you believe life?"

"Oh *that*. Step on it, I'm late for my meeting," she replies impatiently.

After leaving Fran off at her office, I return home where I surprise Cat and jerk first class with oak leaf clusters together on or in bed (Charlie's) as there's a mad rushing and dashing and slamming of doors upstairs when I let myself in the front door. The boy, who rejoices in the apposite name of Randy, comes downstairs first and explains that they were doing homework (in Charlie's room?), and I explain that he can get the fuck out of my house and not bother coming back. To her credit Cat doesn't opt for the homework route and says they were just fooling around but can't stop herself from adding that she wasn't aware that England had turned into a fascist state.

"Come on, Cat, you can do better than that. Agreed upon house rules hardly constitute a repressive regime."

"I'll bet Bonnie Prince Charlie could bonk his precious prophetess on the kitchen table if he wanted to. Probably has, come to think of it."

"No, he can't, and Charlie's twenty-one not fifteen."

The poor girl screws up her face into an alarming life mask of exasperation and says, "Sixteen, last time I heard. Anyway who cares, twenty-one, fifteen, what's the difference? The point is I've got the same ... ah ... urges as the next person, so why can't I enjoy them without sneaking around like a thief in the night."

She's right, of course. (And so are we). Seventeen? Seventeen and a half? Eighteen? With your driving licence? With the right to vote? After your first solo Sainsbury's run? At the onset of puberty in many cultures. Never in others.

Suddenly tired (why is being a parent so fucking exhausting?) and fed up, I say that I think we should talk it over with her mother and add that for the moment at least Randy is jerk *non grata* and she's grounded.

***

I know I don't want to wake up, but neither am I terrifically keen to continue the dream I'm having. Something to do with me trying to get onto a moving train but never quite managing to lift my feet high enough to get onto the bottom stair and being encumbered by a large old fashioned leather suitcase smothered in hotel and steamship-line stickers. And then I'm walking through a vast deserted station (in black and white), and I feel I'm being followed, but whenever I turn around there's no one there.

Panicky, I swim up through layer after layer of clammy fog and then I'm awake: sweating, tumescent and hung over big time. My mouth's as dry as a dog biscuit. Mechanically I gulp down some tepid water wishing I'd passed on the second (fourth?) Armagnac, take painful note of the time – seven fifty-five - and the fact that I'm alone in bed, groan then shudder back to sleep where my hangover can't pursue me.

More disturbing dreams follow, but since I know that they can't be as bad as the uncomfortable reality of being awake, I savour their oddity until, that is, the Python Dream starts when awake is definitely where I want to be, so it's back up through the haze to the surface.

It's now nearly eight-thirty and my head feels marginally better. Rain lashes against the windowpanes, and wind whooshes through the copper beech outside our bedroom window. Through a chink in the curtains, I can see the London sky tired and grey as a week-old bruise. I lie on my back and try to remember details of the second half of last night's dinner-party at David and Sarah's without much success. There was a *moussaka* (there's always a *moussaka* at the Finches), there was Tesco's plonk (there's always that too, for a relatively well-off man David's passing squeaky), there was, I'm sure, an elaborate dessert but I've no recollection of it. Oh yes, there was another couple, Cynthia and ... I draw a blank. He something in the City, she something in software, I think. I do remember that both of them got right up my nose almost before we'd exchanged greetings.

"Do I detect a thinly disguised transatlantic accent?"

I am standing with my back to the fake fire, the man is practically standing on my toes, and I can read the veins in his face like a road map. *His* accent is right off the scale, way north of plummy.

"You do. I'm Canadian."

He says "Aha, a Canuck!" as if I'd just divulged the formula for Coca-Cola. Why the hell does David do this to me? He knows perfectly well there's a certain type of Brit I have trouble with. To wit: the ones who talk about their colonial brethren, wear expensive bespoke double-breasted navy blue blazers with gold buttons, gaudily striped stockbrokers' shirts acquired at one of those fatuous shops on Jermyn Street, and brown suede lace-ups with metal clickers on the toes *and* heels.

"Toronto?"

"No. I was brought up in a one-horse village south of Montreal."

"You mean in the Eastern Townships?"

"Yes."

"Not Knowlton by any chance?"

"Yes. But I haven't been back for years."

"How extraordinary. The Crichton-Stuarts are *great* friends of ours."

They would be. The Crichton-Stuarts were local grandees with an enormous house on the lake and thin noses wedged between morose eyes. He was largely responsible for having my father struck off the medical register. Not that he didn't deserve to be; it's just that he persecuted the poor bastard with the zeal of a Torquemada.

At dinner Cynthia rabbits on about her children - all predictably at schools of unparalleled pre-eminence - and once, looking across the table, Fran slides me a Slow-Down-On-The-Sauce look, but it's too late as I'm already in the bag or thereabouts. The fortunes of the First XI's annual fixture v their ancestral rivals blur and fuzz and recede, and I realise that I've got a hole in my heart where Charlie used to be. No, it's worse than that, it's actually more selfish, more mean-spirited. With Charlie away and gone for good now, any attempts at pretending that I'm anything other than a back number on a hiding to nowhere are futile. I'm not claiming that there's anything remotely unique about my situation, simply that it's unique to me and I don't much like it.

"Wakey, wakey."

I open my eyes.

Fran's standing in the doorway one hand on the jamb, the other on a cocked hip. She's in jogging mode: loose fitting shorts, sockless Nike Airs, maroon sweat and rain-soaked Russell Athletic top, headphones clipped around her neck like some space age talisman. Her cheeks and the fronts of her thighs are blush pink, there are spatters of mud on her calves and her hair is plastered in damp straggles to her forehead. She looks as healthy as I feel unwell.

"Morning. Good run?"

"Not specially. It's pretty dire out there."

Gingerly I sit up in bed. The bedroom lurches alarmingly and then rights itself. I groan and drink some water.

"Bad?"

"Not good."

Without a trace of serves-you-right in her voice she says, "Well, you did take quite a run at the Armagnac. You and John come to think of it."

"Ah ..."

She bends down, picks up an errant sock and tosses it into the bathroom. Then she comes into the room and flinging open the curtains declaims theatrically, "Behold the sceptred isle."

"Thanks, but I'd rather not. John?"

She laughs and replies, "You don't remember diddley squat, do you?"

"Not much after the moussaka. Christ, can't Sarah cook anything else?"

"Well, I once remember an execrable shepherd's pie and then there was the night of the shot-put Stilton soufflé served with vanilla ice cream. John, the man you don't remember, seemed pretty well in control. I suspect he's a pro."

"And I'm not?"

Fran is moving purposefully around the room, picking up clothes, straightening pieces of furniture, organising. I can practically hear her thinking, sorting, marshalling her thoughts.

"Fran?"

She comes and sits on the bed next to me. I can smell her sweat. The wind's rattling the windows and rain drives in breathless enfilades against the panes. Fran takes my hands in hers and kisses them.

"Well, let's just say that you're not in his league. John Staunton's the sort of bloke who can have a seriously boozy lunch, go back to the office and function perfectly effectively. Of course he'll be dead long before he's sixty, but that's his problem."

"And what d'you think is mine?" I ask, unsure I want to hear her answer.

Fran frowns, gazes out of the window and finally says almost diffidently, "I suppose you're in a bit of a muddle: no job, Charlie gone now, Cat might just as well be. Fifty behind you. My guess is that the drinking's a symptom, not the thing-in-itself. By the way, if it was a pre-and post-*moussaka* sort of evening, you won't remember that you started crying last night."

Again stated without a scintilla of censure. Appalled, I now do remember suddenly bursting into tears although I can't for the life of me recall what brought the jag on.

"South Sudan," she prompts helpfully.

"What?"

"The iniquities of tribal warfare to be precise."

"But I don't know a thing about tribal fucking warfare. I find stuff about that part of the world more confusing than all the derivatives and futures gobbledegook put together."

"You didn't last night."

"Oh, Fran, I'm sorry, really I am."

She shakes her head and says crisply, "No need to be. Now, more to the point, what are we going to do about our horny little daughter?"

"Enrol her in nunnery?"

"Ha bloody ha."

"Make sure she's on the pill, loop, papyrus leaves, condom undies, whatever?"

"Whose side are you on?"

I say I don't know, which is no less than the truth.

"Well, I'm not having her using our house as a convenient place for a spot of nooky during her spare between French and whatever they call Algebra these days. Lordy, look at the time. We're going to be late."

I stare at her blankly.

"Keir Buchan, you unholy creep, don't tell me you've forgotten."

"Forgotten what?"

Fran's at the bathroom door half out of her clothes. "That we're supposed to be at Mummy and Daddy's by noon, asshole. Go and make sure Cat's up and about. Move!"

Her parents live in a trad monstrosity near the top of a hill in Dorset. The roast will already be in the oven. Like most fixtures with my in-laws, who I would probably dislike if I could be bothered to, I've simply filed today's event in a blatantly Freudian *oubliette* and bolted it shut.

After I've chivvied a grumbling Cat out of her lair and taken a quick shower, I guzzle some orange juice, eyeball the mail, which is all about as personal as sky writing and check my e-mail.

greetings from rainy cambridge mass okay flight tho sat next to a sumo restler sized born again christian lady with attitude digs fine texan physicist to the left of me korean mathematician to the right cannons nowhere q: did you hear the one about the english nymfomaniac a: she was halfway across the irish sea before she learnt a 21-inch murphy was a television sorry about that miss you charles le solitaire.

Christ almighty. Restler? Nymfomaniac? Charlie has successfully resisted the best efforts of rafts of private tutors, a clutch of well-intentioned teachers in a chichi London preparatory school, more in a top-of-the-second-division public school and a world-class university, to teach him how to spell. It seems bright biochemists needn't be bothered and anyway he claims that he doesn't even try on e-mail.

Now we're in a traffic jam inching towards the Hogarth roundabout. Fran's driving, I'm leafing through the sports section of The Guardian and Cat's asleep in the back seat. Idly I wonder how many man-hours are lost to traffic jams in the average western lifetime. Fran, I know, will be in a lather as her parents are nothing if not creatures of strictly observed timetables and unless we get very lucky we're now doomed to be late. Her father, Kenneth (never Ken) Barker, gets migraines if he's kept waiting for his meals. When this happens Muriel develops debilitating stomach cramps out of sheer apprehension for the discomfort her inefficiency and thoughtlessness has inflicted upon her husband. Needless to say the trick's to get the nosh on the table on time.

Finally, like a snake sloughing off a painful skin, we struggle free of the traffic, and Fran guns the Volvo down the M3. Soon we've left behind the depressing straggle of mid-sized factories, shopping malls, depots, used car lots, and pseudo-suburban enclaves and are bowling through the Hampshire countryside. The weather remains atrocious. The rain drives down out of a livid sky. I flick on the radio: Man U tipped to beat the Gunners, Bath to extend their hegemony over Gloucester, David Cameron may or may not be losing his hair, a team of researchers in the States have concluded that snowflakes may be carcinogenic, the stock market continues to rise, the pound to fall, or is it the other way around?

"Keir?"

"Hmm?"

"What about something nice? *Carmen* for example."

I ruffle around in the glove compartment and find our Jill Gomez CD of the highlights of the world's most listened-to opera. We haven't got three bars into the overture before the peanut gallery protests.

"Daaaad?"

"Yes, Cat?"

"I thought we agreed you wouldn't play that stuff when I'm in the car."

"Sorry," I reply sweetly, "but it seems to me you forfeited any bargaining rights you might have had at about one forty-six yesterday afternoon."

"Of which, more later," Fran adds grimly, and Cat shuts her trap.

By the time Carmen has been topped by the feckless Don José we've left the motorway and are cutting through the New Forest. Here an eerie mist clings to the fern and bracken covered moors and the rain continues to pour down. Stoic brown ponies with black manes stand with their backs to the driving rain, their tails blown horizontally along their rumps by the wind.

"Darling, when are you going to start looking for a real job?"

Surprised, I glance across at Fran. She's concentrating on the road and doesn't return my look but I sense there's more than traversing New Forest chitchat to her query.

"City Lit doesn't qualify?"

"What d'you think?"

I *know* City Lit doesn't qualify. I know taking bored house-persons and flirtatious *au pairs* through *The Sun Also Rises* and *The Lord of the Flies* for the next fifteen years is not the work of a serious person. But what is? Or rather, what am I qualified to do that is?

"Well, I guess I've been waiting for the summer to be over and Charlie to go before I started looking, but I've got to confess I'm feeling remarkably demotivated."

"I can understand that, after all you've had rather a serious kick in the teeth, but you know how much lead-time job hunting takes and ..."

"Fran, are you telling me you're worried about money? We've ..."

She looks at me over the tops of her trendy green glasses and says evenly, "No, not at all but I could be very worried about *you* if I put my mind to it."

"Me?"

"The same."

"Listen, last night was an aberr ..."

"I've already told you I don't care a toss about last night. I do care about the look in your eyes."

"What look?' I ask, twisting around in my seat to see if Cat's listening in on this. Fat chance. She's snoring quietly with a thumb in her mouth, her index finger curled beneath her nose and her phone which is softly spewing tripe into the atmosphere. I would say seriously uncool for someone's who's rushing the rights of passage fences as fast as she is.

"The no-one-at-home look I sometimes catch, that one," Fran replies.

The rain has stopped abruptly and great rents in the cloud cover are appearing overhead. We've left the New Forest and are heading west along the ridge of the South Dorset Downs. The views on either side of the road are spectacular: the English countryside at its plump, self-referential best. We are now officially late.

How am I going to answer Fran? Of course, I've not failed to see the look in question. And didn't Charlie's squeeze say something similar way back in Riva? I myself have from time to time been alarmed by the thousand-yard stare in the eyes of the person in the mirror. And there's no denying that I've been out of touch, distant, since having been given my marching orders and setting off down life's back nine. It's as though events were happening (or not happening) to him - that vaguely familiar but not really felt figure - not me, whoever he might be.

"I'll be all right, honest. I just need to get my bearings, get a second wind. I guess it's a longer haul that I thought it was going to be."

Fran favours me with one of her patented don't-shit-me looks. "But what d'you *feel*? I mean, what's going on inside to make you look so ... so damn miserable?"

"Not much, but that may, I think, be the point."

"Where are we?"

Cat has woken and like her grandfather is undoubtedly famished.

"Nearly there. We just went through Portesham."

"I'm starving."

Five minutes later we arrive at the Barkers'. The house is on the outskirts of the intolerably bijou village of Abbotsbury where Fran's parents have lived for nearly a decade since Kenneth's retirement from a senior but far from top position in the Loans Department of a bank in the City.

Lunch is served before I can get my G&T to my lips. Kenneth's not such a bad egg really. He's a deeply conservative (both upper and lower case) man of some self-confidence although of late I've noticed a wary flicker in his eyes as wave after wave of Internet, World Wide Web, Google, modem, CD-ROM, DVD, Tweet, Twitter, virtual reality, faxing, IMAX, Skype, internet banking, digital remastering, Big Bang, e-mail, iPod, Facebook, streaming, and so on and on have clattered down the pipeline, irrevocably altering the warp and woof of life lived well into the twenty-first century and leaving him beached and bemused in their wake.

Kenneth went to a minor public school, joined his bank straight from school, uncharacteristically did a two-year stint in Cairo where he met his future wife, but otherwise lived a settled comfortable life, taking the seven-thirteen from Sutton to Tower Bridge station for the thirty-five years of his working life. Muriel is another, sadder kettle of fish. Once a handsome serene woman, she is now a desiccated Gordian knot of nerves for whom contact with even her close family, let alone the outside world (her bridge four a miraculous exception) is painful. Fran puts this down to chronic insomnia and a hormone imbalance. Personally, I'm inclined to blame extended exposure to Kenneth who treats her like a well-bred (she's from a notch further up the social ladder than he is) Helot. Fran has a relatively uncomplicated relationship with her parents although I think she spoils them.

As predicted, as preordained, the roast lamb has been cooked to within an angstrom of its life while the potatoes, beans and broccoli are criminally underdone. However by way of compensation, Kenneth, who knows and likes his wine, produces some excellent claret and it's not long before any deficiencies in the fare are forgotten as the remnant of last night's over indulgence is overtaken and merges seamlessly into today's. Soon I'm on automatic: I respond to questions asked of me, even pose some of my own, but I might just as well be on Betelgeuse so little am I interested in the ritual going on around me.

The sun comes out and a light mist rises from the flagstones on the patio beyond the dining room's aluminium French windows, like a special effect in an opera. Beyond that a line of larches trapped in the sun at the bottom of the garden sparkles with myriad raindrops. Everything seems scrubbed to a breathless cleanliness by the recent rain; everything, that is, save me.

Charlie's girl has a point: what the hell is it all about? Surely not Kenneth banging on about Euro-Johnnies sticking their noses up Scottish pheasants' arseholes, nor Muriel picking at her table mat with dry neurasthenic fingers, nor Fran restlessly fussing a line of salt around the stem of her wine glass with the back of a little finger, nor Cat visibly pining for her phone. No, it appears in large measure to be about disquiet. Or at least of late to me it does. An*gst* as the essential loam of being? Well, why not? Why is that any less acceptable than Joy, or Happiness, or Love, or whatever being the linchpin, the glue? I've a notion that it's less acceptable because we've been infected with the bacillus of hope that messes everything up, because hope is for what - a not too unpleasant death?

Cat helps Muriel and her mother clear the table. I've noticed with some amusement Kenneth's transparent attempt not to be offended by his granddaughter's louche appearance. Today Cat's wearing the mandatory microscopic black skirt, black tights, black Doc Martens, black polo shirt, and by way of relief a Black Watch waistcoat. Her brutal hair (ungelled by maternal edict) is a subtle shade of orange. She looks like a cross between a Pict and an extra in a Charlie Chaplin movie and I'm proud of her.

Once Kenneth and I are alone in the dining room he downs a glass of wine in one gulp and says, "I don't get it. Do you?"

"Get what?" I ask disingenuously because I'm pretty sure what he's got his knickers in a twist about, having got mine in the same state many times for precisely the same reason. But not today, today I'm sleeping with the enemy.

"Why someone ... well, someone of Catherine's ... ah ... breeding would want to dress like that."

"Breeding?"

My father-in-law, whose face is now a brisk cornelian, pours both of us another glass of wine and says equably, "Yes, Keir, breeding. It's a common enough word and furthermore it's one whose meaning, in this context, you are perfectly familiar with, so don't bugger me around."

Sometimes the old duffer can be excellent value.

"I'm told it's just a phase. Like the Barbie doll one and the horsey one and all the other ones. Most of her friends are from very similar backgrounds - if not to say stud farms - but they can hardly wait to get home from school and slip into mufti the better to hang out."

He shakes his head and stares glumly into his wineglass. What ghosts is he seeing in there? What evenings at the Gezihra Club in the company of well-bred and understandably dressed English roses are swirling around in the magic lantern of his claret?

"Charlie get off all right?"

When in doubt change the subject.

"He did. We took him to the airport with his girlfriend. He sent his love," I fib smoothly knowing that Charlie might conceivably have done so had he given more than a nanosecond of thought to anything other than his own libido for the last three months.

"Ah, yes, the famous girlfriend. I gather she's a looker."

"That she is."

Just then Cat backs through the swing door into the dining room balancing a tray of rice pudding filled ramekins. I am instantly assailed by a smell so steeped in the bottomless well of my boyhood and youth that tears come to my eyes and I literally gag and have to excuse myself.

"Keir, darling what's …"

"Be right back."

But right back is precisely what I won't be. I splash some cold water on my face in the downstairs loo and then let myself quietly out the front door and am soon slipping and sliding in lambent sunshine along the footpath which angles up and across the Downs from the foot of the Barkers' garden. Soon I'm following the path across an upland meadow dotted with glassy eyed sheep that pay scant attention to me. The sun glints on the sea, and I can see the thin strip of Chesil Beach and beyond that the Bill of Portland. In an effort to dispel the effects of the *petite Madeleine* which Muriel's unconsciously offensive rice puddings has evoked in me, I fill my lungs with tangy sea air and try to think of something, anything, else. But it's no good, the floodgates of memory have been opened and all I can do is go with the flow.

CHAPTER FOUR

It's really the raisins (or are they currants?) that I hate the most. I spoon them surreptitiously out of the gooey mass of coagulated rice in my bowl and place them beneath the rim in the hope that my father won't notice and make me eat them. But he always does, and I always pile them up on my spoon and swallow them in one gulp hoping that by doing so they might somehow fool my taste buds. However, the buds are never duped and the reaction is always the same: a prickly feeling at the back of my throat, saliva filling my mouth, tears brimming in my eyes and then the grim struggle to keep everything down. Then there's the smell of the pudding itself connected as it is in my mind to that of jism and by association my guilt at having jerked off while reading another Mary-Sue's-Nipples-Hardened paperback purloined at Clark's Drug store and smelling fuzzily of cheap paper and linoleum. The odd thing is that Jamie, my twin and senior by some four minutes, absolutely adores rice pudding. I don't think my father's being deliberately cruel. It's just that he's the son of Scottish immigrants brought up on the wrong side of the tracks during the Depression, and then you wasted nothing and did what your elders told you to do. It was that simple.

Or not.

Hamish Buchan was also a dedicated GP and a generous if aloof father until, that is, drink and then drink and an unspecified *too many 'onlys'*

sorrow transformed him into a figure of pathos. His father had been buried alive for three days at Passchendaele and not surprisingly had never thereafter been the same and could ~~only at~~ *Only* best manage menial jobs. Still, he and my grandmother somehow managed to scrape together enough dosh to send their only child to medical school ~~only for~~ *but* both of them ~~to die~~ *died* in a train crash on the way to Niagara Falls on their first holiday in fifteen years, a few weeks after their son had graduated from McGill.

The Kaba *Special* pistol, squat and unlovely as a toad, sits on the dining room table next to Dad's tumbler of bourbon. It's Sunday lunch and the Buchan *paterfamilias* is pissed. Jamie and I are fifteen and too young to feel much other than humiliation at our father's condition. We're miles from pity. Mother sits opposite Dad, her face as imperturbable, as unreadable as one of her husband's prescriptions. Long, long ago she learned to hide her pain and misery and has taken refuge in religion. She crouches in the lee of her duties at the church, her charitable works, her lay activities in the community, her bible classes. Who can blame her? I sneak a look across the table at Jamie who closes his eyes in a silent gesture of resignation and cuts his meat with bowed head.

"James? Keir?"

This will be the question about how many geniuses can we name who have either gone mad or committed suicide.

"Van Gogh."

"Hart Crane."

"Nietzsche."

"Schumann."

"Goebbels."

I hold my breath. Jamie's gone too far but then he always does just as I never go far enough. Dad takes a sip of his neat Jack Daniels and runs a speculative forefinger over the pistol (kept in his top bureau drawer wrapped with a box of bullets in a yellowed oilcloth) which we know he bought in Honolulu on his way to patching up soldiers fighting the commies in Korea. Ho hum, tell us about it Dad, tell us about saving the world from the Red Peril, tell us about a future GP having to hack blasted legs off at twenty below, tell us about the snow in the highlands and the wild drink-fuelled leaves in Seoul.

"James, are you ... trying to be funny?"

"Nope. Surely you don't have to be *good* to be a genius and Goebbels certainly committed suicide. Just read about it. But if you don't like him, what about Tchaikovsky?"

"Jurysstillout," Dad slurs.

And so it goes. Not all Sunday lunches are like this, not all of them are pistol days. Most in fact are characterised by sullen silences punctuated by outbursts of paternal spleen usually directed against his two faithful hobby horses: the Federal Government and, to bait mother, the Anglican Church. This one, however, is a beaut. Is in fact the worst ever and ends with Dad firing off a clip into the dining room ceiling and being carted off by Fabian, our normally seriously under-employed cop, to sleep it off in the village poky.

Afterwards Jamie and I walk down the disused railway tracks towards the lake. A late fall twilight is settling over the land. Cinnamon mares' tails drift across the northern sky. The smell of wood fires is in the air, and over on the hill to our right someone is chopping kindling, the sound distinct and poignant. A motorboat whines and slaps across the lake. We pause to light our fags. The match flares in my brother's cupped hands and his face is eerily lit from below. Jamie, my brother. Jamie, my twin. Jamie.

"Well?"

"Well, what?"

He shrugs and dragging deeply on his fag says, "Well, what did you make of that little performance?"

"Dunno." I mean, what's a fifteen-year-old supposed to make of a father so fucked up and out of it that he shoots up his dining room ceiling after the Sunday roast?

But Jamie's more sophisticated, more worldly that I am. He makes a face and states matter-of-factly, "He'll be dead of cirrhosis of the liver long before he screws up the courage to join the immortals in suicide heaven."

I allow as how he's probably right. He isn't. The truth, like most truths, is less neat and far sadder. Hamish Buchan (ex-MD) will outlive his first born by many years and even then he won't depart in either the coded dignity of madness or the futile defiance of suicide, but alone in an Albany NY flop house drowning in his own vomit.

When we're eighteen, Jamie and I go off to McGill, he to take a BSc with a view to going into medicine, me a BA with SFA on my mind save having a good time. That summer we work for the third and last time at the Boating Club - lifeguarding, tennis court dragging, odd jobbing - but mostly we're into girls and hanging around in seedy bars and taverns. Often the bars and clubs have loud live bands which we love to hate. The taverns are dingy grottoes stinking of spilled draft beer, cigarette smoke and Dettol from the urinals, less favoured by suave dudes like us because still all-male preserves.

The Yamaska Club, Cowansville PQ, August 20, 1981. I've just broken up with Jill Chambers, the girl I've been seeing but not making it with all summer, and I'm feeling pretty sorry for myself. Jamie has Torrie Ryan, with whom he *has* been making it all summer, in tow. We're with the usual crowd: Mary Ritchie, Eeyore Scrivins, Lips Larsen, and Clare Marchand. The quarts of Labatts are going down fast and furious. The girls drink Brandy Alexanders and Tom Collinses. The music is compliments of The Kinky Dicks and is particularly noisome. I dance with Mary, then with Clare, who's supposed to be going out with Lips but seems to be coming onto me but I'm still pining for Jill and am one unhappy cowboy. The strobe lighting bounces off our shirts in a bluish glow. Eyes glitter wildly. The band's going ape shit. Suddenly I've got a screaming headache and I've drunk and smoked too much and I've had it. I find Jamie on the dance floor.

"I'm off," I bawl in his ear.

"What?"

"Tired. Leaving."

Jamie shrugs and fumbles in his pockets for the keys to Dad's Buick.

"No, you keep them."

"What?" he shouts.

"Keep the car," I yell back, "Gotta get some fresh air, I'll walk for a bit, hitch a ride. See you tomorrow."

He gives a thumbs-up sign and goes back to his maniacal dancing. I leave without saying goodbye to anybody. The parking lot is deserted. I breathe in huge slabs of the humid night air. The club with its flashing neon lights looks like a movie set. The Rick's Café of Cowansville, PQ? Feeling slightly ill, I walk out to the highway and set off down the road. There's a full harvest moon that's so bright I fancy I can see the colours of the fields and trees all around me. After about a mile I begin to feel better and wonder about turning back (I could sleep in the back of the car) when I'm pinioned in the headlights of a car coming up behind me slowly.

"Hi, Keir, jump in."

It's Clare Marchand and I gladly clamber into the front seat of her father's T-Bird.

"What's wrong?"

"Not much. Headache. One too many 50's. You know."

"Yeah, tell that to that crazy brother of yours."

She's right. Jamie is a bit of a head case, always has been. But that's precisely his attraction, at least for most girls it is, and God knows he's always been successful with them. I ask Clare if she sees him like that too.

"No way, in fact he scares the pants off me."

Clare's wearing a sleeveless cotton dress with a square cut décolletage, and in the half-light I can see the shadow of her cleavage and the foothills of her knockers.

"What about Lips?"

Clare shrugs. Her tits ripple and I spring a hard-on.

"He's boring."

"I thought you liked him."

"So did I."

Clare slows the car, pulls into a dirt track leading to a field of high corn and turns the lights and engine off.

"Well?"

We kiss. It's a long meandering event that has our tongues dancing and darting around each other like courting swans. Her lips are wonderfully soft and pliant. She tastes of Brandy Alexanders and Export A's.

Finally we break and she smiles and says "I thought you'd be good" and my heart soars.

I'm about to say something foolish when she puts a forefinger on my lips and whispers "Shush, no bullshit" and traces the outline of my mouth with her fingernail. The car is permeated with the dense orange brown of the witch's moon. Somewhere nearby a bullfrog is croaking and the air is full of the high tension thrill of crickets.

We kiss again. The steering wheel jabs into my ribcage and I've got lover's nuts something fierce, which is business as usual after my summer of getting just so far with Jill. Clare seems to know what she's doing, which is more than can be said for me.

"Look."

I do. She's leaning back against her door and slowly undoing the buttons of her dress. One, two, three, four, five. She shrugs out of the arms and her bra seems to be impossibly white against her end-of-summer tan. Then she arches her back and performs a Houdini-like trick that undoes the bra which she lets fall into her lap. Her large breasts with their small dark nipples are free and I realise I'm in the front seat of a Ford Thunderbird with a girl who wants to go all the way.

"You like?"

"Christ, yes," I groan.

I kiss her breasts. Feel the puckered hardness of the nipples and smell the perfume she's dabbed in her cleavage. With one hand she pulls my head down onto her, while with the other she rubs my cock which is straining inside my underwear.

"Clare, please. I can't wait much ..."

"That makes two of us. Come on."

The time it takes to get around the car seems interminable and not a little ludicrous as I fumble through my wallet to see if I still have the rubber I've long ago despaired of using.

Clare is standing in front of the field of ten foot high corn. She has stepped out of her dress and knickers and is waiting for me with her arms held above her head like some pagan earth-goddess. This in a cornfield in Quebec's boring old Eastern Townships not some Swedish free-love den or Neapolitan bordello. I've never seen a woman completely naked in the flesh before and am amazed by the size of her pubic bush.

"You won't be needing that," she says indicating the rubber which I've tried to palm, not being all that sure at what stage one's supposed to don it.

Now she's on her knees. She works at my belt, unzips my fly, pulls my shorts down and runs a hand along the shaft of my cock. Then I'm on top of her, none too certain where everything is down there, but Clare guides me into what seems to be the molten centre of her, and she gives a little cry, and I come almost immediately and can't help thinking how much more complicated the real thing is than its country cousin, and then she's urging me hoarsely on, and I've just enough hardness left to last maybe fifteen seconds. Then I slip out of her, and I'm aware of the harsh friable earth digging into my elbows and knees and of my failure.

"Sorry."

"Whatever for?"

"Well, you know ..."

"Nonsense, you were great," she whispers in my ear.

Bless her.

We pull our clothes on and are soon back on the road smoking up a storm and listening to golden oldies from CKJM Montreal.

"First time?"

I nod. Christ, wasn't that un-earth-movingly obvious?

"I didn't figure Jill Chambers would be putting out ... holy mackerel what have we here?"

We're nearing the outskirts of Knowlton at a place where the road forks: left into town, right through the Bolton Pass and on down to the US border. Lately there have been a number of accidents at this spot and there's been all sorts of talk about putting lights in without anything ever actually having come of it. Ahead we can see a police car pulled over onto the soft shoulder with its orange light flashing. Clare slows to a crawl, and we can now see Bill Stockton, Chief Fabian's assistant, standing by the squad car waving a flash-light in one hand indicating caution with the other.

"Look at that, will you," Clare breaths, pointing off to the left where some fifty yards into a fallow field, shadowy figures are moving around a dark object that looks like a gigantic radiator. Only it's not a radiator, it's an overturned car from the front of which a wisp of smoke is rising into the unnaturally bright night. The police car's headlights probe blindly out into the field. Skid marks on the macadam turn into the two deep ominous furrows in the dark earth. Only now am I aware that the back door of the squad car is open and two people wrapped in grey blankets are hunched in the seat.

Clare leans out of the car and calls to Bill Stockton, "Hi, Bill, looks bad, whose car's that?"

As Bill knocks his cap back off his forehead with a knuckle and opens his mouth to speak, I recognise the two in the car as Lips Larsen and Mary Ritchie, and my insides go black and I feel as though I'm falling forever without end through all of time and space.

"'Lo Clare. Real bad. That there's Doc Buchan's brand new Le Sabre, or what's left of it. We think the twins are trapped in the front seat but we can't get any sense out of Lars and Mary here. Who've you got with you there ... sweet Jesus Lord!"

The next thing I know I'm running, stumbling across the field towards the overturned car which I can see is pretty much flattened up front although the back's not so bad and is presumably where Lips and Mary were. Before I can reach the wreck Bill catches up with me, and then everything's confused as an ambulance screams up the Cowansville road and Marcel Blouin's truck arrives from the village and I'm led back across the field to Clare's car. Then a medic is looking into my eyes with one of those mirror things with a hole in the middle and someone gives me an injection, and then, with no recollection of how I got there, I'm standing at our front door with Chief Fabian waiting for either of my parents to come downstairs to be informed that their eldest son is dead. Somewhere in there, out by the crossroads I think, the word 'decapitated' impinges itself on my consciousness; certainly no one ever suggested that any of us identify Jamie nor that the coffin should be anything other than closed.

In the event it's my mother who comes to the door. I can hear her heavily descending the stairs, and then she's fiddling with the lock and I can see her dressing-gowned figure through the muslin curtain in the glass door. Moths flap and fidget around the light over the door. I can smell the far off brackishness of the summer-baked lake and nearer the sweetness of mock orange by the side of the house.

"Hello Chief, oh, Keir you've not been up to your old tricks ... Oh, no ... no ... please no."

But it's yes, yes, yes until the end of time. My brother's dead, and I'm left to roam the world without my other half and a sense of guilt (why hadn't I taken the car? Why should I, with a fraction of Jamie's talent, not have been the one to make the fatal error of judgement?) so palpable, so immanent as to sometimes render me virtually immobile for hours on end.

At the funeral, at the *double* funeral because Eeyore Scrivins was also killed (Torrie Ryan was cut out of the front seat of the Buick, concussed but otherwise virtually unscathed), I sit between my red-eyed mother who believes in God and my Dad who doesn't and who smells of bourbon and Old Spice shaving lotion, and I understand nothing.

Later it seems that most of the village is packed into the little graveyard. Drizzle hisses on the leaves of a nearby sycamore. 'Ashes to ashes and dust to dust' and Jamie's coffin disappears into the obscene rectangle in the ground, and we go to the edge of the grave and throw nosegays of anemones on top of the coffin, and the world until recently so gracious and full of promise is a strange and terrible place.

"Keir?"

Clare Marchand is standing in front of me beneath a dripping, brightly coloured golf umbrella. I notice for the first time that she's got extraordinary eyes, large and dark and expressive, and then in spite of the circumstances I see her in my mind's eye, naked in front of the towering corn her arms stretched above her head. My cicerone. I can feel myself blushing.

"How you doin'?"

"I guess I'll get by," I say without much conviction.

She shrugs as if she'd been expecting me to say something like that and looks down at her feet (neat in navy blue high heels fringed with wet newly cut grass) and then back up at me frankly, appraisingly. "Listen Keir, no one's to blame, no one except Jamie, that is. You know that, don't you?"

"I should have figured he was out of it."

"Was he? Seems to me he was always way out there on the edge. Some people are like that drink or no drink. Grieve, Keir, grieve for all you're worth but don't blame yourself for your brother's death."

"That's easier said than done," I mumble.

"Of course it is, but it's what you've got to do otherwise you'll both have died out in that field."

I never saw Clare Marchand again. The family moved to the States and she went to university somewhere down there. A mutual acquaintance once told me she'd done Peace Corps work in Ghana, married a civil engineer there and had a raft of children before becoming involved in her adopted country's planned parenthood programme. Dear Clare.

***

I've rambled in a wide semicircle and am now toiling up the steep hill to my in-laws' house. I stop to catch my breath. Dusk is in the air. Soon there'll be tea to get through and then drinks and then dinner and then tomorrow and then the day after tomorrow and then the day after ...

CHAPTER FIVE

The remainder of the weekend passes without serious incident although Fran lands herself in deep shit for having the temerity to suggest that a Labour government might not *ipso facto* lead to the total ruination of the country.

"It's his unwillingness to engage in any kind of dialogue that so depresses me," Fran says.

It's Sunday night and we're back in town. Fran's sitting at her vanity doing the arcane things she does there at the end of the day. She's wearing a flannel nightgown and she looks very young, almost schoolgirlish. I'm lying on the bed alternately reading *The Trial* (with which I'm kicking off my dangerously under-subscribed "Isolation and Loneliness" course at City Lit on Tuesday) and watching Fran go through her paces. The argument in question erupted during a pot-luck meal of cold lamb and soapy macaroni and cheese in her parents' Aga dominated kitchen and was dispiriting precisely because it hadn't been an argument at all, merely my father-in-law's ill-tempered regurgitation of High Tory cant.

I watch Fran kneading cold cream into her neck and seeing me in the mirror she cocks her head enquiringly, and there's something in the gesture that reminds me of the day I first met her in a friend's rooms in Newnham. The talk had been self-consciously literary; Fran sat in the window embrasure with her chin on her knees saying little.

Eager to impress I'd said more than enough for both of us. After one particularly clueless remark she looked at me quizzically and said, "You don't *really* mean that, do you?"

"Remember that tea in Nell's rooms?"

"Which one ... oh ... that one. Of course I remember it. I thought we were talking about Daddy and his Labour bashing."

"We were, but let's drop it. As you say it's not very enlightening fare."

Fran nods, but later as we're lying in the dark and I'm sliding off to sleep she says "God, I hope Labour wins the next election" with a vehemence I've rarely heard her express on any subject.

"Don't worry, it will," I mumble as I slip beneath the waves.

In the morning there's more e-mail from Charlie:

Cocteau n'est pas un homme, il est une omelette. Not bad, eh? Tex turns out to be gay. How was Dorset? Here was dreary so I went to Fenway Park but game rained out after second inning could you phone Cassie and ask her to send me the clock radio I left in the bedroom?

I dig out Cassie's number and call her, but she's not in so I leave a message on her answering machine and continue with the desultory preparation of my imminent Cont Ed debut. But my heart's not in it so I go for a walk on the Heath, but apparently my heart's not in that either, so after a few pints and a sandwich at The Holly Bush I go home and read an article in the *New Yorker* about genetic engineering which bores me insensate, so I take a lengthy nap from which I awake grumpy and out of sorts.

That night after dinner we watch a programme about the nearly extinct Siberian tiger followed by the News, then Fran and Cat go to bed and I drink some single malt whisky and settle down to watch something called *The Philadelphia Experiment II* which I think is about the Nazis having won the war. I awake with a headache and a hedgehog in my mouth and drag myself upstairs to bed.

In other words I've seen off another Monday.

The City Literary Institute, to give the place its full title, is housed in an ugly building not far from Holborn. All Souls it may not be, but I'm all too aware that given the state of the market I'm lucky to have landed any job at all. My class turns out to have fleshed out nicely and is comprised of a cross-section of housewives, widows and widowers eyeing each other speculatively, upwardly mobile accountants, and European *au pairs*. There's also a limitlessly ancient man, twisted and bent into the shape of a question mark who I soon identify as Public Nuisance Number One. He has an East End accent you can stand a spoon up in and is chronically incapable of depersonalising either his questions or his answers. Thus Joseph K's not inconsiderable problems are akin to those experienced by our hero, the unnamed city of *The Trial* is in fact London (Shoreditch to be precise), Kafka's father as described by me reminds the old boy of his own Da and so agonisingly on and on. At the break I try to suggest as tactfully as I can that the idea is to encourage general conversation throughout the class.

Because of his corkscrewed torso the man's drained eyes are aligned on a north south axis, so I find myself bending my own neck in an effort to accommodate him.

"Sain' oim 'ogging the loimlight?"

"Not at all, I ..."

"Oldies got roites too, yer know."

"Of course you ..."

"Aigism, I calls it."

"I think that's going a bit ..."

But he doesn't want to know and limps off to get an insipid coffee (or carve someone up with a bicycle chain for all I know), and I'm left wondering why I always assume people with physical disabilities somehow have to be kind and gentle and full of hard-earned wisdom.

"He was in Science and Ethics. Did the same thing there, spoiled the whole class, he did. Nothing personal, Dr Buchan, but I'm transferring out."

"Of course," I say to the middle-aged woman in a Rastafarian tuque who's whispered this piece of intelligence to me in the crowded corridor outside the classroom. And then something gives, something goes pop inside and I'm buggered if I'm going to slog down here three nights a week to be accused of ageism or any other Ism for that matter by a bitter old man in a moth-eaten cardigan with egg stains down the front. I can't recall having wilfully done something as irresponsible since the night years ago when I walked out of Charlie's Parents' Night after being told that my son was 'ineducable', but I now do something irresponsible.

The Princess Louise is crowded: City folk, young men in wide suits (all wearing ties that look as though they've been designed by Max Ernst on a bad hair day), their bosses in better cut suits and fake Hermès ties, bulgy secretaries drinking Hooch and spritzers, some Japanese tourists, a local or two. Feeling deliciously decadent I get a pint and retire to a quiet corner where I savour my beer, my freedom and the *Evening Standard*. I know the guilt will come later, but for the moment my having abandoned "Isolation and Loneliness" to its own devices seems a master stroke. Maybe I'll get a job in a pub, I speculate as I watch the inevitable wraith-pale, carrot-haired Irish youth pulling beer. But of course I won't do anything of the sort. What I will do is apply for a number of jobs for none of which will I have a chance of being short-listed, let alone interviewed. I'll continue writing the current Chester Dillon, I'll take increasingly long, introspective walks on the Heath and do my best to ignore the small but insistent voice at the centre of my being which has been telling me of late that I'm not really *for* anything and so ... but of course I baulk at the next step.

By the time I've downed a second pint, the childishness of what I've done begins to bite. Later as I tramp through the freezing rain to the Tube station, I imagine myself, once word of my betrayal has done the rounds, as the subject of some sort of universal blackballing plot, shunned by far humbler institutions than City Lit. Unemployable. How can I have acted more like a petulant six-year-old than a fifty-year-old man with grown children and liver spots burgeoning on the backs of my hands? Well I have and that, as they say, is that.

The Tube rattles and sways up the Northern Line, and I watch disconsolately as a tall black youth in trainers, out-sized down jacket and reversed Mets baseball cap sullenly shreds his chocolate bar wrapper and methodically flicks the pieces onto the carriage floor. I say nothing.

The rain continues as I make my way through the poorly lit streets of Hampstead. I've forgotten to bring an umbrella and am soaked through before I'm halfway home. Fran left in the morning for a conference in Harrogate and Cat's not yet home. The house feels large and empty. I soak in a hot bath, then get a beer from the fridge and settle down to watch whatever crap is on offer on TV.

Crap it is.

"Dad?"

I awake with a start. Cat's standing in the doorway looking at me curiously, as well she might since we seem to have reversed roles: me the bored couch-potato, she at least up to something, at least upright.

"Hi there. God, what time is it?"

"Round nine. How was your class?"

I tell a plainly impressed Cat about my recent rush of blood, which in the telling sounds even more naff than it played in real life.

"Just like that?"

"Pretty much. I could see that the old guy was going to be a big time pain in the ass and suddenly I just didn't want to put up with it. Know what I mean?"

Cat, who's still in her school tunic, looks at me curiously as if seeing me in an entirely new light, which I suppose is no less than what is happening. Dad as Rebel Without a Cause.

"Sure I do. I'd say on average I feel like that - I call them depiphanies - once or twice a week.'

And I've no doubt she does. Ever since puberty Cat's been a contrarian, has done things the hard way. So, come to think of it, has Charlie although he didn't bother to wait for his balls to drop to make it crystal clear that he was marching to his own often perverse tune.

Cat flops down on the sofa and asks if there's anything decent on TV.

"Negative, unless Chat Show Roulette is your cup of relentless bad taste. What say we go and get something to eat on the High Street?"

Twenty minutes later, after Cat's changed into civvies, we're seated in a warmly babbling, agreeably animated ersatz Parisian brasserie drinking passable plonk. I realise with a faint suture tug of surprise that I'm glad to be here with Cat, content to be alone with my daughter in a Hampstead restaurant on a wet Tuesday night in September. After we order (*steak frites* for her, *saucisse de Toulouse* for me) and have torn apart most of our neighbours, the conversation veers back to the consequences of my little psychodrama of earlier in the evening.

"So, watcha going to do now?"

"Oh, I'll think of something," I reply weakly.

"Like what?" Cat asks, spearing a ketchup-smothered nosegay of fries and cramming them into her mouth.

Like what indeed? Where, I wonder desperately, has my sense of the excitement of simply being alive and healthy in a world of infinite promise gone?

"Hell-o? Da-ad?"

"Sorry. Where were we?"

"You said you'd find something to do with the rest of your life, and I asked what that might be?"

"To be honest, I'm not sure. I'm feeling a little bit ... oh, I don't know ... out of the loop ... disconnected."

"It shows. You've gone off life as you've known it precisely because life's no longer as you've known it."

I blink as Cat shovels another bundle of fries down the hatch. Her eyes really are an extraordinary shade of blue.

"Is it that obvious?" I finally manage, feeling decidedly put out that what I imagine is my hidden, stoically borne disquiet is apparently as obvious as a neon sign in Piccadilly Circus.

"*Jawohl*. You're classic MLC material all the way."

"ML ... oh, I get it: Mid-life Crisis. Very funny, very droll."

"I wasn't trying to be funny, but I guess I must have sounded a bit flippant. Lots of my friends' parents are going through the same thing. Suzy Retzhoff's Dad hasn't put a foot out of the house for over six months and Jason's Mum ..."

Can this really be happening to me? Can my sixteen-year-old daughter really be sitting there calmly telling me (sounding like some cut-rate Hermann Hesse into the bargain) that not only have I lost the way but that it shows and, unkindest cut of all, I'm actually a member of a readily identifiable sub-sect.

"Okay, okay. Since you seem to be the expert on mid-life crises, why don't you tell me what you think I should be doing?"

But she just shrugs dismissively and scans the dessert section of the menu.

"Cat?"

"Come on Dad give us a break. It's your life."

Is it? Is it really? Well if the truth be known it feels like the tag end of someone else's, not mine at all. The sense of otherness I experience is chilling.

"Dessert? Coffee?"

"Sure, I'll have the *flan caramelisé*. D'you think Charlie and La Cassamassima will survive the great schism? *Mon Dieu, quelle chanson et danse.* You'd think no one had ever been separated before."

Obviously she's gone as far as she wants to go down the stony path of the state of my psyche. Well that's fine by me, but it's unsettling to have one's own daughter - to whom an eye blink ago, wreathed in delicious post-bath scents and curled up in your lap, you were reading *Swallows and Amazons* - read *you* like a Grade One primer.

Over coffee we agree that Charlie and Cassie's relationship is probably doomed to the well-populated scrap heap of transatlantic love affairs.

As we're walking home beneath a now beautiful night sky, Cat puts her arm through mine, something she hasn't done for a long time, and falls into stride with me.

"Dad?"

"Yes?"

"Guess what?"

"Andrew Marr's got Britain's most self-satisfied smirk?"

"Well, yeah, there's that, but also the fact that I'm sorry if I came on a teeny bit strong back in the restaurant but I'm worried about you, I really am."

I'm more moved than I can say. We're standing in a puddle of light beneath a lamppost on the corner of Frognal and Church Walk. I put my arms around her and give her a hug, and my heart's suddenly full to bursting and I've a lump in my throat.

"Thanks Cat. But you needn't worry about me, I'm as tough as old boots."

"Sure?"

"Yup."

"Well, if you say so. Now, what about the rave you and Mum don't want me to go to?"

But she's only winding me up so we go arm-in-arm back to the house and I'm grateful for her solicitude although I can't help thinking that I must be in worse shape than I thought I was.

Later, as I'm in bed dozing off with my book digging into my ribs and my specs adorning my mouth, I'm jolted awake by the annoyingly cheerful warble (whatever happened to the common or garden ring?) of the phone. It's Fran, late after a conference-related dinner. As ever when she phones from these things, I listen for the heavy breathing of the russet bearded fellow Family Counsellor who's plied her with Chianti whatever over ravioli whatever at the San wherever and is lying hairy and horny on the bed next to her. I'm never disappointed to be disappointed, only ashamed to have projected my own occasional peccadilloes onto her.

Fran's had a rough day. Her paper was poorly received, the workshop she went to worse than useless, her lunchtime stroll through Harrogate marred by a downpour, the dinner inedible, the hotel grubby. When she's all grumped out, I tell her somewhat diffidently about my City Lit moment of madness.

Silence.

"Fran?"

"Right here. Keir, d'you know what you've done?"

"Sure I do. I've reneged on my contract."

"Yes, but I was thinking more that you've deliberately ..."

"Hang on. This was no more premeditated than hurricane whatever they're calling the latest one."

"Well, at least allow that you were predisposed to let this irritating old gent get up your nose. So now you're well and truly cut adrift, the better to feel sorry for yourself ..."

"Thanks for sharing that with me, Family Counsellor Fran," I respond testily.

"Oh, Keir, don't. I'm not criticising, just pointing out what your actions look like from the outside."

"Mad?"

"No, just very, very sad."

Ha! What does she know about sad? What does Fran with her cheery, forthright disposition and her touching belief in logical solutions to everything from erectile dysfunctionality to rising damp understand about the world in the evening?

We talk some more but I've lost interest. I'm not sulking, just fed to the teeth and frightened by something, I know not what, stirring inside me.

"I'll try to get away from this damn thing early, maybe take a taxi over to York and catch the Intercity. Bye now. Love you."

"I love you too and ..."

But she's hung up. I replace the receiver, park my book and glasses on the bedside table and turn out the light. I lie in the dark and listen to the familiar sounds of the house. And then with a sickening sense of disbelief, I realise that I no longer care whether Fran loves me or not. For more than a quarter of a century Fran and I have been a number, and now suddenly I am no longer part of the equation, have lost my capacity to be loved. And I'm scared witless.

Morning comes all too soon. I awake bathed in sweat after a sleep riven by hectic dreams none of which I can remember. As if to mock the chaos within, the day has dawned as bright and fresh as a newly minted coin. I linger in bed resentful of the gaily twittering of birds in the garden. I hear Cat haring through her mandatory late-for-school routine and know that I should get up and do fatherly things, but I do not. Cannot.

"Dad, you okay?" she calls through the bedroom door.

"Fine. Lousy sleep though. See you tonight."

A PERFECT SENTENCE

She chirps something I don't catch, clatters down the stairs and out the front door slamming it so hard the ceiling light jumps in protest. Clickity-clack, clickity-clack, squeak of the wrought-iron garden gate (must get some WD-40), clang of gate, receding clickity-clack. She's gone, and I'm alone in the house I bought with the money the mother I hardly knew left me when she died adrift in a fog of Alzheimer's in a distant nursing home. I close my eyes all too aware that further sleep will not be an option. The Radio clicks on, the *andante* of the Mozart clarinet concerto coils into the room, and I am suddenly seized by the need to have done with it all, to be on the other side. Beyond is definitely where I want to be, and I'm surprisingly unsurprised.

The phone obtrudes. An administrator at the City Lit would like to know what I think I'm up to. I tell him that I haven't the faintest idea what I'm up to and suggest that he take a flying fuck at a rolling doughnut. Then I stagger downstairs and into the kitchen where I brew a pot of coffee and take a swig of Poire William from the bottle in the fridge.

Steaming mug of coffee in hand, I wander around the garden observing the flora without interest. The alcohol on an empty stomach makes me feel giddy and slightly unwell. An hour later I am still standing in the garden, a stone cold half mug of coffee in my hand.

Later still I put in a desultory stint at my desk paying bills, trying to balance accounts, sending condescending amounts of money to various charities, scanning catalogues, but I'm aware that what I'm doing is avoiding the only account that matters at the moment.

Normally Hampstead Heath is one of my favourite places. I love its semi-wild vistas ending in distant church spires or sudden breathtaking wedges of London. I love the ponds edged with urban fisher folk who I've never seen catch anything, and the long raking sweeps of open land with dogs racing here and there and wellied owners toiling in their wakes. But now as I trudge across the Heath with the sun blazing out of a borage blue sky, I feel only disgust. The leaves have already begun to turn, and the open spaces have long since been scorched by the summer sun to tawny tracts of grassland more appropriate to Argentine pampas than Central London.

I pause at the men's pond, and it's there watching a few hardy sportsmen swimming about in the gelid looking water that I run out of ways of pretending that I'm anything other than desperate. In fact I despair, which is a long, long way north of being desperate.

In other words, as the crows in the nearby trees caw for all to hear, I might as well be dead.

In other words, I might as well be dead.

In other words.

Dead.

I watch a man with an enormous belly walk to the end of the diving board. He stands there white and bulbous, bobbing slightly while he talks to someone in the water. Then with a cry he dives in producing an untidy splash, and I cannot make any sense of what I've just seen. Large man dives into Hampstead pool. Large man dives into Hampstead pool observed by lost man groping his way towards unbeing. Large man dives into. Large man. Man.

An hour, perhaps two hours later, I'm still sitting on the wooden bench. A line of puffy clouds strung like laundry on a clothesline is moving slowly across the southern horizon. The pool is empty save one capped swimmer just now rounding the last marker.

There is much that I regret, but now that seems unimportant. I remember reading somewhere that suicides, once they have made up their minds, once they know they won't turn back, commonly enter into a state of grace and act with great calm and deliberation.

A PERFECT SENTENCE

So, calmly, deliberately I walk back across the Heath. Crossing the High Street I spot our neighbour, Sam Cohn, going into The King of Bohemia, and we exchange neighbourly waves. What the hell is Sam, a stockbroker in the City, doing up here at two o'clock on a Wednesday afternoon?

I return to the house in a mood of quiet exultation. There will be no notes, no copy of *Malone Dies* on the bedside table, no histrionics. A dignified exit is in order.

The sleeping pills are the remains of a two-year-old prescription I gave up on after a few days. Who knows, perhaps I didn't throw them out with precisely this scenario lurking in the uncharted shipping lanes of my mind. I've never seriously thought of taking my own life before, but perhaps at some darker level the thing has been germinating like a seed in winter soil. Certainly it now feels like an idea whose time has come.

I swallow the entire bottle of pills in three gulps, washing each down with a draught of Talisker. Then I lie down on our bed. Radio 3 will see me out nicely. A maddeningly familiar violin concerto is playing. Bruch? Brahms? Sibelius? Jamie and I walking along the tracks in the twilight ... Cat at dinner last night ... Mother's vacuous stare ... Fran reading on the veranda ... Charlie's girl by Lake Garda sipping her Pepsi through a coloured straw ... time to go ... time to sign off ...

CHAPTER SIX

As I swim up through layer after layer of dense fog I'm aware that there's something wrong, that something is seriously amiss. Lalo's Symphonie espagnole, that's what it is, not Brahms or Bruch. But that was ... oh, Christ, this must mean that I'm still on this side, still breathing in and breathing out.

I open my eyes.

Bare white room. Head banging like a jack hammer. Mouth puckered, dry and tasting of sick. Damn. More failure to contend with. A fitting epitaph: he couldn't even do the goods on himself. Well I was serious enough then, but do I now detect a flicker of relief?

"Keir?"

Ouch! Fran's sitting in a moulded plastic chair by the window with her hands folded in her lap. Behind her is the dark rectangle of the window and beyond that lights twinkling afar.

"Hello, Fran. Where the hell am I?"

"The Royal Free. I'm sorry."

"Whatever for?"

"That I didn't realise how ... well ... desperately unhappy you were ... are ..."

"Well, if the truth be known, neither did I. Not until today that is. It all went ... well, let's just say very fast. What happened?'

Apparently I owe my life to a second consecutive sub-standard workshop at Fran's conference. Normally she's the least rash of people and only very rarely does things on the spur of the moment, but shoddy professionalism Fran cannot abide, so when it became clear that the facilitator of The Semiotics of Body Language was talking through his hat she became the second Buchan to do a bunk in less than twenty-four hours and left the conference in a hurry and a huff.

So it was that she returned to London hours earlier than expected, only to find me out for considerably more than the count with the radio playing Javanese gamelan music and, eerily due to some malfunction of the answering machine, her own voice repeating her message saying that she was on the train from York and would be home in a few hours.

"What time is it?"

"Past seven. They pumped your stomach out."

"They would, wouldn't they?"

Fran stands up. Coming to the bedside, she takes my hot damp hands in her cool dry ones, and her eyes are very large and have clearly been to and returned from somewhere very new. I tell her that I'm glad she came home when she did.

She shrugs, a tiny gesture tinged with pathos, and says, "Are you sure?"

"Very," I say.

And I am although I'm at a loss to explain why. Less than five hours ago I was eager to be dead and gone, and now I'm content, no, I'm actively happy to be alive.

"How d'you feel?"

"Shaky and not a little foolish. Does Cat know?"

She nods and looks away; and I can't help wondering how my daughter will be affected by having been exposed to what I'm told is an act of supreme selfishness but which I have to admit at the time seemed little more than a public service. In the event, a kind of bemused anger seems to be Cat's chief reaction to my bungled attempt to take my life.

"Dad, you're weird. We had a really nice dinner last night, and this morning you said 'See you tonight' and then you go off and guzzle a bottle of sleeping pills ... Jeez!"

Cat and I are sitting at the kitchen table. Fran is fiddling around at the sink. This being England it's raining. On the radio someone's going on about Euro Wets and Welsh cheese.

"Listen, Cat, I've already told you that I hadn't a clue, not the faintest inkling, that I was going to do what I did until much later ... on the Heath ... I was watching some guys swimming in the pool, and I couldn't connect, just couldn't figure out what anything meant in relation to anything else. And I wanted out."

But she's not buying that. It doesn't coincide with her sixteen-year-old *Weltanschauung*.

"People don't just go for walks on Hampstead Heath and suddenly say 'hey-ho, time to go' and top themselves. They don't, they just do not."

"Well that's what I did, more or less, so at least one person does. I'm not saying I'm proud of it, and I'm sorry for the hassle I've caused, but remember you did say I was classic MLC material so you could say that I simply lived up to my billing."

Cat looks at me through narrowed eyes, and I can see that I've frightened her by somehow implicating her in my act of irrationality.

"What's wrong with you anyway?" she asks sulkily.

"I guess that's for me to find out."

And it is.

The following afternoon at Fran's insistence and to my private consternation (I don't think I'm ready for a debriefing) we fly to Venice for a few days in the only city I know that never fails to deliver.

And I am duly enchanted as the *vaporetto* fusses back and forth across the Grand Canal and Fran and I stand in the stern watching the impossible succession of *palazzi* gently brushed by the last rays of the afternoon sun. It's passing odd to think that but for a poorly prepared facilitator at a family counselling conference in Yorkshire I wouldn't be here, or anywhere else for that matter. As the *vaporetto* grinds to our stop, I reflect that the Bard got it wrong; it's luck, not ripeness, that is all.

Our room in an *albergo* near the *Accademia* is high ceilinged and beamed and gives onto a little green canal with a glimpse of the busy Grand one beyond. We dine in a nearby restaurant and afterwards walk to Florian's for a nightcap.

Fran sips her liqueur and stares past me. I drink my beer, look past her and see me sipping beer in the mirror behind her head. We speak at the same time.

"You first."

"No, after you."

Our eyes engage, break off, re-engage. Again we start speaking simultaneously.

"The thing of it is …"

"Maybe we …"

"The thing is you've gone off me, haven't you?" she says sadly.

Her gaze is steady now, blue and unflinching yet brushed by hurt. I'm not ready for this. When are we ever ready for it?

She shakes her head impatiently. "Oh, for God's sake, there's no law that says people have to go on loving each …"

But she's wrong. That is not it, is too simple, too linear.

"No, Fran. It's not that I don't still love you because I do. At least in my own doubtless insufficient way I do. It's the receiving part of me that's on the blink. Oh, I can feel the messages coming in but I seem to have lost the capacity to be moved by them."

She considers this, looks into the depths of her amaretto, runs a slim finger around the rim, and then slowly raising her gaze asks, "Why? What on earth has changed?"

"I haven't the foggiest," I answer truthfully. "It simply came to me that I'm running on empty, that I've lost the knack of needing, and I knew I didn't want to go on being like that."

"And now, how d'you feel right now?"

"Good question. Chastened, confused, frightened, most of me glad to be back from the edge, some small part of me sorry not to have gone over it, got it over with. All of the above."

She nods and taking my hands in hers says quietly, "You know broken things can be fixed, batteries recharged, but you have to want it to happen, you have to be willing to work at it, try to glue the pieces together, make the connections. Are you?"

"I think so but I can't be sure."

It's not much of an answer, but it's the best I can manage at the moment.

So for three days Fran and I gorge ourselves on *La Serenissima's* particular and affecting marriage of stone and sea and sky. We admire the Tintorettos in San Rocco, walk the length off the Lido in a storm, indulge in a usuriously priced tea at Danieli, get lost in the ghetto, lunch on Torcello and pass on the Harry's experience.

On our last night, I awake at three with my heart thumping madly. I lie waiting for the attack to recede, which after a wild ride it does. Patterns of light flicker and dance on the ceiling. I hear the sound of a launch growling along the Grand Canal. Fran is asleep on her back, one thin shoulder outside the covers, short hair half covering her face, her breathing steady and even. I wonder what she's making of all this. Since that first night at Florian's, we've talked about just about everything except my failed suicide. The last thing on my mind had been to lay a guilt trip on her, but I can see that even for someone as balanced as Fran having your partner of many years try and very nearly succeed to delete himself from your life must make you think, must call into question some fairly fundamental assumptions.

I slip out of bed and pad to the window. The ornate lamp over the *albergo's* entrance casts a semicircle of light onto the stone quay and out to the jade green water beyond. A barge laden to the gunwales muscles down the Grand Canal, its running lights eerie sentinels, the helmsman a dark figure hunched over the rudder. Across the way an old woman in a beige dressing-gown waters her geraniums, and I can't help wondering what crippling bout of insomnia has caused her to do this at such an ungodly hour. A black cat ghosts across the courtyard, a distant church bell chimes.

"What's wrong?"

Fran's sleepy voice floats to me out of the darkness.

"Nothing."

"Come back to bed."

I do. She's warm and smells of sleep and Nivea cream and a perfume I can't identify.

"What was it?"

"Bad dream. Okay now."

"Mmm ... I'm glad ...'night."

The flight home takes us directly over our old friend Lake Garda. Miles below we can see the blue Rorschach blob of the lake and the vague smudge which is the town of Riva at its northern tip.

Fran shakes her head and says, "Lord, doesn't it all go so bloody fast."

It's not a question, and anyway she's right. Don't look away lest you miss the main event. Blink and it'll already be tomorrow. I close my eyes and see as clearly as if it were this morning Fran in my digs overlooking Parker's Piece after we've made love for the first time. She's draped on the sofa totally unembarrassed by her nakedness. I'm fumbling around looking for cigarettes and a lighter. Late afternoon summer sunlight streams in through the tall windows and ricochets around the room. Our clothes are scattered everywhere, Fran's bra hangs from the ceiling lamp. I am that skinny long-haired youth scuttling around the room wondering whether my dick's up to scratch and already worrying about not having used a rubber. And now nearly thirty years later we're here, wherever that may be.

The drinks trolley arrives.

"Keir?"

I guess Fran's got more than red, white, or rosé on her mind.

"Yes?"

"Listen, I know what you're thinking ..."

"Well, that makes one of you."

"Don't. I know you think I'm an unimaginative, bean-counting sort of family Counsellor, and I certainly wouldn't deny I'm a pragmatic person, but that doesn't mean I don't understand, no recognise, that there are more things in heaven and earth than are dreamed of etcetera, etcetera ...'

"I've never for a moment thought ..."

"Be quiet and listen. As you well know, what you did last week is wholly alien to me, unthinkable, and yet you did do it. You tried, very nearly successfully, to take your own life, and I've got to take that on board, accept at least some of the responsibility because it's not as though we've been living on different planets, not as though we haven't been in this together. I don't know what the future holds for us - right now I'm not getting the most positive of vibes but perhaps I'm reading that one wrong too – however, I want you to know that I can think of nothing sadder than our continuing together because you feel sorry for me ..."

Fran's voice trails off. The plane continues to roar westward, now over the neat decimalised quilt of rural France. I tell her how busy I am feeling plenty sorry for myself and assure her that she's in no way to blame for my emotional outage.

"Who or what is, then?" she asks intently.

I shrug. Nothing just happens for Fran.

"Search me."

"I wish you'd let me."

But it's too late, and I think we both know it.

Not long afterwards as we're free-falling down towards Heathrow through an impenetrable cloud, Fran, who has never liked this part of the miracle of modern mobility, holds my hand tight while I, knowing as I do what dying is like, am not afraid.

***

Get a load of this: the actor Robert Taylor's real name was Spengler Arlington Bough! And this: Stewart Granger's real name was … wait for it … James Stewart!!! How was Venice? Spent last Saturday pm in the Isabelle Stewart Gardner museum fab JS Sargent Whistler after to Durgin Park with Tex for lousy chowder please accept C's invite if only for my sake also pick up clock radio luv C.

Sure enough, among our telephone messages there's one from Cassie asking us to dinner at a date of our choosing. As Fran says, under those conditions it would be hard to refuse (which is what we both would prefer to do) even if it weren't for Charlie's pathetic plea that we go. What can he conceivably gain from our spending an evening with his girlfriend?

And so one night at the end of October we take the Tube to Covent Garden. Unused to an efficient Northern Line, we arrive with half an hour to spare. After locating Hanover Place (an alley near the stage door to the Opera House), we go to a nearby pub where I get stuck into a large whisky.

"Come on, it won't be that bad."

"Oh yes, it will."

"Nonsense. She's a perfectly nice girl, and it's sweet of her to ask us to dinner."

"Maybe, but I'd rather be watching football."

"But you don't even like footie."

"My very point."

I fear the worst as we tramp up three poorly lit, foul-smelling flights of stairs.

"Sorry about that. The folks downstairs are very partial to curry."

I'd forgotten just how attractive Cassie Laporte is. She's wearing black leather trousers, a white sleeveless polo shirt under which she's very clearly in what Cat refers to as full SS (*sans soutien-gorge*) mode. Her shoulder-length hair has been fluffed and frizzed into an extraordinary pre-Raphaelite happening.

Fran kisses her and hands over some potential daffs and says how much she likes the new hairstyle.

"Do you? I'm not sure about it, but a change was in order."

I give her the bottle of wine I'd picked up at Oddbins and we exchange social pecks.

"Why thank you. Be it ever so humble, but come on in."

The room into which we advance is entirely lit by candlelight. There must be twenty-five or thirty tapers flickering in sconces on the walls and candlesticks and saucers around the room, and the effect is enchanting. There's a sofa covered with a colourful Rajasthani throw, a low beaten-brass coffee table, some squishy paisley covered cushions on the floor, a pretty kilim, and the usual suspects (Steinberg on NYC and the rest of the US of A, Ansel Adams on Yosemite National Park, Munch on angst) on the walls. It's charming and totally unlike the fifties appointed (Melamine and blond wood) studenty horror I'd for some reason convinced myself it was going to be.

"Oh, and this is Lance."

A tall figure has materialised in the archway leading to what is obviously a galley kitchen. He's wearing a denim shirt, jeans and cowboy boots and bears an uncommon resemblance to the youthful Sam Shepard. We shake hands with him while Cassie explains that she and Lance go back a long way (I'll just bet they do) and that he'd appeared from the States unexpectedly this very morning.

Of course Lance speaks with a creamy Southern drawl, lives alone somewhere on the Washington State coast and writes acclaimed short stories when he's not going out with the fishing fleet, improving the environmentally correct log cabin he built with his own hands, or brushing up on his Sanskrit.

Actually he turns out to be a nice, if seriously jet-lagged guy with a good line in self-deprecatory humour and some very funny stories about life in a fishing village in the Pacific Northwest. There's lots of wine going around, and after a few glasses I find myself mesmerised by the play of candlelight on Cassie's amazing head of hair and get caught staring by Fran.

Dinner is served at a scarred pine table in the kitchen and is *pasta* free (how did she know I loathe the stuff?) and delicious (leek soup, chicken diabolo, saffron rice). Somewhere in there I take a trip to the loo which is through the bedroom. Uncomfortably I think of Charlie. Charlie and his lady shagging, to be exact. Double bed with gaily striped duvet neatly in place, vanity made of tea chests, full-length Victorian mirror, obviously home-made curtains, ditto complicated looking cupboard and storage arrangement. Unframed poster from the Hockney exhibition at the Royal Academy. Lance's backpack is propped up in the corner. American Airlines identity disk with the Hanover Place address as Destination. Well *he* knew where he was going even if she didn't. I take a leak, slosh some water on my face and realise that I've shipped a fair few *décis* of wine.

After cheese Lance yawns and stretches and says, 'Nine am, my time. Think I'll turn in if y'all don't mind.'

Fran and I look horrified that it could conceivably be ten o'clock and make appropriate leaving sounds. But Cassie won't hear of it.

"Lance can kip in my room. I'll use the hide-a-bed. Off you go stud."

So Lance says what a pleasure it's been and toddles off to bed, and we have coffee and Calvados (which I need like psoriasis) in the living-room and listen to some country and western, which I usually dislike but which sounds okay to me now, and then I'm smoking a joint and listening to Cassie complain about Charlie's telephone habits.

"I mean, he phones two, three times a week, and he knows I'm bad on the blower. He gets up like at three in the morning to catch me before I leave for work. Not my best time. And then there are the letters."

"What letters?' I hear myself asking fuzzily. Across the room, Fran seems to be trying to tell me something.

Cassie takes a huge drag on the joint and says, "That's just it, he wants me to write all the time. Real letters not e-mails."

"Real letters?" I'm losing it fast.

She makes a face saying "Yeah, you know, stuff written on paper, stamped, mailed and all that, and they've got to be gushy. I'm not much good at that either."

I feel immensely sorry for poor pining Charlie checking out Boston museums and rained out baseball games while the Sam Shepards of the world breeze into town and his girl may or may not be telling the truth. Waiting for the postman.

We leave soon after that. Brassy, brutish Soho flashes and jangles outside the taxi like a diorama by way of George Grosz and the *Big Issue*. Not having smoked dope for some twenty years, I'm feeling pretty ropey.

"Serves you right."

"No doubt."

"Why, Keir, why?"

"Why what?"

"You didn't much like the stuff way back when, so why tonight?"

"Seemed like a good idea at the time. Damn, we forgot to get Charlie's ... uh ... radio thing."

"I imagine he'll survive just fine without it," Fran opines frostily.

Later making superhuman effort to connect, I ask her what she made of the evening.

"Perfectly pleasant until, that is, you decided to go native." She replies tartly.

"Come on, Fran ..." I barely manage before a tidal wave of mission-specific nausea rolls in and I have to ask the driver to stop, and I stagger out of the taxi and execute what my children used to call a technicolour yawn near the gates to the American Ambassador's residence in Regent's Park.

Returning unsteadily to the taxi I mumble "Certain elements of refurbishment, ma'am". Fran chortles, and I know I'm forgiven by her if not by me.

**

In early November I finish the current Chester Dillon and send it off to the publishers. It's not bad as such lightweight fare goes, and certainly we can use the money, but I'm fresh out of ideas now. Anyway, for the moment at least, I've had enough of the bumbling jackass of a detective.

Ever the activist, Fran signs me up as a driver for Camden Meals on Wheels, so three times a week I do the rounds of the nether reaches of the borough with a Trinidadian wonderfully named Dawn Hyacinth, whose speech I'm only now beginning to understand so broad and complex is her West Indian accent. Not,

I admit, what you'd call a notably full and active life but it's all I can manage at the moment, and when all's said and done, many lives are a lot less interesting and almost all are infinitely less comfortable. I still wake up in the middle of the night with my heart doing its damnedest to get out of my chest and I still haul myself around the Heath in all weathers often looking and feeling like hell. And yes, I still have regular weekly therapy sessions with Harvey who claims I'm doing very well, whatever that might mean. And from time to time I catch Cat peeking at me with a mixture of perplexity and apprehension, but she needn't worry because having been that route I'm no longer interested in it. As she herself would say, 'Been there, done that, got the T-shirt.'

One day in mid-November Charlie's e-mail waxes desperate: *No jokes today. Worried sick about Cassie. Can't get through will phone tomorrow eight am yr time.* I relent: why did the barmaid champagne? Because the stout porter bitter. Ha, ha, ha!

Not bad but actually it doesn't really work because the unfortunate girl would hardly need to *sham* pain if some oaf of a porter really took a hunk out of her.

Once again, poor Charlie.

I phone Cassie and sure enough there's no answer, no nothing, not even a recorded message. But isn't she allowed to take a break, take Eurostar to Paris, pop over to Amsterdam to purchase some especially plosive dope, visit friends in Scunthorpe? Still that's not the point, and I know it. As far as Charlie's concerned she's AWOL, and that's all there is to it. Cat claims her brother's well out of it, and when I ask why she just shrugs and says, "La Cassamassima's one tough *hombre.*"

"What's that supposed to mean?"

"That I think she got pretty badly burned by her Etonian cad or whatever he was and is fucked, if you'll *pardonnez mon anglais*, if she's going to let herself be burned again."

"A: pardon not granted. B: Charlie's not a cad."

Cat bestows her pained Stephen Sackur coping with a low-wattage junior minister look on me and replies, "I don't think she's ready to be loved the way Charlie loves her, or thinks he does."

"And how might that be?"

"Oh, you know, Exclusively, Bespokedly, By Appointmentedly, that way."

Fran agrees. She looks at me over the top of her book (Elena Ferrante's latest) and says, "Cat's spot on. I don't think the timing's right for her - I know it isn't for him – but that doesn't explain why she doesn't answer the phone."

"I'm sure there's a perfectly good reason."

"Yes, dear."

As I knew it would the phone rings at precisely eight the next morning. Charlie sounds crazed, and the thought crosses my mind that he's stoned or thereabouts. Or maybe just hung over. Either way he gets right to the point.

"Dad, would you mind going down there, to Hanover Place I mean, to see if ... check out ... oh, I don't know ... to see what you can see? She should be there, like Tuesday's her day off. Maybe the phone's out of order or disconnected ... for some reason but her cell's not working either. Please, I'm at my wit's end."

I try to calm him down and assure him that I'll go down to Covent Garden right after my dentist appointment in the morning. I want to say something cheerful without sounding unfeeling or, worse, condescending, but the boy's in no mood to be humoured, so I pass him on to his mother and head for the shower.

The dentist is brutal, and I leave with a temporary crown in place and my head feeling as if I've just walked into a Mike Tyson jab. Also the right side of my face is frozen into what feels like the grin of a precocious half-wit.

I take a bus to Marble Arch whence, since it's a beautiful soft-edged fall day, I decide to walk the rest of the way. I angle down through Mayfair marvelling as I always do in that part of the world (or indeed in my own neck of the woods) just how much money there is in the world and just how few people have real access to it. Soho's raunchy bustle is more pleasing to me, and I stop for a coffee and a gawk at the passing parade. I reflect that almost everyone looks as though they're up to no, or at the very least not much, good - even PA's, temps and office boys on their breaks.

And then to my utter amazement I realise that I'm looking at my father-in-law who is on the far side of the street engrossed in the menu of a Lebanese restaurant in which I happen to know he wouldn't be seen dead. Kenneth's wearing the Pop-Up-To-Town uniform of his caste: matured and aggressively polished brown brogues, cavalry twills, slightly loud checked sport's jacket, graph paper Viyella shirt, V-necked fawn pullover and striped tie surely denoting membership to some laddish coven.

I'm about to finish off my coffee and go across the street for a friendly natter when something in his manner stays me. In fact I raise my *Guardian* and peek around it feeling like a character in an Inspector Clouseau movie. But that's okay because it seems Kenneth has the same flic in mind. I don't remember ever seeing anyone look so transparently shifty. He's moved down the street and is now standing in front of a building of singular unattractiveness with painted in windows (unlike its neighbours it sports no advertisements for anything at all) and a short flight of stairs leading down to double metal doors one of which has a small one way window in it. Kenneth's got his hands clasped behind his back and his handsome white haired head is swivelling back and forth like one of those toy dogs some people insist on putting in the back windows of their cars.

Hello, hello, what have we here?

And then I finally get it: Daddy's on his way IN. Daddy's going to spend some quality time ... hey presto! He's gone! Disappeared like Alice down her rabbit hole. Gone in for a spot of slap and tickle with Maytai or Sharon (or both of them) before the two fifty-five from Charing Cross, and I'm utterly beguiled. I didn't think the old boy had it in him. I wait a few minutes and then walk past the building. The place oozes sleaze, badness. This isn't your Girls, Girls, Girls, your Adult Videos and Poppers, your Live Pole Dancing. This is the real deal: come for cash. That one Kimberly Philip Tickell is licensed to sell beer and spirits on the premises is the only concession to the passing public, otherwise the building might just as easily be one of the many disused ones in the area. And my septuagenarian ex-banker of a father-in-law is in there probably lashed to a bedstead with his Old Fartist tie and his cock in some twelve-year-old Malay girl's mouth.

I'm still lost in admiration for mankind's infinite variety as I press the Laporte, C buzzer at Cassie's building in Hanover Place. There's no reply, then I remember that it was out of order when we were there before, so I give the door a shove and it turns out to be on the latch. There's a pile of junk mail on the floor and instinctively I bend down and tidy it up. RNIB, Mencap, Age Concern, Save the Children, letter for Mr. G. Patel from India, letter for Ms. Cassie Laporte from ... Charles K. Buchan, 12 Main St., Cambridge, Mass., 02138, USA. Wishing I'd not agreed to this particular mercy mission I go on up the steep stairs. The Patels are cooking up a storm: quiddity of curry hangs thick and sub-continental in the airless stairwell. Once at Cassie's landing I listen at the door. Not a sound. I knock hoping against hope that she won't be there so that I can get away with leaving a note.

I knock again, softly so as not to be heard.

Not a peep. Just fine by me. I go down on one knee in the gloom and begin writing a note: *Dear Cassie, Charlie asked me to stop by* ...

Just then the door opens and Cassie is standing in a blaze of sunlight with her wild eerie of hair lit from behind and seemingly on fire. She's barefoot and wearing a mid-thigh length T-shirt (Imperial College Rowing) and has clearly just woken up.

"What the fuck ... oh, hello, Keir. What on earth are you doing down there?"

"Your mail," I say sheepishly handing her Charlie's letter which she takes with a faint wrinkle of her nose.

"Well don't just stand there ... come on in ... Christ, what time is it anyway?"

"Past twelve. I don't want to bother you ..."

"You're not. I'll fix some coffee."

As I follow her through the sitting-room (full ashtray, *two* empty wine bottles), I can't help noticing through the open door to the bedroom one slim brown foot poking out from beneath the duvet. In the kitchen Cassie busies herself with the coffee while I sit at the table and try not to look shocked.

"You look shocked," she announces.

"Well, I'm not."

She shrugs, "Have it your own way. Sugar?"

"No thanks. Listen, Cassie, I only came here because Charlie phoned this morning saying he hasn't been able to get through and he's ..."

"I forgot to pay BT and they cut me off. Plus I lost my cell last week and haven't got around to buying a new one. Like end of mystery."

"I see, well will you ... could you ... give him a call from a box, or better still come and have dinner with us and call from our house?"

"Thanks but there's no need for that, they reconnected me late last night."

She stretches mightily. I hear the shower go on in the bathroom and then a lovely haunting voice singing something in a language I don't recognise.

"Amharic. Ethiopian to you. Why can't Chuck just relax? Let the cards fall as and where they may? Like can't he see that this ... hounding me is ... oh, I don't know, counterproductive?"

"I guess not. He's in love."

Cassie shrugs again, lights a cigarette and blurts out almost angrily, "Know what I think ... I think Charlie's like in love with being in love, and I know he's three thousand miles away."

I don't know what to say, so I look at my hands which aren't a whole lot of help. It's true that Charlie's made a meal out of his obsession for this girl, but then why the hell shouldn't he? It's not every day that a guy falls in love, and it's only once one falls in love for the first time.

"Hi, Miriam, this is Keir, Charlie's dad."

The foot which I'd glimpsed in the bedroom is attached to one of the longest, tallest, drop-dead gorgeous Sallys I've ever set eyes on. Miriam's over six feet tall, slender as a haiku, with copper brown skin and enormous fly-away eyes set in a face of chiselled, patrician beauty. Her black hair is cut very short and gelled.

We shake hands. Miriam asks to be remembered to Charlie. She's in a hurry, so she gulps down a cup of coffee, gives Cassie a whisper of a kiss, me a smile to die for and disappears.

"Wow!"

Cassie makes a funny face and says, "She's nice too."

And then I surprise myself by asking her if she'd like to have lunch with me.

She observes me from behind half closed eyes as if trying to measure me against some interior yardstick and then says pensively "Sure, why not?" and adds, "on one condition though."

"Shoot."

"We don't talk about Charlie."

Silently I beg my son's forgiveness and attempt to lessen the guilt by asking her to promise to get in touch with him.

"Okay, you've got a deal. I'll phone this evening. In the meanwhile I'd better get dressed."

I wander around the kitchen. Stare out the window. See if I can read any of Charlie's letter (I can't). Flip through the Oxford University calendar on the wall. Yesterday's entry: M. for dinner. Today's: recover. I try not to think about the two of them together (fail).

Then Cassie calls from the bedroom, "Get yourself a beer and while you're at it bring me one too. Hair of the mastiff and all that good shit."

I get two beers out of the fridge and dither at the half open bedroom door. What am I supposed to do put the bottle on the floor like an offering to Santa?

"Oh, for heaven's sake come in, I won't bite."

Feeling awkward I push the door open with a knee and go into the room. Cassie's sitting in front of the mirror brushing her hair. She's wearing a short leather skirt but has nothing on top except her hair. Her breasts defy gravity and her large sloe-coloured nipples stand out from their areolas like acorns. I hand her a San Miguel.

"Cheers. Be with you in a sec."

Ten minutes later we emerge into the wan afternoon light. Groaning, Cassie squints and scratches around in her handbag for dark glasses.

"Phew, that feels better. Well?"

I say that I know a passable French place not far away.

"Lead on McBuchan, I'm famished."

She puts an arm through mine, and as we set off through Covent Garden's crowded lanes I realise that the ache in my mouth has gone.

CHAPTER SEVEN

The restaurant is just as I remember it, which is to say under-lit and over-priced. The *maitre d'* offers us a table by the window but Cassie baulks at that so he leads us to a booth at the back of the room.

"That's more like it. I always feel like Exhibit A at tables like that. God, I could eat a camel."

After we've ordered and the waiter has gone through his tiresome wine-serving shtick, we clink glasses and Cassie says brightly, "Here's to you, Dr Buchan."

"And to you,"

"Guess what?"

Her green eyes don't just look, they lay siege. I duck under her gaze and ask what's on her mind.

"Lots. First, I'm not a dyke, neither is Miriam for that matter ..."

"Look, it's none of my bus ..."

"Shush. Just to let you know. Last night was by way of a change of pace. Second, as I said, way back when in Italy, you've got the saddest eyes I've ever seen in any man."

Thinking I was going to get another breathy revelation, I'm taken aback by this and remark weakly that I don't feel particularly sad.

"Then you must be in denial because they," she asserts pointing two fingers at the offending organs, "can't lie. Unlike their boss."

"What's that supposed to mean?" I ask, unable to keep the pique out of my tone.

"Nothing very complicated. We all lie - some more than others - but our eyes cannot. That's all. Listen, Keir, I think it only fair to tell you that I know about ... well ... about your ... ah ... troubles a little way back."

"Which troubles?" I query genuinely mystified.

"Oh, all right, your suicide attempt. So you see it wasn't just the eyes."

"Fucking-A. Pardon my French, but Charlie should know better."

"I agree, but I can't unknow what I know, can I?"

"Of course not. Anyway, I'd probably have told you myself - it was a rather singular experience to say the very least - but it wasn't Charlie's shameful little secret to divulge."

Cassie nods. "He's always been a bit of a blabber-mouth. Like why?"

"Why what?"

"Why did you try to top yourself? I mean you've got a great wife, nice kids - even if Cat's being a bit of a dip shit these days - a lovely house. You're a good looking, amusing guy ... I reckon most folks would be more than happy to be in your shoes."

I sigh. Why is it so difficult for people to grasp that suicide has very little if anything to do with bank balances and pretty houses or even relationships and all to do with a hole in your being and the inescapable feeling that tomorrow is simply one day too far?

"Let's just say that, trite as it may sound, all of a sudden nothing made sense, nothing tallied."

She looks at me sideways as if to say 'get real' and chirps, "But nothing *does* make sense, everybody knows that. Things just are. Ah, grub."

Our starters arrive and Cassie weighs into her *salade tiède* with youthful gusto while I tinker with a *pâté de campagne* that has lost its way and am grateful for some pickled onions and gherkins that haven't. At the booth next to ours, a piss artist of about my age is having a little snooze with his head cradled in his arms while his companion, a sleek thirty something, continues to eat her lunch without apparent concern.

"Where are you?"

"Right here and glad to be so," I reply honestly.

"Good. Now, what on earth are we going to do about those eyes of yours?"

I say that I don't feel as sad now as she seems to think I am and suggest that whatever she's seeing in there is the afterglow of whatever it was that led me to think I'd be better off dead than alive.

"If you say so. Know any funny stories?"

"No, but I would like to know more about Cassie Laporte."

Our main courses come. I order another bottle of wine and she tells me about growing up in a blurred succession of one-reactor towns all over the States. She talks about the trauma of her mother walking out on husband and daughter and later her father dying in her junior year at college.

"There I was, twenty years old, without a relative in the world. Oh, I guess my mother must have been somewhere, but I sure as hell hadn't a clue where, nor did I care. There weren't any grandparents, and Daddy's younger brother was killed in a car crash so there wasn't any joy there either. Like I remember sitting on my bed in residence and crying my eyes out and wondering what I'd done to be dealt such a shitty hand."

"I can well imagine. So that's when you came to Europe?"

"No, not immediately. I dropped out of college - none of that stuff seemed relevant any more - and took some practical courses, but then the insurance settlement came through and suddenly all I wanted was out, so I sold everything and got on a plane to Athens."

The restaurant is nearly empty. Our legless neighbour has gone, supported by his long-suffering companion. Waiters are laying tables for dinner, eyeing us resentfully. I mime for the bill and ask Cassie where she met her former husband.

"Mykonos. Where else? My fault really. I mean, Darius Lascelles had 'Jerk on the Make' written all over him only I didn't want to know. Loneliness is a great seducer."

"And he took you to the cleaners?"

"Pretty much. I was incredibly naive. Still, I hadn't yet got the money for the only house Daddy ever owned, so Darius could hardly get his claws on that and I've still got most of it left. My little nest egg."

I ask what her husband did for a living when he wasn't fleecing innocent college drop outs but she's had enough and heads off to the loo while I settle the bill and finish the wine. Outside it's already dark and the evening's as dense and brown as a Franciscan habit.

"Well?" she asks.

An empty taxi trawls by. I don't hail it.

"Well, what?"

Cassie tilts her head to one side. I can't see her face at all clearly, but I've the impression she's amused by something. Presumably me.

"Well, Dr Buchan, what happens next?"

"Your call," I reply, dimly aware that I've just crossed over into new, perilous territory.

"Oh if it's my call, that's easy. We go back to my place and fuck."

"Listen ..."

"You asked."

And then it comes to me with all the force of a revealed truth that there's nothing I'd rather do than go back to this singular woman's flat and make love to her on the same bed she shared with the divine Miriam last night and with my son on so many nights before.

"What about Charlie?" I ask conscious that I'm about to complicate my life and the lives of the people around me beyond redemption.

She clicks her tongue and shrugging impatiently replies, "Believe me this has nothing to do with Charlie, but nothing."

A surge of vain pleasure invades. Charlie's odd man out. Charlie's on the shelf anyway. This is not about Charlie. This is about me and Cassie. I'm not cutting my son's grass. Well, not really. And then for one vertiginous moment I almost do the right thing.

Almost.

"Listen, Ca ..."

But she shakes her head and encircling the back of mine with both hands pulls me to her and kisses me with such savage, urgent need that I'm lost even as her tongue flickers around mine and she grinds her pelvis into me.

And so we hasten through the evening streets, and I am aware of nothing save my imperative need to screw my son's girlfriend.

We don't even make it to the bedroom. Once inside her flat Cassie, who's already wriggled out of her jacket on the way up the stairs, pins me against the wall, and we kiss hungrily. With trembling hands I undo the buttons of her blouse and her breasts bloom up and out, and the size of her hardened nipples astounds. Deftly she undoes the buttons of my shirt. I curl my hands around the hem of her short skirt and on up and encounter cold tight bare buttocks and then her moist sex.

"Jesus!"

She emits a cigarettey chuckle - "A girl's got to be prepared" - and works at my belt and zipper and then sinks to her knees and lifts my shorts over and off my erect cock. She buries her head in my groin and her lips close around the head and I run my fingers through her amazing hair.

I sink to my knees now and pull Cassie's skirt over her head and for a moment we pause like that: our arms in the air and our fingertips touching, teepee-like, trembling on the brink. Then she smiles a smile for all seasons and pulls me into her and leaves her hands imprisoned between us, and soon we find a sort of wild rhythm and presumably because of all the wine I've drunk, I take a long time and she's come and returned for seconds by the time I finally explode inside her like all the July the Fourths ever, and I think if this be wrong what then can right be?

The Patels are at it again. Thick aroma of curry curls under the door and wafts over us as we lie, now uncomfortable, in Cassie's tiny hallway.

"Well, well, well."

I try to prop myself up on my elbows, but I've rubbed them raw on the sisal matting and involuntarily flinch as I roll off her. Can this be me? Can this be the on-the-shelf, salt-and-pepper-haired Keir Buchan - still wearing his natty Argyll socks but otherwise bollocky naked - lying on the floor of a darkened hallway next to this woman half my age, whose bush I now see is the same colour as her hair (ever since Garda I've wondered about this but it's not the sort of question one puts to one's son) and with whom I have just had deeply satisfying sex?

"Well, what?" I ask anxiously.

"Well, very impressive, very impressive indeed."

"Lucky dip," I say with false modesty because the truth is that right now I feel strangely empowered as though I could always find the answers to her questions, endlessly discover new rivers to the sea for both of us.

"Who'd have guessed," she muses brushing the back of her hand softly up and down my cock. "Who'd have thought 'ole sad eyes would turn out to be such a tiger?"

Of course what I want to ask is how good? Better than Charlie? Better than my son who you once claimed was dynamite in the sack? Better than Lance? Miriam? The Etonian con man? All the unnamed others. But I don't. Instead I run my fingers over her amazing nipples delighting in their otherness.

"Freaky, eh? I used to be embarrassed by them, hated gym and swimming classes because I got teased about them in the showers. Brrr talking about showers."

Cassie's idea of a shower redefines the meaning of the event for me. She applies soap expertly, slipping and sliding over hill and dale with languorous authority (you just know she's done this before, but that's fine, that was practice for now) and knowing touch.

"You're in pretty good shape."

"For an old fart?"

"For an anyone. You like?"

She's soaping my crack and flirting with my anus, then she inserts a finger and I am surprised how pleasurable it is. No one has ever done that to me before.

"I'm not sure."

She laughs and moves on saying lightly, "I see we have some catching up to do. Plus, we're going to have to do something about your handle."

"My handle?"

"Your name, dummy."

I ask what's wrong with my name although I know the answer full well. It reeks of the manse, of tight-fisted Scots bean counters and sad men in lonely highland crofts.

"It's okay. Well sort of okay, but I don't want to share it, let alone you, with ... well, all the others."

My heart leaps. We're talking the future here. We're filling hours, days, weeks and months with trysts, assignations. We're talking lunches seguing into indigo afternoons of endless lovemaking. And she doesn't want to share me, wants me to herself. It doesn't get much better.

"So, what's my new name going to be?"

She holds me at arm's length with her head tilted quizzically to one side and finally says, "Dunno yet."

"Well let me know when you've decided, so I know what to respond to."

"Responding doesn't appear to be one of your problems."

We've finally made it to the bed. Cassie's wet hair is plastered in a single thick braid down one side of her head and around her neck. She's kneeling beside me, not touching just looking, which is in itself apparently an erotic act as my cock stirs and thickens under her frank appraisal.

"What's your pleasure *Señor* No Name?"

"Your call," I say for the second time this afternoon.

She laughs her throaty laugh and asks, "Would you have walked away if I hadn't kissed you back there outside the restaurant?"

"I doubt it," I reply untruthfully, knowing full well that I wouldn't have had the balls to do what she did.

She smiles into herself and runs her hands over my stomach and on down and remarks thoughtfully, "So we seduced each other?"

"Who cares as long as it happened?"

"Quite."

And then she's on top and settling and rising around our fulcrum with ever increasing urgency, and all of a sudden I come and she pumps on until she too comes in a series a long rasping moans pitched somewhere between loss and gain.

"Bull's-eye."

"I'm glad. I nearly didn't stay the course."

"But the point," she purrs in my ear, "is that you did. Many don't."

The phone shrills not six inches from my head. Groaning, Cassie swivels off me and picks up the receiver. Charlie's voice. Christ almighty so much for the manifest joys of modern technology. Surfing the betrayal highway.

"Hi Charlie ... uh ... well, yes it was reconnected last ... I was just about to give you a call ..."

I make as if to get up but Cassie stays me firmly with a hand on my chest as if to say 'not so fast my slippery friend, we're in this together'. And of course she's right and who knows where 'this' will take us.

As I lie listening to the muffled sound of my son's voice and observing the taut beauty of his girlfriend's ass and the long clean line of her flank, I'm possessed by a strange joy which transcends the morality (or lack of it) of the moment and refers only to itself.

"Yeah, he dropped by around one o'clock ... took me out to lunch in fact ... awesome *riz de veau*. Charlie, will you listen to me. BT cut me off just like that, and I didn't think it was such a big deal if we didn't speak for a few days ... plus I lost my cell."

It's physically painful to hear Charlie's still slightly immature voice as he remonstrates with the woman he loves for not loving him.

"Hang on, that's unfair and you know it. I've written lots and no I haven't been seeing that asshole Felipe, who's not an asshole at all ... actually Miriam came to din ..."

But Charlie's got the bit between his teeth (I can see him with his hair falling over his slightly nerdy glasses and his fingers fiddling with a pen), and he's off on another rant. Freighted words like Betrayal, Promise, Love and many others limp grievously into the room, and I have to control an alarming impulse to grab the phone and put the poor bastard out of his misery. Because I now know in my bones that even if I get run over by the No.16 bus this evening, he and Cassie are through or, as Cat and her pals would say, toast.

"I told you I wasn't going to make any promises ... I mean, I don't *belong* to you. We'll sort it all out when you come back for Christmas ... see where we stand ... it's only a few weeks away now."

Cassie has rolled onto her back. Her breasts fall away from the centre of her chest with its constellation of freckles. I remember the tiny tattoo that she had near her navel last summer at Riva. It's gone. She's holding the receiver in one hand while with the other she taps out messages I don't understand on my stomach. On the wall to her left there is a print of Whistler's mother that I hadn't noticed before. As ever, Ma Whistler is not amused.

"Don't Charlie, just don't. I'm going to hang up now. I'll phone you tomorrow ... bye."

Cassie sighs and replaces the receiver as an anguished transatlantic plea for more time, a rewind, a respite is cut off in mid-flight.

"Fucking-A."

To my surprise (and it has to be admitted chagrin), Cassie's eyes are muzzy with tears. I hadn't figured her for a weeper but of course given the right chemistry we're all weepers.

"What's he want?" I ask, knowing the answer.

Cassie shrugs and rocks forward on the bed with her head in her hands. The embossed curve of her vertebrae stands out like a necklace of pearls.

"Me is what he wants," she whispers through her hands, "all of me."

"He's young," I say, "he's young, and he still thinks that's possible."

She takes a big gulp of air, holds it in and then lets it out slowly with a tiny sibilant sound like air going out of a balloon.

"And you, I take it, do not?"

I hadn't thought that my unconsidered remark would enjoy more than a half-life's existence, but I now realise that I've been ill served by my own glibness.

"Well,' I reply warily, "I guess I can imagine a situation where two people possess each other so equally as to cancel out all sense of being possessed."

"Only imagine?"

Cassie plays for keeps which I'm beginning to realise is one of the many things that I so like about her.

"Fran's a pragmatist and I'm a sort of romantic realist which adds up to an odd cocktail. Let's just say that there are gaps."

"Am I a gap?" She asks amusedly.

"No, you seem to be to be all presence."

She sighs again and lies back with one hand crooked behind her head and the other absently doodling on my thigh. I should go.

"Damn," she announces to the ceiling, "damn, damn, damn."

"Stop being so hard on yourself, it's not your fault."

"Of course it is. And now this. What a fucking mess."

"This?"

She wags an index finger back and forth between our two bodies like a metronome and says, "Yes this. I'm guessing that something more than physical attraction is going on here ... or have I missed the point?"

"No, or at least not for me you haven't, but neither does it follow that it has to be a mess."

"You've got to be kidding me," she snorts.

No, it's me I'm kidding, because I know she's right.

"I'm late," I say changing the subject.

She shakes her head and turning to me places a finger on my lips and whispers that what she has in mind shouldn't take too long. Later I dress hurriedly and say good-bye. Cassie remains on the bed smoking pensively.

"Will I see you tomorrow?"

"I certainly hope so. I finish work at four. D'you want to meet at The Bunch of Grapes?"

"I'll be there. Are you okay?"

She nods and replies, 'More than. Know what? They're looking better already.'

"What are?"

"The eyes."

"And so they damn well should."

I clatter down the stairs and out into the busy night-bright streets feeling as elated as a small child who's been to a birthday party to which he didn't even think he was going to be invited. The weather has turned and more rain is falling. I'm lucky to find a taxi. The driver's of the chatty variety but after a few non-committal grunts and jejune 'oh, really's he twigs and shuts up.

In hindsight I discern an inevitability to today's events. Nothing remotely like what has transpired was on my mind when I set off on Charlie's errand this morning, but now that it's happened it feels as though mine was a treachery coded to happen. It's as if some genetic quirk in me, some flaw was bound to lead me to this. Ah, the sweet comfort of inevitability. I'm exonerated because it was fated to happen. Keir the antinomian.

There's an accident at Swiss Cottage and the traffic's grid-locked, so I pay the driver and head up Fitzjohn's Avenue. Passing the stately bourgeois houses on the way up the hill I glimpse snapshots from these strangers' lives - a man pouring wine in a candle-lit room, a family grouped around the flickering blue Cyclops of a telly, a woman arranging her hair in a mirror - and I'm grateful for these vignettes of normalcy. It seems as though some people have got it right and there's an odd fugitive comfort in that. I may have got it wrong, but it sure as hell doesn't play like it right now.

The garden gate squeaks. Our house is ablaze. As far as I can see every light in the building is on. (Trying to curb my children's Canadian-style electricity profligacy has been one of my many losing battles).

"Anybody home?"

I can hear the familiar cadences of a BBC newscaster coming from the study.

"Hi, Dad. We're in here."

I park my umbrella in the stand by the door, check my face in the hall mirror for tell-tale signs of the tangled web of deceit I'm in the process of weaving, and go into the study.

"Hello there, old man."

I stand in the doorway rooted to the champagne-coloured carpet over the choosing of which Fran and I had a silly row. My father-in-law, who's sitting in my chair, is turned expectantly towards me. He has a drink in one hand and his dumb Jeffrey Archer half specs in the other and is wearing the V-necked sweater I'd seen him in only this morning.

"Dad, you okay? You look as though you've seen a ghost."

"Hi Cat. I'm fine, just fine. Evening Kenneth."

"Evening, dear boy. Popped up for a decent haircut and toddle around the RA, but I came over a bit dizzy. Fine now, but Frances insists I stay the night."

The devious son-of-a-bitch *has* had a haircut, and I spot a Royal Academy catalogue on the coffee table. I'll just bet he came over a bit dizzy. On the box a commentator dredged from the BBC presenter stockpot is reading his auto cue with a perplexed look on his face. I pour myself a whisky and collapse on the sofa next to Cat.

"Where's Mum?"

"Late."

"When will she be back?"

She flashes me one of her smiles and replies deadpan, "At the office."

Business as usual with my daughter. I sneak a look at her grandfather: a liver spot mottled hand with signet ring on right pinkie, taps an impatient (what's he waiting for, his dinner?) tattoo on the arm of the chair, freshly coiffed hair is neat and spiffy as a choirboy's, over-polished brogues wink their smug social message. I wonder if he ... no, I can't allow myself to wonder about such matters ... bad for the old blood pressure.

"Must call Charlie. Saw Cassie today, her phone was disconnected, lost her cell, was all."

"Oh, yeah. How is she?" Cat asks disinterestedly.

"Seemed fine. I'll be right back."

Upstairs I phone Charlie, but he's out, so I leave a message containing all the information he already knows and gild the lily by saying that Cassie looks great, that we talked a lot about him over lunch and ... oh yes, for him not to worry.

After Fran has returned from work, fussed and flurried over her father, we have dinner in the kitchen. Then we watch a programme entitled *Towards a New Morality* and Kenneth, who's done ample justice to the wine, goes on about disappearing standards, the decline of decency and the demise of the gentleman's agreement. Heady stuff.

"How did you find Daddy?"

Fran's in the bathroom, I'm lying half-dressed on our bed. I close my eyes, and Cassie floats into view as I last saw her, flushed and drowsy after our third fuck (or was it the fourth?) of the afternoon.

"Keir ..."

"What? Oh, you know, a bit pissed ... busy day must have worn him out ... you know."

"I suppose so. I wonder if I should be concerned about this dizzy spell?"

But it seems she doesn't want to know my views on the subject because she turns the shower on, and I hear the door to the shower stall click shut.

I tap out Cassie's number.

"Hello?"

"Hi, it's me."

"I hoped you'd call."

"I miss you," I say, somewhat surprised to realize that it's the truth.

"Tell me about it."

I hang up and lie on the bed listening to the twin sounds of the wind and rain clawing at the windows and the domestic sluicing of Fran's shower. And I am gripped by a funk as dense and complete as any I have ever experienced. What the hell do I think I'm up to? What male menopausal, pre-prostatic madness have I succumbed to? Back off Keir, back right off. Put this afternoon down to anything you want to, put it down to global warming, rogue meteorites, the Bermuda Triangle, whatever, but don't get in any deeper, don't destroy the lives of those you love simply because you've fallen for a redhead with world-class tits and legs that don't give up. But why the hell not? Fran's more interested in her job than me, Charlie's in America and is already just an ex-boyfriend as far as Cassie's concerned, Cat's perfectly content to be discontented just so long as she's left in peace with her phone. And yet.

"Sorry?"

Fran's standing in the bathroom door. She hasn't put a nightie on, a sure sign in our vocabulary that she wants to make love. I panic. I haven't showered since this afternoon. Doubtless Cassie's smell, her herness, clings to me like a signature, an olfactory mugshot.

"I asked what you had for lunch."

"Lunch?"

"Yes, lunch. You know the meal squished in between breakfast and dinner."

"Uh ... oh yeah ... a veal and spinach thing. Gotta take a shower."

This is dumb if not to say incomprehensible because I'd had a salmon steak. Why do I feel I must lie about something that need not be lied about? For the practice, of course, to get it right when it really counts. I brush past Fran and her quizzical stare. I can't have taken more than a half dozen showers before going to bed in the nearly thirty years of our shared life.

After we've made love, I lie on my back with Fran's breathing a frail thing of beauty rising and falling in the dark next to me, and I know what I must do.

CHAPTER EIGHT

"Ivor!"

"Come again."

It seems knowing the right thing to do and doing it are two very different matters. Cassie and I are sitting in the half gloom at the back of The Bunch of Grapes. It's four-thirty and outside it's already as dark as perdition. Traffic rumbles and grumbles along Knightsbridge.

She scrunches her nose and repeats, "You're an Ivor. As I was falling asleep last night it suddenly came to me, but I wasn't absolutely sure until just now when I saw you at the bar getting the drinks."

"What clinched it?"

"No idea. D'you mind?"

"Of course I don't. I was getting fed up with Keir anyway."

She says "Good," and then adds mock heroically, "I dub thee Sir Ivor, Seneschal of my Body, Lord of my Heart."

My heart does a somersault, and I take a long pull on my pint to slow things down. It's hard to believe that not twenty-four hours ago we were little more than acquaintances: she Charlie's former (I know, I know) girlfriend, me the nosy parker who'd caught them OTJ in church. And now we're sitting close together in a West End pub and it feels as though I've known her half my life.

"D'you mean that?"

"What?"

"What you just said, seneschal of my body and so forth?"

"Oh, I expect so," she replies matter-of-factly.

I sense she wants some space, so I tell her about my father-in-law's penchant for seedy Soho clubs and his turning up unexpectedly at our house last night.

"I really think that in his own mind he did come up to town for a haircut and a shot of culture."

Cassie's eyes sparkle mischievously and she says, "Tut, tut, tut. Surely people in grass skirts shouldn't throw lawn-mowers?"

I blush and argue hotly (methinks too hotly) that there's a world of difference between a seventy-one year-old ex-Loans Department Manager - pillar of the community, sacristan, etcetera etcetera - getting blow-jobs in Soho dives and what she and I are doing.

"I couldn't agree more. In the former scenario only the poor little Thai girl gets hurt, but in the latter case everyone almost certainly does."

Stung, I bridle, "Well, if that's what you think perhaps we should quit while we're ..."

But she's having none of my petulance and kisses me, and the years between us are consumed, and I feel youthful and both needed and needing which I haven't for years.

Next to us the *Evening Standard* behind which lurks a rhubarb hued Colonel Blimp quivers with righteous C of E indignation and then he's had enough; folding his newspaper with deadly precision and much huffing, he lumbers off (surely a hip replacement looms) with a final withering look of disapproval in our direction.

Cassie chuckles and says, "Screw you Jasper," and then adds seriously, "Listen, I didn't mean to sound all soppy and know-it-all back there, but we can't pretend that we're not playing with fire if not to say nuclear fission."

She's right. Since yesterday I've been in a sophomoric daze and unwilling to think further ahead than the next few hours, let alone days and weeks. Still, I suppose at some level I have grasped that nothing can ever again be the same, that in most profound sense imaginable, our lives and those of the people in our solar system will be forever touched by what we do. Ha! Make that have done.

Forever. It's a big word.

Even if Cassie and I walk out of each other's lives when we've finished our drinks (as I know we will not), a thing will have been done never to be undone. Suddenly with so much irreversibility, so much of the irrevocable in the air, I'm scared witless and say so.

"I know. Like I get waves of it too, but then I think how comfortable this all seems and the anxiety just sort of goes walkabout. Come on, Sir Ivor. Let's go to my place, I've been wanting you like crazy all day."

***

That evening when I get home there's more e-mail from Charlie:

Old refrigerators never die they just lose their cool, ha, ha. Thanks for going down to CG. Riz de veau? C says everything's more or less copacetic, I'm not convinced. Apparently all is to be reviewed at Xmas. D'you think there's another guy? I gather we're staying put for Xmas so if C and me are still a number as I hope and pray we will be can she stay with us for the duration? Thanks again Chuck le Wreck.

C and I, goddamnit. Fran and Cat are still out, so I phone Cassie and read her Charlie's message.

There's a hollow pause and then she says, "Oh boy, it sure as shit didn't take long, did it?"

"What didn't?" Knowing the answer.

"For the world to get in our faces. Can you imagine Christmas *à la* Charlie? Everyone sneaking around the place like characters at some Edwardian house party. Like thanks but no thanks."

I mumble "I'll think of something" knowing that there is nothing to think of, and then I hear the garden gate squeak (the geese of Hampstead?) so we hurriedly agree to meet tomorrow, and I hang up and sit thinking of Cassie and wishing I were with her. No acne-pitted bobby soxer ever felt more put upon, more cruelly parted from his heart-throb than I now do.

Fran and I have dinner alone in the kitchen. I have trouble focusing on Her Day, mine having been so nerve tinglingly alive, so imbued with precisely that density and complexity of emotion, that sheer sense of nowness I'd despaired of ever experiencing again.

"No sign of the hunky Lance at Cassie's?"

"What?"

"Oh, for God's sake, do I have to repeat every question I ask? What's got into you?" she asks testily.

"Sorry. No, no sign of Lance, but I'd be surprised if there isn't someone in the offing or nearer. I mean, I don't imagine the lady's given up men altogether."

Fran nods and sighs, and I suddenly feel about as worthless as a dung beetle. What has this fine woman, to whom I owe so much, done to deserve what I'm going to do, have already done to her?

"Oh, by the way I'm going to be doing some research at the British Museum most afternoons for the next little while. Probably won't be home much before seven, maybe later."

Fran studies me thoughtfully and then says equably, "Fine. What sort of research?"

"Oh, stuff for the next Chester Dillon ... Wren churches and ... and the Great Fire ... things like that."

"But I thought you'd had enough of all that, were going to take a writing rain check."

"Well so did I, but a good idea just ... well, sort of popped up out of the blue a few days ago, and I don't want it to go to waste."

Fran nods. We tidy up and then she goes off to her study to do some paperwork. Later I fall asleep in front of the TV and am awakened by Cat who's gently prising the channel selector out of my hand.

"Dad, you're developing some thoroughly bad habits."

Aren't I just.

In the days and weeks that follow I can't get enough of Cassie nor it seems, gratifyingly, she of me. We're both aware that we're living an interregnum, that come Charlie's return to London at Christmas - or sooner if we're not very careful, which we're not particularly - we'll no longer have the luxury of not making decisions, of sticking our heads in the sand, of pretending that the present situation is running on anything other than borrowed time.

"Monday seems an eternity away."

"I know."

It's Friday evening and time for me to leave. In fact I'm already late and have just phoned Fran to tell her I'll meet her at David and Sarah's where we're invited for what will undoubtedly be another *moussaka* dinner.

"What'll you do?"

Cassie shrugs and says just this side of sulky, "Dunno. Miriam wants to see a flic, so we'll probably take one in. Felipe's talking up a club somewhere under the Westway, so ..."

"Felipe the non asshole?"

She darts me an almost challenging look and says, "Yes, that Felipe. D'you expect me to stay at home crocheting all weekend?"

I do and I don't. Of course I'm jealous of the air she breathes and the clothes she wears, let alone any friends she might want to see, but I'm still enough in touch with reality to understand that it's ridiculous to expect any girl half as attractive as Cassie to go into voluntary purdah for me or anyone else, for that matter. And yet.

"Of course I don't. Can we meet on Sunday? Fran's going to the office to try to clear her desk and ..."

We're on the landing. We kiss. Behind us the phone rings, and Cassie pulls away saying "*Ciao*, Sir Ivor, call me" and stepping back into her flat closes the door. I wait until I hear her saying "Hello? Oh, hi, Charlie. No, I'm alone but ..." before I go on down the stairs and out into the night.

Dinner is not *moussaka* but another virtually inedible Greek dish called koko something or other comprised of bits of offal wrapped around other bits of offal. However, not even this concoction can chivvy me out of the good humour that has taken hold of me. And I even manage not to drink too much. David, who's normally about as observant as a wheelbarrow, remarks on my high spirits as we stand by the mantelpiece sipping coffee and roasting the backs of our legs by the gas fire. On the sofa in front of us the ladies are comparing daughters; the Finch's seventeen-year-old Samantha makes Cat look like Hildegard of Bingen.

"What's your secret, old man?"

"Secret?"

"Well, you must be doing something right, I haven't seen you in such fine fettle, so chipper for ... well, for donkey's years."

"I think being made redundant has helped," I remark only half-jokingly.

"More like a spot of nooky on the side if you ask me, nudge, nudge, wink, wink, say no more."

Although a nice enough fellow (when not fucking my wife), David's an interesting case of arrested development in as much as he's still grieving for the demise of Monty Python's Flying Circus and regularly returns to our college for brain numbingly boring (I once foolishly accompanied him) quasi-Masonic black-tie dinners in hall.

He explains about a friend of his at work who's having an affair with his secretary (I ask you), and I tune out and am visited by a vivid mental image of Cassie as she was not two hours ago concentrating hard on the sex we're having, as she always does.

At breakfast on Sunday Fran announces that she's damned if she's going to work and that her paperwork can wait. I'm nonplussed not least because I've arranged to meet Cassie at Highgate Cemetery at noon.

"But I thought you wanted to get the backlog cleared up."

"I do, but I just don't feel like it today."

Hating myself I say, "You'll hate yourself tomorrow morning."

Fran moans and clatters some dishes into the dishwasher. A squirrel hops across the lawn. Can this really be me?

"You're right, I'd better get it over with. What'll you do?"

Relieved, I shrug and reply, "Oh, you know, mooch around."

Cassie's late, so I stand by the gateway to Highgate Cemetery. From under my brolly I watch straggles of pilgrims crunch around the gravel paths.

"Going my way, sailor?"

I haven't seen her approach. She ducks in under the umbrella and kisses me and everything is simple, everything adds up. She looks terrific.

"Missed you."

"And I you. What did Charlie have to say?"

She appraises me coolly, then shrugs and replies, "Nothing new. I told him to quit phoning. How was your dinner party?"

"Dull. Did you go to that club?"

"Nah. We had a Chinese in Lisle St …"

"We? You and non asshole?"

Cassie pauses. Everywhere, overgrown tombstones slumber beneath blankets of dripping ivy. The rain thrums on the umbrella. Skewering me with her green eyes she speaks slowly, measuring her words, "Don't do that, Ivor, just don't do it. I will not be cross-examined by you or anybody else. You'll just have to trust me. Got it?"

Miraculously I have and say so.

"Good. Maybe I should have called you the real thinking woman's crumpet, not Ivor after all."

"I don't follow."

"I think it's what some wag called Jeremy Irons. He was in this movie Charlie and I saw way back when where he has an affair with his wet son's girlfriend. *Damage*, haven't you see it?"

I explain that I've probably seen two movies in a cinema in the last decade and that I regularly fall asleep during the incomprehensible videos favoured by my family.

"Well, you didn't miss much. Charlie, who knows about these things, said it was one of Malle's few duds."

"How does it ... well ... end?"

Cassie chortles and tightening her grip on my arm says, "That's just it, I haven't a clue. We left after three-quarters of an hour. Middlebrow hokum is what Charlie called it. Ah, behold the great man."

The rain is running down Karl Marx's massive bronze brow and rivulets of water course through his grizzled beard. Bunches of flowers are strewn at the foot of the granite plinth. WORKERS OF ALL LANDS UNITE. Well, why not? Nobody else is going to help you. With a forehead like that the man looks as if he could think for the entire world which I suppose in a sense is precisely what he did, incorrectly if the end of the last century's events are anything to go by.

Later we warm ourselves by the fire at The Flask in Highgate. Cassie devours an enormous plate of chilli con carne while I pick at a Ploughman's and wonder out loud how anyone can remain as slim as she is while eating as much as she does.

"Genes. Daddy was a string bean, and there wasn't much to my mother either in more ways than one come to think of it. Listen, I've got two days time off in lieu which I'll lose if I don't take before Christmas, Why don't we get out of London, go somewhere for a couple of nights?"

In London, out of London, on the Orinoco, in orbit around the moon, it makes no difference to me just so long as I'm included in the game plan, just so long as I'm along for the ride.

"Fine by me. I feel a bout of out-of-town research coming on. Where were you thinking of going?"

"Well, nowhere pretty and ruched and terminally cutesy and bijou and Cotswoldy. Nowhere with a splendid cathedral or sea or walks of breathtaking pastoral beauty or half-timbered houses. In other words somewhere neutral, somewhere which will allow us to be the main event. Know what I mean?"

I do, and not for the first time since meeting her I'm amazed by the sheer uniqueness of Cassie's angles of approach. Far from being the regulation college drop out with a great body and a headful of received stances by way of Jay McInerney and Time Magazine I'd originally mistaken her for, she's the real thing, a genuine one-off.

"What about somewhere really exotic like Stevenage or Leighton Buzzard ...?"

"Where," I query, delighted by the name of a place I've never heard of before, "might Leighton Buzzard be?"

"I'm not sure really. I don't think far. Beds or Bucks."

"Well, it's got my vote, wherever it is. Leighton Buzzard. Perfect. Know what?"

"I think I can guess, but we can't."

"Why not? Fran's not expecting me ...."

"This," she replies coldly, "has nothing to do with your wife."

"But ..."

"It's not a 'but' situation. Lance is coming back from wherever he's been and is staying the night. He's on his way back to the States, and since I don't get to see him much these days I'd like to spend some time with him, that's all."

I do my best to appear cool about this, but I can feel 'sulk' spreading through me like a virus and I try, unsuccessfully, to banish the image of the handsome Lance from my mind. I drive Cassie back to Covent Garden singularly failing to convey a sense of mature acceptance of the fact that there might be other people in her life. I pull over near the entrance to Hanover Place. The sun is shining now, steam rises from the wet pavements.

Cassie gets out of the car and coming round to my side takes my face between her hands and says evenly "Lance is gay" and then she's gone.

***

"Research? What's with this research mania?" Fran asks at breakfast two days later after I've told her as casually as I can that I'm going to be out of town for a few days.

"It's no big deal, there're just some facts I want to check ... atmosphere to soak up ... you know,"

Fran's in a hurry. She gulps down the last of her coffee and giving me a peck on the cheek says, "Actually I don't, but you seem to. You do remember that I need the car?"

"I do."

"And that Mummy and Daddy are coming for the weekend?"

"That too."

"Well, suit yourself. I've got to dash.'

Together we walk down the path to the road. Fran starts the car and puts on her glasses and then, not knowing I'm going to do it, I lean in the window and kiss her hard on the lips. She recoils involuntarily (we haven't kissed like that for years), looks at me curiously (God alone knows what she sees, probably an ageing lecher), then puts the car in gear and accelerates up the hill without her usual wave out the window.

I return to the house aware that I'm going to have to put a good deal more thought into the mechanics of deception if Cassie and I are going to stand a chance of avoiding detection. Someone of Fran's intelligence, not to mention intuition, is not going to swallow vague research projects in obscure parts of the country for very long. But all that's still in the future, still out there in the realm of the unimaginable. The imaginable is Euston Station at four forty-five this afternoon.

"Hi, Dad."

"School closed for renovations?"

"Har-di-har-har. Spare till ten. Yuk, this coffee's *vraiment dégueulasse*."

"That would be because it was made a good two days ago. Cat, have you seen a movie called *Damages*?"

"You mean *Damage* starring, if that's the word, the lemur-faced Irons J.?"

"That's the one."

"I have, and it sucked big time. Why?"

"Oh, it came up in a conversation. D'you remember how it ends?"

"Sure I do. Anorak dweeby son catches the star-crossed lovers OTJ, backs horrified out of flat, tumbles over balcony to death, we get to see yet more of the Ironic tush, plus hint of full frontal. Crap cubed. See you tonight."

"No you won't, I'm going to be out of town for a few days."

Cat stops theatrically in her tracks and turning around with exaggerated slowness says, "You out of town without Mum? No way José."

"Nonetheless, it's true."

"Well, I hope she's worth it. *Ciao.*"

CHAPTER NINE

She is.
I see Cassie as soon as I arrive in Euston's great booming concourse. She's wearing an ankle-length black coat and her oriflamme of hair burns like a beacon amidst the mouses and greys and blue and silver rinses all around her. She's browsing through the novel section of W. H. Smith's as I come up behind and put my arms around her and bury my face in the fragrant warmth of her hair. It comes to me with a childlike *frisson* of pure joy that I'm not going to have to share her with anybody or anything for the next two days.

The train slips out of the station and gathers speed along the dark cuttings and sooty tunnels leading out of London. Cassie sits very straight with her eyes closed and a hand lying lightly on my thigh. I like that.

"Tired?"

She nods without opening her eyes. "I'll be all right. We stayed up pretty late, you know, the way you do."

"How is he?"

Cassie sighs deeply and for some reason I know the answer. Lance has Aids.

"Yes. Apparently he's been HIV Positive for a few years, but now it's the real full-blown stinking McCoy. Poor bastard."

"I am sorry."

She nods again distractedly. Tears glisten in her eyes, and two furrows of mascara run down her cheeks.

"So am I. I wasn't going to mention it but since you guessed, why not? The good news is that he's convinced that he's going to lick it. Some do, don't they?"

I tell her truthfully that I don't know much about it, and then she puts her head in my lap and for the rest of the forty-five minute journey to Leighton Buzzard sleeps soundly while I stare out of the window and am unable to stifle the mean-spirited thought that Lance could have come out of the Aids closet on someone else's watch.

In Leighton Buzzard we check into the unremarkable Swan Hotel on the High Street not, however, without the discrepancy in our ages being celebrated in the water-weaselly eyes of the man-child who books us in.

"Mr and Mrs?"

"No, that'll be Dr Buchan and Ms Laporte," Cassie announces firmly as the youth avoids her imperious gaze.

The room is innocent of ruched curtains, and the town turns out to be in absolutely no danger of being labelled cutesy, let alone bijou. A brisk walk reveals a main drag with the usual complement of Bootses, banks, building societies, Oxfams, estate agents, fast food outlets, and newsagents all bedecked with hideous logos and smothered in ugly signs. There's a prettyish Fire Hall with a clock tower and what looks like an old church with an unusual spire. Pubs abound as do, for some strange reason, barbershops of which we count five in a two-hundred yard radius.

The pub is crowded and permeated with the essence of small town High Street pubness: odour of bitter spillage and years of ash droppings (of yesteryear) ground into burgundy and sludge-green floral pattern carpeting; tired amalgam of pork baps and mushy peas seeping from the kitchen and the far tinny whiff of quietly gurgling urinals and russet-tiled floors regularly sluiced with Jeyes.

But somehow it's okay, somehow it's just what the doctor ordered. A group of middle-aged men at the bar talks football and telly and laughs the beery brays of middle-aged folk talking football and telly at the bar. The slot machines whirr, beep and jingle. Next to us a table of kids listens to a whey-faced youth tell a story which from the sound of it could land him in deep shit with the Race Relations Board. The girls are over made-up and bored out of their brains; the guys (all of whom have availed themselves of the services of the town's barbers, baroque punk seeming to be the flavour of the month) are on the cusp of drunk.

"Here's to us."

We clink glasses. Noticing us, one of the girls - herself not much younger than Cassie - whispers something to her chum, who looks us over and nods. They both laugh.

"Don't worry, they're just jealous."

"They've got a funny way of showing it," I object.

"Hey, what's got into you? People are going to look, and we're just going to have to get used to it."

I'm elated by the implied futurity although at the same time I'm suddenly assailed by one of those chilling tastes of time foreshortened that are like the scent of our winding sheets, the memory of our own deaths.

"You okay?" she asks, plainly concerned.

I try to explain, but she's too young (at twenty-five you don't wake up at dawn with your heart going like the Little Engine That Could seeing yourself in a wicker rocking chair on the veranda of the Ocean View old people's home just a few hem-length changes away) and I don't want to put a damper on the evening, so I change the subject and then get us another round.

Later we buy plaice and chips in a brightly lit shop on a side street and a bottle of white wine in an off licence run by an albino Indian, then scuttle past the reception desk trailing a spoor of deep battered fish and vinegar-laced chips behind us like a bad reputation.

We eat on the bed watching a program about wildlife in Serengeti, then it's the News at Ten and Cassie tidies away our debris, runs a bath and drifts around the room undressing in absent-minded stages.

"Well?"

"Well, what?" she asks.

"What d'you make of the Buzzard of Bedfordshire?"

"Perfect. Just what I had in mind. A backdrop rather than a place. Are you okay here?" she queries, suddenly solicitous.

"I'm fine just as long as you're where I am, or I'm where you are, whichever comes first."

She stands between the TV and the bed with her head on one side gazing at me with a little smile playing around the corners of her mouth.

"What's so funny?"

"Not a thing. I was just thinking how glad I am to be here with you on our honeymoon. Oh, shit, the bath!"

She dashes to the bathroom and, cursing like Lenny Bruce, mops up the overflow while I lie on my back savouring the moment, realising as I do that for the first time in as long as I can remember I am actively, presently happy. I also understand what I've known at a gut level for some time without acknowledging it. To wit: there is nothing I will not do to ensure Cassie's continuing presence in my life.

The French expression *nuit blanche* perfectly conveys the seamless passion of that first night at The Swan in Leighton Buzzard. Afterwards, I can in no way differentiate between one lovemaking and the next, and yet I retain a memory of pleasure given and taken at a level of intensity beyond anything I have before experienced. We must have slept from time to time because I've a recollection of waking to the feel of Cassie's tongue and lips and her knowing fingers that seemed to move like thinking fire over my body. Finally, as queasy dawn creeps into the room and after a last juddering, seemingly life-threatening fuck, we collapse in an exhausted tangle of limbs and fall asleep in each other's arms.

I am awakened by the wind causing the old-fashioned frames to rattle and bang with a noise that is exactly like that made by the windows in my bedroom in the big old house in Knowlton when the wind was up and the lake a restless pewter presence glimpsed between the bare branches of the trees. With that inevitably comes the perfectly realised image of my brother as I last saw him, wildly dancing at the Yamaska Club the night he died. And not for the first time since that terrible night I wonder how my life might have differed had I not lost my womb-mate so early in the game. I have always considered that my almost permanent sense of otherness, of not quite being complete, can be linked to that premature rupture, that first grisly master class in loss.

"Ivor?"

Being called Ivor gives me inestimable pleasure because it's her name for me, her way of colonising me.

I open my eyes.

Wearing jeans and a canary yellow sweater and looking like several million bucks, Cassie is sitting in the armchair by the window with sections of the newspaper strewn all around her.

"Have you been up long?"

"Hour or so. I'm hungry."

Ah, youth.

A PERFECT SENTENCE

After breakfast (at which I feel scrutinised by businesspersons, middle-aged couples and toddlers alike), Cassie suggests we make a morning of cruising the local supermarkets.

"Whatever for?" I ask, more surprised than I can say.

"I'll tell you on the way."

After asking for directions at the desk, we head off for the outskirts of town where the supermarkets hang out. On the way, Cassie picks up the story of her childhood. After her mother took off, her dad, who was devastated, made a point of getting transferred from one nuclear plant to the next even more than he had before.

"It was as if he were searching for something out there in all those Salems and Senecas and Gravel Necks. Or maybe it was the chain-link-fenced anonymity of it that attracted him. I don't know. What I do know is that over a period of five years we moved nine times. New schools, new houses, trailers, bungalows, apartments, new friends, if that's the correct word for the succession of unrelationships I endured. Like, just as I'd break into a desirable clique, just as I was beginning to get asked to slumber parties, have dates, be normal, Daddy would come home from work and announce we were moving on, and we'd pack up the Econoline and hit the road. And believe me we're not talking The Romance of the Road here, there was nothing remotely *Thelma and Louise* about it."

We're threading our way through Tesco's parking lot. An ancient, rain coated couple is being bullied by a cart with attitude, a make-up less mum in sweats irascibly yanks a small child around like a rag doll (the baby had her up all night, her eldest is on the carpet for truancy, Sean didn't get back from the pub until after eleven, sozzled) and a gargantuan couple in lurid tracksuits dip knuckle less paws into a jumbo bag of onion flavoured crisps balanced on top of a cart laden with what is obviously more of the same healthy fare.

Cassie darts a look at me and bursting into laughter exclaims, "You look as though you've got a bad smell under your nose."

"Sorry about that, but I'm a Sainsbury's man," I proclaim, ever the wag.

Once inside the store we meander through Fruit and Vegetables and I can literally feel her unwinding as we linger over Cox, Empire, Gala, Braeburn, and Granny Smith apples, admire the impressively full range of lettuces, pause by the potato carousel heaped with red Romeros, Idaho bakers and dark earth encrusted new Nicolas.

"The thing was that with all that change in my life, all the coming and going, the only constant, the only parameter seemed to be the supermarkets. Oh, the name of the chain would change from state to state - A&P, Grand Union, whatever - and the layouts sometimes differed although you'd be surprised how similar they are, but still there was all that order, all that predictability out there and it filled a need."

I find myself unconscionably touched by Cassie's story. It's not hard to imagine the lonely teenager shopping for her sad, rootless father in a string of supermarkets in reactor towns all over America, and somehow it makes her present poise and self-assurance all the more understandable. And the funny thing is I too can now feel the soothing effect of these neatly husbanded lines of produce (we're in Coffee, Tea, etc.), these ordered rows of the bewildering array of articles it apparently takes to keep *Homo sapiens* alive and kicking at the narrow end of the twenty-first century. There's a thought: the supermarket as therapist.

"D'you do this in London too?" I ask as we dawdle down the aggressively hygienic Dairy aisle.

"Certainly I do. I guess you must think I'm nuts."

"Not at all," I answer as it happens truthfully because this seems a much saner and cheaper way to centre oneself than guzzling tranquillisers prescribed by an overworked NHS doctor or paying a total stranger eighty quid an hour to listen to you talking about yourself.

After Tesco we hit Safeway and then move on to Waitrose. Mercifully, as I'm getting supermarket lag, there doesn't seem to be a Sainsbury in town.

"Thanks for indulging me."

When the cloud cover has cleared and a winter sun burns weakly out of a sky the colour of blindness, we go for a walk along the tow path of the canal which skirts the town. We're alone on the bank. Here and there peeling barges are moored to bollards, a few ducks go about their business, some crows exchange raucous greetings, a single-engine plane potters low over the fallow grey fields and disappears beyond the Chiltern Hills.

Cassie disengages and walks backward ahead of me looking at me curiously as if suddenly trying to assess my role in her life. It's chilling to think that what she sees is a man with greying temples wearing a designer donkey jacket and olive green cords, limping slightly (shredded ligaments: Knowlton High vs. Granby, circa 1975) as he walks along a canal in Bedfordshire on a Thursday afternoon in December in the year of someone else's Lord two thousand and thirteen. That's me: Keir - aka Ivor - Buchan PhD, ex-Lecturer in English Literature at the Open University, and present ... what? What about cuckolder of his own son? No, they were done, they were through, but I know that no amount of double-speak will ever quite be able fully to expunge the guilt of having moved in on Charlie's patch so damned fast.

"Guess what?" she asks.

"I give up."

She has stopped as I have, and we stand like that, a few feet apart, before she says, "I've gone and done a rather stupid thing."

"Like?"

"Would you believe fallen in love?" she says almost sheepishly.

I ask "What's so stupid about that?" while a fireworks display is going on inside my head and my heart is revving like a drag car waiting for the green light.

She sighs, a long sad sound that seems to go to the very quick of the human equation we've engineered and whispers, "Probably just about everything except the fact itself, which seems very right. Still, I'm happy about one thing."

"Namely?" I inquire still trying to keep the almost unbearable elation I'm feeling out of my voice. (Why, for fuck's sake? The woman I love has just said she loves me).

"That I *can* fall in love. I was beginning to suspect I lacked the necessary equipment."

"You mean you don't, didn't ... well ... love Charlie?"

She shakes her head, tears brim in her eyes and the vivid green blurs to North Sea indeterminate. "Not really. I liked him a lot. I loved many of his ways. I enjoyed going out with him, well most of the time I did, I could have done without some of his tantrums, but, no, I never loved him. And he knew it."

"So then ... so then I haven't messed him around," I blurt out and am instantly ashamed of the words which seem to have issued from some unlovely nook of my psyche.

She shakes her head and whispers, "Come on, Ivor. That's hardly worthy of you."

"You're right, that was pretty tacky. Jesus, though, why does everything always have to be so complicated?"

She shrugs and looks sightlessly at some spot over my head. "Search me."

We go on down the tow path locked together as if our very closeness might shield us from a world which allows such dangerous affinities to flourish. We stop. Cassie frames my face with her hands and gazes at me with such intensity that I blink and try to avert her gaze, but she won't let me and says evenly, "Complicated or not, know that I love you more than I would have thought it possible. I thought I could keep it at the Great-Sex-With-An-interesting-Older-Man level, but I can't. I'm a goner."

What is it about the power of those three banal words? I tell her what she already knows, and I'm filled with a sense of arrival, of having reached a place of rare worth.

That night after a surprisingly good Indian we go to the hotel's Hunters' Bar (complete with baleful stuffed hind or hart, or whatever it is) for a nightcap. The place is full of an older, more agrarian crowd than was in last night's pub. We sit opposite each other, and I don't care a toss how obvious it is to the assembled Leighton Buzzardians that I'm old enough to be the father of the stunning redhead in whose fond gaze I now luxuriate and with whom, with infinite pleasure and no little anticipation, I shall shortly be retiring to bed.

"Remember when I hit that guy on the way to Riva?"

"Of course. Why?"

"The way you fixed him up ... I mean, that was the first time I saw you ... as yourself ... as someone other than the girl who was going out with my son."

"And," she giggles throatily, "shagging him in that chapel."

"And that too."

"God, that was *so* embarrassing."

"I must say at the time you didn't seem all that fazed to me." I retort almost testily.

Shaking her head she says, "Well I was. Like it was hardly the best way to impress you."

"I didn't think you were aware of my existence."

"Oh, I had my eye on you all right. Make no mistake about that."

"Meaning?"

She shrugs and after taking a sip of her drink says lightly, "Nothing much. I just thought you were sexy and funny and yet you had those really sad eyes. An interesting combination."

"And now?"

"One and two as billed, three fast improving," she answers lightly.

Back in the room I say that I've got to phone home, and Cassie nods and disappears into the bathroom without a word.

Cat answers the phone, "Oh, hi Dad. And how is Fifi Laframboise?"

"Very funny. What's up?"

"*Nada*. Here's Mum."

Fran and I chat about not very much - a dentist appointment, weekend menus, a possible Christmas present for Charlie - and all the time I'm trying to figure out how on earth the next few weeks (let alone months and years) are going to play.

"How's the research going?"

"Sorry?"

"The research you're supposed to be doing. Where the hell are you anyway?'

"Ah ... Taunton."

"What ..."

However, I've had enough. "Bye, Fran. I'll be back tomorrow, latish."

I lie on the bed staring at a stain on the ceiling the shape of Italy, minus Sicily. I can hear the hiss of the shower and above that Cassie singing a Beatles song already famous long before she was born. Fran's voice is still ringing in my ears, and I feel the full weight of what is happening - what will happen - pressing down on my chest, driving the breath from my body. Everywhere the options are closing down, bang, boom, bang, like so many of those metal shop blinds in European towns at the end of the day.

At one point I could do x, y, and z. Now it seems only z remains. And z scares me every bit as much as it excites me.

"Where're you?"

Cassie is standing by the bed wrapped in a towel tucked under her armpits.

"Right here," I reply absently.

"Well you look like a gazillion miles away. What's up?"

"Everything and nothing. Tell me something, how d'you see ... well, the future ... our future ... ah ... unfolding?"

She dips her shoulders and says "I don't. I'm trying to handle the present as well as I can" and starts wandering aimlessly around the room.

"You don't see, *foresee*, anything?"

"Oh sure I do: Charlie'll come back in a few weeks, we'll have an unpleasant pow wow in which I'll tell him we're through, I'll feel guilty (some), he'll be heartbroken and probably not take it very well, but he will go back to the States after Christmas and find some Seven Sisters lovely, and by the spring I'll just be the girl who helped him lose his virginity. Beyond that it's not really my call, is it?"

"I guess not. But what do you want? How would you *like* things to work?"

"Ah well, that's a different question. Let's see, I'd like to be with you, I mean really with you, until ... no ... for as long as it takes."

"How long is that?"

She comes to a stop at the foot of the bed and looking at me intently says, "Dunno. As I said, I'd like to spend some real time with you, lots of it if that's the way it works, but I'm aware that you may want out when you've discovered what I'm really like."

That's not the way it is, not at all. Right now it feels as though I could never, ever get enough of her, and indeed I cannot imagine my life having anything resembling meaning without her. All else seems unimportant, marginal, although something in me - presumably the bourgeois householder and paterfamilias as opposed to the Byronic lover - wants not to rock the boat until Christmas has come and gone.

Cassie laughs when I tell her this and says, "Love on the back burner?"

"No, just meltdown postponed."

She nods and sits down on the bed next to me. Her shoulders are still pink from her shower, and she smells of gardenia soap. Way off in the distance a siren wails its message of pain foretold. That's out there, here's here, and I ask no more of the world.

"I guess a few weeks can't make too much of a difference, but in the meantime ..."

Nuit blanche followed by *nuit douce*. Long night of lovemaking tender as a tropical sunrise.

Euston Station.

"Will you call?" she asks waiting with me in the taxi queue.

I'm already late (for another side-splitter with my in-laws) but I'm glad taxis are thin on the ground, meaning as it does more time with Cassie before she walks home.

"Of course. This hurts, I miss you already."

"Ditto. Kiss me."

We've all seen it: the mismatched couple (he the bearded Middle Manager in a belted trench coat, she his almost pretty PA) smooching in the Sunday night taxi queue as the lost weekend inches to its bathetic conclusion and the lonely bedsit and family routine loom. But now I'm living it, now I am that man, devouring the tall girl with the extraordinary hair, folding her in an embrace which will have to last until the next filched meeting, the next edition of lies.

A taxi arrives. I give my address to the driver, Cassie brushes my cheek with the back of her hand, whispers '*Vaya con Dios*', turns abruptly and walks up the IN ramp and out into the night. As the taxi swings left into the Euston Road I catch a glimpse of her dark-coated figure striding like a Cossack princess down Gordon Street, and seeing her like that - so self-contained, so independent - I'm buffeted by a gust of emptiness so powerful as to bring tears to my eyes.

"You okay, guv?"

"I'll be fine. Thanks all the same."

The taxi inches along Camden High Street and glumly I observe the passing parade in all its awfulness. Nothing is better calculated to depress than the sight of trendy Camden Town gearing up for another night of force-fed frivolity. Already swirls and eddies of drunken youths clutching cans of lager surge along the litter-infested pavements, pubs and clubs spew cloned revellers into the streets, homeless bundles of clothing with the eyes of concentration camp survivors fuzz in doorway after doorway, music from hell throbs into the night. We stop for a red light at the Kentish Town Road intersection and a human wall of wan and wasted youths crosses the street in front of us.

"Makes you fink, dunnit, guv?"

"I find it best not to."

The driver gives me the once-over in his rear view mirror, then the light changes and we're pockitty-pockitting up Chalk Farm Road.

I reflect that Cassie's right. When she gives Charlie his marching orders he can certainly be relied upon to overreact. Sadly, I recall the phone call from the headmaster of his school informing us that our son was in the third day of a hunger strike and that it was time for us to come and talk sense into the boy. I ask you, a hunger strike in an English Public School in 2006!

"But, Dad, I didn't cheat, honest. Hells bells, I don't *need* to cheat."

Being his parents we believed him but nothing short of a full apology from the maths master in question would do for our Galahad. For three whole days and most of the nights Fran and I argued with, wheedled, beseeched our visibly deteriorating son to relent, but it was as if a mental portcullis had come down and we could have been talking to a blank wall. Just when it looked as though we were going to have to have him force fed, the master - a Mr Waugh as I recall - cracked and admitted making up the whole thing as revenge for Charlie having cruelly exposed him as incompetent in front of the entire Upper Fifth. It turned out that Waugh was the cheat: he'd forged a degree to get the miserably underpaid temporary position in the first place.

And now of course there is this summer's jolly boating incident which I've cravenly failed to address and which I now promise myself to do something about come Christmas.

"Left or right, guv?"

"Left. Just beyond the lamppost."

Home. The taxi disappears and I loiter on the mist-shrouded pavement not yet able to face the music inside. As usual, every light in the house is on. Kenneth and Muriel's Mondeo Estate is parked behind our car. I push the gate open with a foot. No squeak. Fran must have been in one of her domestic modes while I was away.

The next bit plays very slowly. The front door is unlocked and I unsling my overnight bag and step into the front hall where a number of garishly coloured sporting bags and a Duty Free plastic one have been tossed higgledy-piggledy in the corner by the grandfather clock. I don't understand. The Barkers are hardly Nike people (nor do they toss anything anywhere) and they've just driven from Dorset not flown from anywhere. I can hear voices coming from the study: Kenneth's grating whinny, Cat's giggle, Charlie's ...

Christ almighty, these are Charlie's bags. Charlie's done a runner. I think of turning and escaping myself but it's too late; an anxious Fran has appeared in the doorway. Seeing me, she smiles through her frown and says, "Welcome home, stranger."

CHAPTER TEN

The scene in the study is pure Chekhov by way of a *New Yorker* cartoon. Kenneth and Muriel are sitting on the sofa, Cat is perched on the arm of a chair ostentatiously reading the newspaper while Charlie looking like death heated up lounges in an armchair, half-empty beer bottle in hand.

"Hi, Dad. Return of the not-so-prodigal-son."

We embrace. He smells of travel and trouble. I hear myself saying all the appropriate things, but the truth is I'm a stranger observing other peoples' comedy of manners. Charlie explains that what with his Prof out of town until the New Year and once again not being able to contact Cassie, he'd decided on the spur of the moment to come home early.

"I've been going out of my Christly mind. I still can't get beyond her dumb answering machine, so I think I'll head on down there ..."

But Fran, who's standing in the doorway with a troubled expression on her face, is not having anything to do with that. She interrupts him saying, "It won't hurt you or Cassie to wait for another hour or so. Why don't you go and freshen up while I put some dinner together."

It's not a question, and he knows his mother well enough not to argue, so he shrugs and allows as how a shower might not be a bad idea. Still perusing the newspaper Cat asks sweetly how he managed to change his airline ticket.

Charlie blushes and I know he's going to lie. Cat knows it too, that of course being why she asked.

"I got lucky. I sweet-talked the girl at the ticket counter. Where've you been, Dad?"

"Here and there. Airlines don't play ticket games at Christmastime. You mean you bought another ticket, don't you?"

"Well, sort of. But I sold the other half to a guy, honest. Dad, I had to come home now. I just had to. Don't you see?"

Oh, sure I see. Don't think you can tell your old man a goddamned thing about obsession, my boy. Don't think I don't know all about being driven to do unreasonable if not to say immoral things by a love for your love who doesn't love you.

As soon as I'm sure Charlie's in the shower, I dash upstairs and phone Cassie from our bedroom.

"Oh, God, here we go," she moans.

"I know. I'm sure he'll be down there later tonight. Be ... be, oh, I don't know, gentle with him ... he ... well he looks simply awful."

"He would. Jesus wept! *Ciao*." She says abruptly and hangs up.

I stand looking at myself in Fran's full-length mirror. This can't be happening to me, indeed it seems scarcely credible that events can have escalated to the point where very shortly Cassie and I are going to have to stand up and be counted ... or ... but there's no or, and I know it.

"Dad?"

"Hi. Come on in."

Apart from worrying himself ragged about his girl, Charlie's obviously not been eating anything remotely like a balanced diet. He's skinny to the point of emaciation, he's got bags the colour of overripe bananas under his eyes, and the eyes themselves leak the agony of lost love (I can tell that he knows without accepting) into a night which will take no prisoners.

"I'm really sorry about the ticket business. I didn't mean to lie, but it was the only way I could swing it on such short notice. I'll pay back the difference, promise."

I put a comforting arm around my son's thin shoulders (the image which appears in my mind's eye is of a picture in my illustrated Canadian history book of a *courier de bois* in the act of cheating some scantily dressed Iroquois), tell him not to worry about the money and ask him - Cassie aside - how he's been doing.

"But that's just it Dad, I simply can't Cassie-aside-it. She's almost literally all I can think about. Still, I have to admit that Kilmartin's pretty impressive, as is MIT in general, but the truth is I've sort of not really been there. Know any jokes?"

Charlie and his jokes.

"Well it's not exactly a joke, but did you know that Marx knocked up one of his wife's housemaids?"

Briefly, Charlie's face lights up with pleasure and he laughs, "Jeez, talk about alienated labour."

Dinner's a bizarre event. There's a tension in the air that cannot be alleviated by Kenneth's lugubrious stabs at interest in his grand children's lives, nor my overcooked bonhomie. Charlie's clearly dying to be gone, ditto Cat, Fran's ragging some worrisome thought and says little and Muriel might just as well be at her bi-weekly bridge game back in Dorset.

After dinner Cat and Charlie leave together, the olds retire to their room and Fran and I watch a documentary on a Mad Cow epidemic except neither of us is really paying much attention to what's going on.

"Keir, what d'you imagine is going to happen down there?"

I don't know what to say.

"Please, answer me." Fran says frostily.

"Sorry. I presume she'll tell him it's over and that'll be the end of that," I reply realising with horror that I've just put the cart before the horse.

Fran groans and says, "How on earth d'you know that?"

I shrug and mumble lamely, "Just a gut feeling I've got, dunno why ..."

Fran rolls her eyes. "Well, even if you're right, who says that'll be the end of anything, you know Charlie as well as I do. He's liable to do anything if she gives him the heave-ho ... Lord, what a mess ..."

Isn't it just? And by the way it's when, not if. On the screen stacks and stacks of cow carcasses burn in pits. It looks like a scene from a movie about the Thirty Years' War. Trouble in the food chain. Trouble at home. Trouble everywhere except in my love's arms. *Oh, western wind.*

"Where have you really been?"

Fran's looking at the telly, but I can see from the set of her jaw that she's more than a little interested in my reply. So am I.

"I told you. Tonbridge. Why?"

She looks at me and I feel as if I've been cut in two, as if all the love, not to mention the plain old effort and friendship and shared experiences of our thirty-year relationship have been reduced to so much rubble, so much bad faith.

"And I don't believe you," she replies evenly.

"Well, if that's the way you want to ..."

She shakes her head sadly. Her eyes have gone out. She gets up and leaves the room without another word. I watch more herds of cows being incinerated, then experts pontificating, officials excusing, investigative journalists making themselves reputations for fierce honesty, farmers bleating, more cows staggering drunkenly, tongues lolling, eyeballs swivelling. I'm sick at heart and wish I could turn the clock back, go back to before things went wrong, but that would mean a Cassie less world and therefore an unconscionable one. A Party Political Broadcast pole axes me, and I drop like a stone into a sleep peopled by cows with human heads who talk a language I cannot understand but which nevertheless makes sense to me because it tells me I've done something wrong.

I awake in stages. The telly's a blue out. The grandfather clock in the hall chimes three times. And then I realise I'm not alone in the room which is suffused by the etiolated light of the TV. Charlie's chino-clad legs thrust out from the depths of the wing-backed chair next to the sofa on which I've crashed. There's a curious sound which at first I fail to recognise but then identify as that of a grown man crying.

"Charlie?"

The weeping continues.

"Come on, old son, I know how you must be feeling ..."

"No, Dad ... no ... you do not know how I'm feeling," he manages to grind out between sobs.

He's right. I know how *I'm* feeling which is lousy but also somehow darkly elated. I can only guess how it feels to have the only god you care about fail. Charlie continues crying and I can think of nothing useful to say. He leans forward in the chair and buries his face in his hands. I can see his shoulders racked with convulsive sobs. I am afflicted by what I can only describe as a kind of deferred non-guilt. I feel for him but I know that if it weren't me it would be someone else, so everything's really for the best in this cruellest of all possible worlds.

"Charlie, perhaps if you could just ..."

He turns to me, and I'm shocked to see the desolation etched on his gaunt features. With a visible effort to control himself he swallows and says grimly, "Perhaps nothing. It's over, puff, just like that. I wish I were dead."

"What did she say?"

"Not much. "Bye-bye. It's been great. So sorry. I met Ganesh on the landing.""

"Ganesh?" But I know all too well who Ganesh is, fear the worst and feel my stomach go into free fall.

"Ganesh Patel from the flat downstairs. He went all coy on me, but he allowed as how there's been a guy around, some older geezer, so she lied about that too because she swore there wasn't anyone else. Fucking-A."

Your move, Keir. But it isn't because Fran has appeared in the doorway and now does what I should have done long ago. She kneels in front of Charlie and puts her arms around him and hugs him, and mother and son are locked together as in a *Pietà* as old as sorrow itself.

I lie down fully dressed on a bed in the spare bedroom. I'd give anything for another Party Political Broadcast to blast me out of the horror of this wakefulness, but I'm far from such blessed release, and I lie in the dark wishing I were in a different room halfway across London. I try to read the future but all I can see is a battlefield strewn with walking wounded below while above Cassie and I float up and away like one of those beatific couples in a Chagall painting.

"Keir?"

Fran's got her receptionist's voice firmly in place. I'm in for a rough ride.

"Yes?"

She's standing in the doorway and somehow I can tell that she won't come any further into the room. I'm that bad.

"I'm worried sick."

Oh, for Christ's sake, we're all worried, we're all fucked beyond the talking about it, it goes with the territory, it's part of the confidence trick known as the human condition.

"About?" I ask disingenuously.

"What d'you think? Charlie. Us. Whatever it is that appears to be happening to our lives."

"First things first. Where is he?"

"Gone for a walk. You saw him, he's in a frightful state," she answers distractedly.

Trust Charlie to go trudging off to the Heath at three in the morning like some latter-day Werther.

"He'll be all right. He's not the first person in the history of the universe to have to contend with unrequited love," I offer unable to delete the coldness in my tone.

"Of course he isn't, but surely there's something we can do even if you and I are coming apart at the seams ourselves?"

"Are we?"

Fran breathes in angrily and snaps, "I wasn't born yesterday. I don't know what you're up to, but I can guess. I do know that you've been lying to me. If you want out just say so, and let's stop all this bobbing and weaving although it would be nice if we could get through this festive bloody season before you leave if that's what's on your mind. But that's up to you. Oh, by the way, which was it Taunton or Tonbridge?"

Leighton Buzzard if you must know.

The days that follow are a nightmare. Charlie either trails around the house moaning and sighing like a jilted Russian landowner or disappears for hours on end without saying where he's going, often returning trashed. At first Cat takes the piss, but she eases off and then stops altogether when the penny drops and she realises that her brother is quite literally beyond responding to her barbs with anything like the sort of spirit she requires.

"It's like punching blancmange, *quel* nerd. If this be love, *donnez moi un break.*"

Fran, who's always frantically busy around Christmas (it seems that many of her families respond poorly to the hoopla surrounding the son of God's birthday), isn't around much and when she is the frost which descends (on me - to the kids and Charlie especially, she's sweetness itself) is palpable. And me? What does ex-Prof Keir Buchan do? How do I react to the barometer falling in Hampstead?

Not well.

By Wednesday I can no longer bear not seeing, smelling, touching, breathing the same air as Cassie, and I phone from one of the few remaining phone boxes on the high street.

"I've got to see you."

There's a pause. Do I detect another voice in the background? I do. It is James Naughtie wittering on about some incandescent issue or other on Radio 4. Cassie and I speak in a kind of code as if we can hide behind obliquity.

"I know, me too. How is he? It wasn't much fun."

"I'll bet. He's ... ah ... distraught is too mild a word ... sort of out of it. And he's out a lot. Fran's rumbled ... well, me."

"Us?" she queries plainly alarmed.

"No. I think we're talking woman's intuition plus I fluffed my lines. Where can we meet?"

"Not here. I reckon Charlie's snooping around. I'm sure I saw him yesterday."

We agree to meet in an hour in the little park on the Embankment where Rodin's understandably glum worthies of Calais hang out. And so I take the Tube to Charing Cross and walk the short distance to the park in a delicate winter light that fills me with an inexpressible feeling of potentiality, of a future with a future, even though I know in my heart of hearts that this can only be at best a mirage. Still at what point does the untruth of a mirage reveal itself to be its deepest truth?

I pause at the gate to the park. Cassie is sitting on a bench reading a book. I'm happy as never before. Nothing else matters. Just then she looks up and seeing me waves and smiles a smile of such unfeigned delight, such youthful joy that I feel blessed to be part of it, the reason for it even. We embrace beneath the doomed burghers' stern gaze and kiss as if we've been separated by a civil war, not a few measly seasonally adjusted shopping days.

"Oh, my love, let's not do that too often. Let's not allow the world to get between us like that."

She's right, what can we have been thinking? How could we have imagined that we could do other than merely subsist outside each other's ambit? It seems that, like some vast tectonic adjustment, the logic of our being together has finally clicked into place.

Locked together we idle along the Embankment. The river is running high, brown and brave to our right, and ahead the great imperial sweep of London curves away in the jonquil-coloured morning.

Sweet Thames! run softly, till I end my song.

A tugboat bustles upriver. Gulls shriek and dive. Across the river the hideous Royal Festival Hall lords it over the smaller no less ugly Queen Elizabeth one. We stop. I press her up against the parapet. Her eyes seem greener than ever. The wind worries her hair. We kiss again, and she tastes of espresso and cigarettes.

"What a joke: one large house in Hampstead, one flat in Covent Garden and nowhere to go."

"Wrong."

She smiles, it seems almost shyly, and says, "I was hoping you'd say that."

The hotel we fetch up in is just off the electronic end of Tottenham Court Road and is like thousands of its ilk: lobby full of luggage and ladies with large stomachs in belted raincoats and snow white trainers, *décor* by numbers, staff friendly and inefficient. My fib that our luggage is lost is met with a barely perceptible shrug and a well-bitten fingernail indicating where I should sign. Not having enough cash to pay the outrageous amount the place is asking for what will be a very indifferent room, I proffer my Visa knowing full well that by doing this I am in effect coming out of the closet. In a month's time (where will we be in a month's time?), Fran will know that at eleven fifty-six on

Wednesday, December 11, 2013 I checked into a double room at Bedford Court Hotel on Bayley Street. Well, so be it. Anyway, as she said it's high time I stopped bobbing and weaving.

Nor, it transpires, is it before time that we reach our room. I've no idea how many times we made love that afternoon. Suffice to say that by the time twilight nuzzles up to the window and lights are going on in the building across the street my cock is chaffed and raw and I see Cassie wince as once again she settles onto me with a sigh.

"You okay?"

She nods and says she's never been more so, and then she pushes her hair up in a pile and holds it there as she rotates her hips around me, and beyond her I can see a plain bespectacled girl watering a plant across the way. Then I'm pure pleasure as I come, and she rides on and then collapses with a singing sigh on my chest. We lie there in the dark while outside the city rumbles through the afternoon and wise men are not happy.

In the shower I ask Cassie if she'll come away with me. She stops soaping my chest and holding me at arm's length looks at me with a steady gaze. The hot water sluices over us. She's achingly beautiful, and I'm suddenly afraid that I've blown it, that I've misread the tea leaves and that the last thing on earth she wants is to go anywhere with a man twice her age.

"Where to?" she queries cocking her head to one side.

It's not an acceptance, but neither is it a refusal.

"Wherever people like us go."

"We're not like other people."

"Touché. Well?"

She bows her head (the water parts her hair evenly down the middle of her skull), and when she looks up her eyes are mirthful as she says, "I thought you'd never ask, but it had to come from you because you're the one with the most to lose."

And the most to gain I think as I gather her gratefully to me. For a while we stay like that, two bodies moulded together in the shower stall of a second-rate London hotel. Lovers about to set sail into swift uncharted waters.

"Again, where?" she asks.

I hadn't got that far, but it suddenly comes to me that what we should do is get in the car (well *a* car, even bad old me can't do that to Fran), take the ferry across the Channel, turn right at Calais and just blow. *Thelma and Louise* minus the topping of the dreadful would-be rapist. *On the Road* without the neurosis and the booze. *Route 66* without the white Corvette. No specific destinations. No deadlines. Hit the road Jack. Everybody's escapist fantasy come true.

"Sounds great. When do we leave?"

"Just as soon as I can get organised," I say briskly although I know what that will actually entail doesn't bear thinking about and anyway I've a notion I'll be doing the cowardly thing.

CHAPTER ELEVEN

An eighteen-year-old Fiat Tipo is hardly the stuff of roader dreams, not quite the wheels in which one fantasises about taking off for parts unknown: top down, waif lover by your side, pint of bourbon in the glove compartment, groovy music pumping into the indigo desert night. Still the price was right, and for a compact it has a nice roomy feel to it.

It's December 24. Cassie and I stand on the deck as the ferry steams out of the harbour. The sky's an intense blue and the Channel choppy beneath a stiff onshore breeze. Gulls wheel, hover and side slip over the marbled wake as Dover and her tattle-tale grey cliffs recede. I put my arms around Cassie and feel the curve of her back as she leans into me, and I can't help thinking of all that I'm leaving behind: my partner of some thirty years, my children, my comfortable middle-class life. All that, but as they say, you makes your choices.

"How're you doing?" Cassie queries.

"Hanging in there," I reply with little conviction.

"It can't be easy," she murmurs softly.

"I'll be fine."

However, the truth is that the last ten hectic days of subterfuge and frenzied organisation have taken their toll and I'm stretched as tight as a guitar string, emotionally and physically drained. There had been the car to buy (at a Kar Mart on the

A-40), finances to arrange (the Chester Dillon account is gratifyingly flush, I'm giving the house to Fran but will hang on to what's left of my redundancy payment) and once I'd admitted to myself that I would be unable to say goodbye to (let alone attempt an explanation of the inexplicable) the three people I'm about to desert, there were awkward letters to write.

Dear Fran. What? I'm afraid it was bog standard I'm-sloping-off-with-a-much-younger-woman fare. I'm sorry. Not your fault. Wonderful years for which I will be forever thankful. All true but which won't cut much ice with Frances Ann. I cannot *not* do what I'm doing, also true, but neither will it mean much to her because she believes implicitly that unless they are certifiably insane, human beings have not only the power but the moral duty *not* to do silly things. No forgiveness requested because none deserved.

Dear Cat. I think I've always suspected I'd do something like this. I promise I'll keep in touch. Look after your mother and try not to give her a hard time. Nor Charlie for that matter. Don't think too ill of me. *Merde* for your GCSEs. I love you.

And so to: *Dear Charlie*. Mortified that I'm the old geezer. No excuses it just happened. For what it's worth Cassie swears every which way that she was going to bust up with you before we got going. Best to try to forget about it, get on with your life. Great things ahead, no point in looking back. Believe it or not, I love you.

Of course, the letter to Charlie will be a total waste of energy, so much chaff in the wind as he's into a world-historical tailspin from which only time, the sole healer of broken hearts, will deliver him.

Three envelopes on the hall table, my house and car keys weighing them down. Familiar click of the front door, ditto the now oiled wrought-iron gate. I don't look back, and then I'm walking down Frognal towards a world in which none of the old coordinates will obtain, a world filled with missing things and the unnerving sense of my having done both the right and the wrong thing at one and the same time.

"A penny for them?" Cassie asks.

"How would 'I love you' do?"

"Splendidly. Listen, Ivor, you do know you're allowed to be to be like ... a little sad. Like it's not every day that a guy ... well ... you know ... does what you've just done."

"Thanks. And I *do* know. I'm mostly happy, honest. And what about you. How's Cassandra Laporte coping with jettisoning her London persona?"

She shrugs her shrug and replies airily, "I'm copacetic. The job was becoming a bit of a drag, flats come and go, I can live without the Patel curry factor in my life and recently I've been feeling a hit of the old wanderlust coming on. So as far as I'm concerned the timing's perfect. And for the record I think it's romantic and exciting to be here now with you, and I'm looking forward to whatever tomorrow and the next day and the next may bring. One thing though."

I knew it. Here comes the fine print, here comes the actually-I-think-you're-a-crashing-bore-and-I'd-rather-be-with-someone-my-own-age bit.

"Yes?" I query anxiously.

"No promises, no lies."

Relieved, I start, "Fine by ..."

But she interrupts me. "No, I'm serious. Like you probably think I'm being naive and showing my extreme youth and all that good shit, but I really mean it."

I say that I can see she's serious and add that I respect her for it while privately wondering just how much honesty even the most heaven-sent of relationships can bear.

It seems she can read my mind because she says, "Oh, I'm not talking about the small stuff, the fibs and white lies and such. It's just that I couldn't bear it if one or other of us ... well ... started to feel less strongly than the other and didn't say so. I've been that route before and in the long run everybody gets hurt more. Think of poor Charlie."

I explain that I've been doing my level best not to think about my son, add that I read her loud and clear, and give her my word that if I wake up one morning loving her one heartbeat less she'll be the second to know.

She kisses me and says "Good" and that appears to be the end of that. I see the vivid blue canopy of the sky, the heaving Channel and the line of the almost vanished cliffs of Dover reflected in her sunglasses, and I'm suddenly visited by a great comber of panic. Do I really think that the years can be so easily rolled back or, worse still, ignored? How long do I imagine she's going to stay interested in, let alone in love with, me?

Perhaps sensing my discomfort - or merely reading it in my eyes - she takes my head in her hands and kisses me again, long and hard and direct, and already I feel better although I now have an inkling how Faust must have felt when he made his admittedly considerably more momentous bargain.

Abbeville, some hundred kilometres south of Calais, is a government-issue northern French town, and it's there that we spend the first night of our flight into ourselves. We have a drink in a scruffy little café populated by characters from Central Casting. The proprietor, who stands behind the bar with a dead *Gauloise* dangling between his lips, appears unable to utter more than three words without saying *putain*. Two louts work a pinball machine with silent fury, and a woman in frayed plaid *pantoufles* sits running her hands through her sparse carroty hair muttering to herself. A mangy Alsatian snoozes by the door occasionally farting softly.

I enquire about hotels and the patron assures me that only at the nearby Hôtel Terminus will we have a chance of getting a room on Christmas Eve. It turns out that the Terminus is the sort of dump I haven't been in since my student days, but Cassie doesn't appear to notice the depressing little cubby hole of a room with its clashing wallpaper, sagging bed and cigarette-burned plastic shelf over a sink reeking of urine.

That night a dense fog rolls in from the Channel, and by the time we leave the hotel in search of dinner we can only see a few feet in front of our noses. Other pedestrians loom out of the swirling gruel and then are gone. Cars inch by, their headlights sucked up by the ravenous fog. Happily we find a brasserie without an eighty euro Christmas Eve menu where we have an adequate dinner and are informed by the waiter that in his considered opinion Abbeville is the least attractive and most boring town in north west France.

Groping our way in what we think is the general direction of our hotel we stop at a bar for a nightcap. Central Casting's at it again, only this time we appear to have stumbled onto the HQ of the town's underworld. Shifty looking men confer in lowered tones in upholstered booths, two bored hookers flounce about, a sleaze bag with long slicked back hair and a fake camel hair coat draped over his shoulders holds court at the bar.

Cassie sips her drink and whispers, "Where's Gérard Depardieu?"

"Off making a flic somewhere else, lucky sod. Come on, let's split."

However, just then a dwarf bursts into the café brandishing an old-fashioned service revolver that seems like a canon in the tiny man's grasp. The café goes absolutely silent apart from inter-galactic beeps coming from the electric game machines. Oddly, I notice that the midget's shoes look more like leather hoofs than normal footwear. The manikin roars "Roxanne! *Ich liebe Dich!*" and stretching his short arms as far as they can go places the barrel of the revolver in his mouth and pulls the trigger.

The detonation is ear splitting. A shocked silence ensues, and then there's a mad rush for the door. The fog seeps in through the open door while the nearly decapitated homunculus, apparently not yet quite dead, writhes and twitches on the floor.

An ashen faced Cassie turns to me and croaks, "Like, how boring can you get?"

We spend most of Christmas Day in bed, reading, doing NY Times crossword puzzles, making love, dozing. Finally towards the end of the afternoon, we rouse ourselves and, bundling up against the cold, go for a walk through the deserted streets of the town which proves to be every bit as uninteresting as billed.

"My God, can you imagine living in a place like this?"

Cassie demurs. "Sure I can. You forget, I was brought up in dozens of dullsvilles just like this, and I've got to admit that part of me still kind of hankers for the simplicity and ... what? ... innocence of small-town USA."

"You'd be climbing the walls in no time flat."

"I'm not so sure. You know I'm not nearly as ... I don't know ... worldly ... complicated ... interesting even ... as you seem to think I am."

I tell her I think *all* people are complicated including the boring ones and that she's plenty interesting for me, and we move on.

That night, like murderers drawn back to the scene of the crime, we go back to the bar where the midget killed himself. It turns out that the man was from a German travelling circus who had recently been betrayed in love by the other two-thirds of his act. Eerily, most of last night's cast are still in place, and Cassie wonders out loud whether these folks have family.

"People in glass houses," I reply.

She nods. "Fair enough, anyway right now you're family enough for me."

"And you for me," I say and while it's true I can't help wondering what my former family are up to. At that moment I experience a sudden panicky sense of the sheer irreversibility of what I've done. It passes but I am warned that there will be moments when the critical mass of my past, of my pre-Cassie life, will haunt me.

We have a sandwich and a beer before returning to the hotel where our neighbours are screwing noisily in something that might be Serbo-Croat. Cassie gets a fit of the giggles before we join in the fun and the Hôtel Terminus is definitely where the action is in Abbeville on Christmas Day, 2013.

The next morning after a brief tour of Amiens and its cathedral we drive to Paris where we stay with Jim and Cheri Spivak, friends of Cassie's from her SUNY days.

Jim's a farm boy from upstate New York who did well at Cornell and joined the Chase Manhattan bank which, after few years in the Big Apple, sent him to Paris. Cheri's his high school sweetheart and not terribly bright. Jimbo's all Sulka shirts and red felt braces while she's into Hermès scarves and Charles Jourdan shoes. They've been in Paris just long enough to have developed the irritating habit of pretending not to remember certain key English words. (The bank is paying for private French lessons). I suppose I shouldn't have let them piss me off - they're young and keen and at least not anti-everything un-American - but they did. Thanks to a generous housing allowance they live in an elegant block of flats off the rue du Bac and as far as I can make out, think nothing of it. I don't imagine they're any worse than others of their breed, but I'd soon had a bellyful of the Michelin stars, vintages (sorry, *millésimes*) and the impending fortnight in Mégève, so it isn't long before I take to going for long walks around the city.

"Oh, come on, they're not that bad."

"Sure they are," I insist.

PATRICK STARNES

Cassie and I have met at a wine bar on the Ile de la Cité. A light snow is falling, and although it's only a matter of hours since we parted I feel an adrenaline jolt of pleasure as I see her striding across the bridge with the collar of her bomber jacket turned up against the gusting wind and a dusting of flakes on her bright green beret.

"Well, I don't think they are. Maybe you're just a teeny weeny bit jealous that he's doing so well so young?"

I thought we'd get to that sooner or later.

"But that's just it, he's not doing well, or at least not in any way that matters, he's not."

She takes a sip of wine. The snow's coming down much harder now, and I can only just make out the equestrian statue of Henry IV across the street.

"What ways *do* matter?"

"Not his way. He's got a degree in financial sleight-of-hand, a veneer of general knowledge, an inflated salary and he thinks he's got the world by the balls."

"Maybe he has. Like maybe for him he has what he wants."

I'm angry with myself for being drawn into what I sense are dangerous waters (what do I know what matters to another generation?), but that doesn't stop me saying prissily, "There's no foundation. It's all done with smoke and mirrors. He hasn't paid his dues."

Cassie studies me coolly from behind half-closed lids, then clicks her tongue and says, "Whatever. Please, let's not fight."

"Agreed."

"Good. Promise you'll be a good boy tonight."

Jim's taking us out to dinner as special clients of the bank. Frankly, I hope his boss turns up at the next table and the creep has to explain how Chase's European operations will be bettered by expensively wining and dining a pair of lovers on the lam neither of whom have ever even had an account with the bank.

"I'll do my best."

Which I do, but it's not enough. I crack when I realise Jim's labouring under the misapprehension that Evelyn Waugh is a woman.

"Waugh's first wife was another Evelyn. Perhaps that's what you're thinking of?"

Jim's drunk a good deal of château whatever and blinks owlishly at me for a while before saying, "Of course. *Garçon, encore une bouteille, s'il vous plait.*"

Cheri, I'm only now twigging, seems to have designs on me doubtless because she's pretty sure that's how you're supposed to behave when your friend appears on your doorstep with a fifty-something lover in tow. She practically dunks her tits in my *velouté de concombre* in her eagerness to play the worldly coquette.

"Oh, I just adored *The Winds of War.*"

I haven't a clue what she's on about until Cassie remarks sweetly, "That's your Wouk, Herman, as opposed to your Waugh, Evelyn."

Jimbo can't let that pass unquipped upon and says, "Time you *woke* up hon ... get it?"

Cheri squeals with delight and says, "Jimmy's just the best punster ever, aren't you hon?"

He nods modestly and asserts that the pun is indeed the highest form of flattery. I've had enough, but through the twinkling grove of crystal and candles and flowers I observe Cassie eyeing her host speculatively as if trying to assess whether he's worth it or not. At length she says, "Isn't it imitation?"

But Jim's lost the plot. "Isn't what imitation?"

"Isn't it imitation that's the highest form of flattery, not punning?"

"Sure, that's what I said. Hey, Ivor, you ever been to the Tour d'Argent?"

Too many hours later, lying on the hide-a-bed in the Spivak's library, I can literally feel Cassie thinking. From the bathroom across the hall issues the sound of Jim noisily divesting himself of his share of the evening's three-hundred pound tab.

Aaaaaargh! Blaaaargh! Youuuargh!

"Jesus!"

Cassie laughs and says, "I think maybe you were right after all."

"About?"

"They *are* awful. Funny, because they were quite good value way back in Albany. Can they have changed that much?"

"Perhaps it's you who's done the changing."

"Perhaps. Let's leave tomorrow."

She brushes my cheek with the back of her hand. When she's asleep I lie listening to her breathing and watch the last of the snow dither out of the smoky orange sky. Yes indeed, time to move on. Then the midget's despairing 'Roxanne! *Ich liebe Dich!*' comes back to me, and I see what's left of the poor man jerking spasmodically on the floor. Eventually, I too fall asleep although the jilted lover's lonely (why did he choose a café full of perfect strangers as his final audience?) suicide pursues me into my dreams.

* * *

"Rigoletto!"

I swerve to avoid a furry creature which has scuttled across the snow-covered road ahead of us. We're somewhere in eastern France, but judging from the dark brooding hills half buried in clouds we could just as easily be driving through Transylvania. Dusk is falling and the pine trees weighed down by fresh snow look like massive chess pieces waiting patiently to be played.

"What about Rigoletto?"

"Let's call this car that. Me and Daddy always had names for the jalopies he drove. I remember a High Five, a Fantod and a Tinkerbell."

I say Rigoletto's okay by me, which it is. However, mention of the opera has reminded me of the time we took Charlie to see Aida for his eighteenth birthday at the Met. I'm besieged by a whole raft of Charlie-and Cat-related memories and go through a petty bad bit where everything seems passing pointless even my love for the woman curled up on the seat next to me as we travel through the Prussian blue of the winter's evening.

"Anybody home?" Cassie chirps.

"Sorry. Spot of *Weltschmerz*."

"Of what?"

I'm sometimes taken by surprise by what Cassie does and doesn't know.

"Literally world-pain. The blahs by any other name."

"Like Blue Monday on Thursday?"

"Something like that. What about a pit-stop, there's a village up ahead."

The village turns out to be a one-holer: five or six houses huddled around a *dépôt de pain*, a bleak café, and a W.W.I monument to the glorious fallen. After Cassie has rated the loo a surprising B-plus, we have a pastis sitting at a deal table by the window. The proprietress, a tall woman with a stoop and defeated eyes, serves us wordlessly and returns to her newspaper. Cassie places her hands on mine and asks if I'm all right.

"Getting there. I'm sorry to have been such a pain back there, but that was quite a nasty attack of the wobblies."

"Don't apologise, everyone's entitled to slippage."

She leans across the table and, pulling me towards her kisses me, and I see our reflection in the plate glass window beyond '*sèira V shciwdnaS*' and I am a chord resolved. The lady behind the bar looks up and smiles, and there's something wholly affecting about such a reaction to our public display of intimacy out here on the edge of nowhere.

"Thanks."

"But I *enjoy* kissing you," she announces.

"Well, for that," I reply, "and for being patient."

"Patient schmatient. Guess what?"

"What?" I ask hopefully.

"Oh, you know, the usual only more so every second I'm with you."

"Well, me too, and I raise your 'more so'."

The following night we celebrate New Year's Eve, an event we discover we both consider to be the most unpleasant fixture in the calendar, by having dinner in a nondescript restaurant in a nondescript suburb of Geneva and returning to our equally nondescript hotel by eleven o'clock.

In the morning we decide to head for Italy, but that evening we're trapped by a blizzard in an alpine hamlet somewhere in the Val d'Aosta. There's a hotel in the village, so we spend three days there with an interesting assortment of fellow internees (including a very old man who claims to have been King Zog of Albania's valet) and the sojourn takes on the character of an adventure rather than an inconvenience. Even after the storm has blown itself, out we have to wait another day for the ploughs to clear the roads.

Our original intention had been to head to Rome, but after ten minutes in Florence Cassie's hooked and insists we stay put. We spend two nights in a draughty *pensione*, then answer an ad on a notice board in the British Council and luck into a studio apartment overlooking the Piazza del Carmine. A visiting American art historian has had to return home on short notice and someone is needed to take over the last three months of her lease. The place is perfect: a clever entrepreneur has taken an old block of flats, gutted it and built well-designed and appointed studios which, if rented for a reasonable length of time, go for a third of the price of a room in a *pensione* with gelid marble floors and an unreliable supply of hot water. There's even a parking space for Rigoletto, so we pay for three months in advance and move in immediately.

"I feel I'm living a dream."

Cassie's standing by the window looking down on the piazza. The dying sun is an orange orb poised over the *terracotta* roofs of the buildings across the way. The room is suffused with a golden light which seems somehow to come from another age, another culture even. The moment is perfectly shaped.

"Just as long as I'm in the dream."

She looks up, smiles her smile and says quietly, "Of course you're in it. After all, it's your dream too."

CHAPTER TWELVE

We soon slip into an amiable routine. We get up late and after a coffee and a *cornetto* at our local café, Cassie bolts (she runs chronically late) for the British Council where she's taking Italian lessons while I return to the studio to squeeze out a few more pages of the thriller which is slowly emerging out of the ether on my laptop. For the foreseeable future we're solvent, but I certainly don't want to cut myself off from that source of income. Anyway, I've always enjoyed the discipline of writing and even if the Chester Dillon line is hardly high art (Cassie's thinks I should try my hand at something more weighty) I extract considerable pleasure from working on it.

Around noon I generally stroll over to the Piazza della Signoria where we meet at Enrico Rivoire's elegant establishment for an *aperitivo* after which we either return home for a light lunch or go to one of the numerous cheap and cheerful eateries in the area.

Afternoons are spent roaming around the city, hopping from church to church, visiting and re-visiting museums and galleries, reading the newspapers in cafés and inventing lurid scenarios for our neighbours' private lives. Evenings we are generally at home listening to music - Cassie's taken to opera in a serious way - reading and cooking increasingly ambitious dinners. On weekends we often set out in the car to track down Piero della

Francescas, sometimes if the weather is good enough, taking picnics.

In other words, it is the best of times. Which is not to say that we don't have our fair share of disagreements, tiffs, misunderstandings, poutings, because of course we do, but they're always about inconsequential matters and always short-lived. Indeed, it's almost as though we need these flare-ups (I soon find out that Cassie comes by her red hair right royally) as decoys, safety valves to protect the delicate reactor at the core of our relationship.

However, having Scottish blood, part of me has trouble accepting such good fortune. And in this it seems I am not alone for once in a meadow with a Tuscan hill town as backdrop Cassie confides that she sometimes feels guilty that she's as happy as she is.

"I kind of feel that there's something wrong with being so ... oh, I don't know ... lucky, blessed even, if that doesn't sound too jerky.'

I say that it doesn't sound the least bit jerky and allow as I sometimes feel the same. What I do not mention is that I'm old enough and ugly enough to suspect that in the fullness of time the world will contrive to extract its pound of flesh, blood and all. But for now the world is our oyster, Florence is a fine place to be and the future is now.

At the end of February I receive a written letter from Fran. I've been in contact through Blakeney Talbot, our solicitor, concerning the transfer of the ownership of the house and have arranged for him to forward any snail mail without divulging my whereabouts. Even then, I only supplied him with a *poste restante* address so anxious am I that we be left to ourselves. We use our phones exclusively for dictionaries and Google.

It's a mild morning and I sit on the balustrade of a bridge with a splendid view of the river and the Ponte Vecchio beyond. Seeing Fran's familiar handwriting gives me a turn. For some thirty years that script has been a presence in my life: notes, reminders, shopping lists, love letters (in the early days), postcards when on trips with her parents or the kids, recipes, address book entries, all the freighted components of a shared life.

The arrangements seem fine to me. I'd thank you for the house if I didn't think that A: I deserve it, B: I imagine you're giving it to me in the mistaken view that doing so will somehow lessen your guilt. Ungenerous? Of course, but that's how I feel towards you, that's how it is with me these days.

Where to start? Well, even now months after you walked (slithered like the snake you are) out of my life and the lives of our children, I can still hardly contain my anger. Know one thing: I shall never, ever forgive you for what you have done.

I stop reading. A sculler in a cerise zephyr glides downstream. Fran's rage fairly crackles out of the densely written missive. I realise that I'm surprised she's so furious. But why? What did I expect? A polite thank you note? Still, Fran as a Fury is hard to come to terms with because I now see that I've somehow managed to convince myself that after the initial shock had worn off she'd be the tolerant, forgiving Fran of a thousand former dust-ups and reconciliations, certainly not this unyielding Ice Princess.

Now, let me tell you what you have done. Simply because you have been unable to keep your pecker in your pants (don't you dare talk to me about love) you've destroyed our family. You've betrayed me (I'll survive, albeit badly scarred), you've betrayed your son in the most grotesque manner imaginable (he's still here and in a terrible state, but more of that later) and you've abandoned your teenage daughter at precisely the time in her life when she's most in need of stability and some role models that don't change with the weather. I honestly didn't think I was capable of hatred, but I now know differently and that saddens me more than I can say. It's like some essential loss of innocence. If I could hurt you, I would, and that realisation for an essentially tame, civic-minded person is devastating.

Predictably, my parents (Daddy really) have not been slow to slot into a we-told-you-so mode and talk a load of rubbish about bloodlines and family-trees and writings on the wall and so forth, but providing them with the ammunition to rub my face in all that has not further endeared you to me. Still, I can live with it. What I am having a great deal of trouble assimilating is that your son, the real loser in all this, for reasons best known to himself refuses to actually blame you for what has happened. When I broke the news to him (i.e. gave him your sleazy, self-serving letter) he understandably went stratospheric, but not against you, against your whore if you please. He said she was always cheating on him (your turn will come, boyo, your turn will come) and that she was a witch and a bitch and much more (in graphic detail), all of which makes my ears burn just remembering it. They say that the line between love and hate is easily crossed and on the basis of my own experience and what Charlie is expressing I would have to say 'they' have a point. Still, while I don't think your slut is anything other than that, I blame you and you alone for what has taken place. Don't get me wrong, Charlie's mad at you, mad as hell, but as I said he doesn't seem to think it was your fault. I suppose the poor boy was/is so in love with the creature that he can empathise with someone else falling for her. By the way, tell the lady (sic) that she'd better not come across Charlie in a dark alley. For the record, he refused point blank to return to the States and mopes around the house looking tragic, doing nothing and losing weight by the day. Make you feel proud of yourself?

As for Cat, well, she was devastated. Oddly, for someone as independent and brassy as she is, she was ashamed and had real trouble facing her peers at school because, as you can imagine, the tom-toms were beating in no time flat. Everyone knows, and worst of all they commiserate. She's better now and, not that I imagine you much care now that you're living out your post-menopausal fantasy, she seems to have come clear through her bolshie period, has dropped most of that rat pack and is focusing on getting into Oxford.

Which brings me to me. I'm not going to claim I never loved you. I once did, wholeheartedly and almost faithfully, which I imagine is more than can be said for you as I can't believe your chum Ruth was a one-off. We had some good times: you were a witty companion, a fair-to-middling lover and an adequate father. In retrospect I can see that your being made redundant was probably the beginning of the end for us. The End was Charlie going off to MIT leaving you to horn in on his girl. God, you utter creep! A surprising thing has happened: along with the anger I have recently come to recognise another emotion operating in me, to wit, relief. Yes, relief. Relief that I'll never again have to put up with your childish sulks, your deeply hypocritical attitude towards my parents, your tantrums, and recently your excessive drinking. Relief that I can go to a dinner party without having to worry about who you're going to be rude to. I put up with all that and much more because I believed I still loved you, because you were the father of my children and because I thought that's what troupers did. Well, this trouper's taken her last bow and believe me it feels great.

So there you have it. Blakeney is drawing up divorce papers and doubtless you will hear from him in due course. Let me guess, you're in Tuscany or, if not, there ... no Tuscany it is. Right?

Right.

Fair-to-middling?

The sun is shining out of a blue sky in ever so fucking obvious Tuscany. It's hard to believe such an uncompromising letter could have come from the pen of Fran, a woman not much given to extremes, but I've only myself to blame for having roused the virago in her. I re-read the letter and am surprised how little I am affected by it. Of course she's got it pretty much right although as usual I cannot bring myself to agree that something which feels so right can be all that bad. Trust Charlie to make such a meal of it, and why won't anybody take on board the simple fact that he and Cassie were through before I embarked on my sin-laden horning in? I suppose it must be because it doesn't make as good copy: Dad the Corrupter of Youth plays better than Dad the Accidental Opportunist. Cat being so upset is a surprise, but I'm glad she's extricated herself from her hang-around-somehow-managing-to-look-both-bored-*and*-pissed-off-at-the-same-time set.

It seems I too am relieved. Fran's letter and her brutal honesty have made it official as has her perfectly understandable desire to get a divorce. Characteristically, she's supplied the full stop at which I for some reason have mentally baulked, and I'm grateful to her for it.

I rip the letter into pieces and toss them over the edge, watching as they flutter down to the tawny braid of an Arno swollen by winter rains.

Full stop.

Cassie's sitting smoking at a table in a wedge of sun in one of Rivoire's windows. Steam from her cappuccino spirals up and away. She's engrossed in a textbook, the tip of her tongue a red button in one corner of her mouth, her forehead creased with concentration. It comes to me then that love isn't *like* anything, is not susceptible to the simile, can neither be parsed nor qualified, it simply is.

She looks up and seeing me waves and blows me a kiss.

Oh, yes.

Over lunch I give her a bowdlerised version of Fran's letter and cannot resist asking if Charlie's accusation that she cheated on him was true. She takes a sip of her wine and then staring at some point above my head says slowly, "Well, things may have overlapped a bit. It was hard to tell what was ending and what was beginning, but once we were a number, no, I was faithful."

"Then ..."

"Listen, Charlie was jealous, insanely so, come to think of it. Like he was always imagining things, inventing demon boyfriends, imagining trysts that never happened. A perfectly innocent friend from my Barcelona days once showed up and for a while in there Charlie behaved pretty badly. To be honest he got to be a complete drag about it all, and finally I had to explain that I wasn't his chattel. I'm not anyone's, not even yours and you at least I love. *Basta*! I'm going to be a pig and have some of their *Crostate di fragole*."

Your turn will come boyo, your turn will come.

* * *

In February we take the train to Ravenna, Cassie having decided that life would not be worth living without having checked out at least some of that lovely city's Byzantine mosaics. The trip is hexed from the word go. We get into a hassle with some stout-thighed German ladies over seats. A waiter drops a plate of spaghetti in Cassie's lap. After Forli the heavens open and rain sluices down out of a sky the colour of bad dreams. Ravenna itself is shrouded in a marrow-chilling fog. Our room gives onto a half-empty pseudo canal and smells of drains and stale cigar smoke. We have dinner in a noisy *trattoria* full of American college kids, and after an argument about nothing in particular we turn in early.

I awake in the middle of the night. Cassie stirs and mutters in her sleep. Way off in the distance a foghorn sounds, three blasts and then after an interval a final, long, infinitely mournful sob.

There's nothing like waking in the early hours of the morning in an unfamiliar hotel room, next to a woman half your age, in a town gripped by a pea-soup fog to get the old intimations of mortality working overtime. My funk lasts until I fall into a thin sleep and dream of wind and rooks in a graveyard above Sligo and my father dead in an Albany flop house.

In the morning Cassie takes one look out the window – the rain has not let up and the fog is even denser than before – shudders and announces that she's staying in bed. So I tramp around the city, get lost and sodden and return to the hotel out of sorts. That night we have another indifferent meal and wonder why we've come to Ravenna in the first place, apart from the mosaics.

Again I awake in the middle of the night. Drowsily I move over to touch Cassie, but she's not there. Still only half awake, I sit up in bed. The bathroom light is on, but the door's closed, and I can hear a low chanting sound coming from the inside. Alarmed, I slip out of bed and listen at the door.

"Cassie?"

The chanting continues uninterrupted. I open the door. She's sitting naked on the toilet with her head between her knees and her arms clasped around her shins. The crooning continues and then she runs her hands through her hair and very slowly raises her head and looks at me. Except she's not looking at me, she's looking *through* me. Her normally lucent eyes are blurred and absent, and finally I get it.

The syringe is on the sink beside her. I am truly surprised. Cassie smokes the odd joint (I don't know and don't ask where the stuff comes from) but I'd no idea she did hard drugs.

"'Lo, Ivor."

I've not had much experience with drugs so I don't really know what stage she's at nor what to do. I stand swaying in the bathroom doorway, a faintly ludicrous figure, my eyes squinty in the bright light, my mind in a muddle.

"Don't be angry ..."

I'm not angry, just afraid and confused but I manage to croak, "Why?"

She shrugs and says, "Dunno. Woke up and felt sad and lonely so I thought I'd do something about it. Silly really. You go Up and then you go Down, and then you're back where you started. Oh, fuck, why doesn't anything last?"

Because it doesn't. Because that's the hand we're dealt. All of us. Because, sublime paradox that easily sees off all the other paradoxes, that's the only constant.

I say "Some things last longer than others", but she's lapsed back inside herself and reverts to the crooning that I now recognise as a bizarre version of "Rockaby Baby". I kneel beside her and put my arms around her. She starts crying, and her whole body is convulsed by great shuddering sobs which seem to come from the very depths of her being and speak of an ancient sadness the existence of which I'd had no inkling. But why hadn't I? We've all been impelled into an alien world from the warmth and safety of the womb and so have accounts at the same bank. Every last one of us, saints and sinners, simpletons and rocket scientists alike. So why should she be any different? Perhaps because I love her so much, I can't bear the thought of her being subject to the same fear, the same terror as am I.

Finally when she's cried herself out I manage to get her to bed where she falls instantly into a deep slumber. At first unable to get back to sleep, I pace up and down until with oyster-grey dawn seeping into the room, I return to bed and finally doze off.

"Ivor?"

The voice comes from a long way off. I fight to remain dissociated from it, coddled as I am in a dream world where loss is a metaphor.

"Good morning."

I open my eyes. Cassie's sitting at the little desk by the window. The fog is still with us. She's dressed and looks as bright and fresh as a new coat of paint. Then I remember and groan.

"As well you might. I'm sorry about last night, I really am."

"You frightened the shit out of me."

"I frightened the shit out of *me*. It won't happen again, promise."

I sit up in bed. Someone flushes a toilet, the plumbing gurgles and clanks.

"What was it?"

She shakes her head impatiently. "Does it matter?"

"Not in the least. I'm just curious," I reply.

"Heroin. Miriam gave me a hit as a going away present. Like she does a lot of stuff."

"And you don't?"

"You know perfectly well I don't. It's a common misconception that you get hooked simply by having the crap in your house or whatever. I used to do a bit of it, the dire Darius was a minor pusher, but that's the first time I've shot up in ... oh, I don't know ... ages."

She's right. I've always assumed that with hard drugs it was a question of zero tolerance, one strike and you're out, doomed from the first euphoric rush to a vicious spiral of addiction ending in a squalid death in a doss house. Well, that's clearly not the case here, but there's also no getting away from the fact that I'm taken aback by Cassie's admitting she's used hard drugs. Suddenly I feel old, disposable, out of place, like a stranger arrived in a city bereft of signs, known landmarks, familiar sights.

"What's wrong?"
"Someone just walked on my grave."
"Come on, let's go home," she says firmly.

***

In early May I finish the Chester Dillon and send it off to the publishers on the same day that Blakeney Talbot writes to inform me that I'm a divorced man.

"Well?"

"Well what?"

We're lying on a gently sloping field with a distant view of Volterra. All around us the meadow is carpeted with a profusion of wild flowers.

"What's it feel like to be an ex?" she asks cheerfully.

I point out that since she's been down the divorce route herself, she should know what it feels like.

"Well, actually I don't."

"Come again."

"Darius and I were never divorced. I just split one morning when I'd had enough. So technically at least, I'm still Mrs Darius Lascelles although given the company he kept and his talent for making enemies I'm more likely to be a widow than anything else."

I'm surprised she hasn't mentioned this before, but when I say so she shrugs and says, "It's not something I much enjoy thinking about, let alone talking about. As you know, the whole thing was a train wreck from the word go."

"But what made you go with him in the first place?"

Cassie squints into the middle distance, sighs deeply and says softly, "I've already told you, I was very lonely, he was good looking and … like charming in that dreadful English upper class sort of way … at first … you know."

"I suppose. And what finally made you leave him?"

"A right hook."

"You're joking."

"I'm not. He was a *very* bad actor."

"And you haven't seen him since?"

"No, thank God. I once met a school pal of his who'd bumped into him somewhere or other. Apparently Mr Lascelles was still frothing at the mouth at my having left him and vowing vengeance if he ever lays eyes on me again. Enough, let's talk about something nice, or better still let's *do* something nice."

A few weeks later we can't get a table at our favourite restaurant because the place has been overrun by a group of Japanese tourists from the Kobe White Water Club. And the next day Cassie returns from her class in a towering rage because she's just seen some tanked-up college kids throwing a Frisbee around the Piazza della Signoria.

"It was gross."

"Well, it's going to get worse before it gets better. Maybe it's time to move on?"

"That's just what I was thinking. Would you mind?"

"Not at all,' I reply truthfully, "just as long as we do the moving on together."

She smiles and says "yes please, always and forever" with such conviction that I can only believe that it will be so.

For someone who has, until my recent self-imposed exile, lived in precisely two houses in nearly twenty-five years of what has been a preternaturally bourgeois, settled life, I take to the nomadic existence on which Cassie and I now embark with surprising gusto. I imagine most middle-class, middle-aged punters like myself have had, at one time or another, the yearning to drop it all: the mortgage, the car servicing and MOTing, the shopping at Sainsbury's, the Department meetings about not very much, the worrisome children, the in-laws, the squeaking garden gate, the whole shooting match. Just say *sayonara* to all that and blow, wander where the wind or the road or your fancy takes you. Juvenile, puerile, elitist, unrealistic, irresponsible and much, much more it may be, but believe me it's fun. And if you happen to be able to arrange your moonwalk in the company of a stunningly beautiful woman with a lively sense of humour and an active libido, well, so much the better.

CHAPTER THIRTEEN

We spend June and July meandering through the South of France, mostly sticking to small villages in the interior. Sometimes if we particularly like a place or find a hotel which is good value, we stay for three or four days, but for the most part without any sense of haste we keep on the move, and the unplanned, footloose, quality of our travels lends a will-o'-the-wisp charm to them. Furthermore the vivid colours, the hot summer sun, scorched skies, swallows swooping across evening skies, the nervy thrill of cicadas, the tawny land and sleepy villages, genista, lavender, eucalyptus, cypress and pine exuding their complicated aromas - all contribute an exotic romanticism to our flight.

"Sometimes I feel so full of my love for you that there's nothing of *me* left. It's strange and wonderful all at the same time," she says her hand in mine as light as a child's.

We're sitting on the balcony of our room in a modest hotel in the countryside outside Carpentras. The last light has faded in the west, and now the sky is spread out like a vast magician's cloak. I can see the pale oval of her face and the whites of her eyes framed by the dark mass of her hair. I too am consumed by love and when for the thousandth time, I tell her so she squeezes my hand and says, "Maybe in misplacing ourselves we make room for the other."

Perhaps she's right, perhaps loving is precisely about losing that sense of self which in other situations we so cherish. Certainly nothing in my past (not even the heady days of my courtship with Fran) has prepared me for the sheer emotional excess I'm experiencing.

At the end of July Rigoletto coughs and expires somewhere in the hills above Aix-en-Provence and has to be carted off to hospital in the unlovely outskirts of that most lovely of towns. Because of the Festival the place is full to the rafters, but with scarcely credible good luck we manage to secure not only a hotel room but also tickets for *Così fan tutte* that same night.

After the performance we walk down through the old town to the bustling Cours Mirabeau where we have a coffee in a café beneath dusty plane trees rustling in the hot summer breeze. Even at that hour the bars are crowded and the air is full of the babble of a dozen languages. Waiters, most looking as if they would prefer to be elsewhere, weave amongst the tables while barefoot gypsy girls try without evident success to flog sprigs of white heather.

Cassie, who's been captivated by the opera (her first live Mozart), is full of questions many of which I can't answer (like whose side is WAM on?), and it occurs to me that one of the many pleasures to come my way since we've been together has been seeing how eagerly she has embraced the lavish cultural feast on offer all around us. By her own admission formerly something of a popcorn and *Jurassic Park* kind of girl (although for all that remarkably well read), now it's she who's first to forge up the stony path radiating the midday heat to the obscure Romanesque chapel alluded to in a footnote of our guidebook.

I see Kenneth and Muriel before they see me. But it's all wrong; my ex-in-laws hardly ever go Abroad, certainly not to the South of France in deep midsummer. In fact ever since I've known them they've gone to the same hotel in St. Mawes (same room, same sheets for all I know) for the last two weeks of July. So what the fuck are they doing pootling down Aix's main drag at eleven-thirty on a hot summer's night? Panicky thought: maybe Fran, Charlie, Cat are with them too? But no, they seem to be on their own unless they're with the equally counties couple ahead of them. That'll be it; old friends (Rog and Pru) from the bank days who have a renovated *mas* nearby and have been trying to get them to visit for years. Kenneth, red-faced and much frailer than when I last saw him, is wearing the summer uniform (we've seen the winter one in the badlands of Soho) of his sect: grey worsted trousers with cuffs, brown corduroy brothel creeper Hush Puppies, a limply hanging wrinkled off-white linen jacket, a striped City shirt, natty ascot and a vanilla-coloured Panama with sweat stains around the brim.

Muriel ... but now I've been sighted. Like wind-up toy soldiers they've come to a stop by our table. Muriel's mouth hangs open like a gargoyle's, Kenneth turns a shade redder and puts his arm around his wife's shoulders as if to protect her from the manifest danger of being confronted by her asshole ex-son-in-law after dark in a foreign city.

I've not only been sighted, I've been sighted with a hand three-quarters of the way up one of Cassie's slim brown thighs and she with one of hers tucked down the side of my crotch.

"Keir!"

"Hello, Kenneth, Muriel. Lovely evening."

I make no attempt to disengage from Cassie.

I can see that Muriel's not going to be able to say anything. Kenneth on the other hand would like to say a whole lot (and doubtless have me horsewhipped into the bargain), but just then the distaff side of the unit ahead turns and whinnies "Come along you two, *do* stop dawdling" and the Barkers shuffle dutifully on, soon to be swallowed up by the crowd.

"Your ex's folks?"

"Yes. How did you guess?"

"Dunno. Maybe Charlie once told me their names. Like they look quite ... ah ... heavy going."

"Oh, they're not that bad, just living in the wrong century."

Later after we've made love in our poky room, which is seemingly slap in the middle of some train tracks, we lie on the sweat-drenched bed balefully observed by a long-suffering Christ skewered to his cross.

"Ivor?"

"Yes?"

"D'you think about them a lot?"

"Who?" I ask knowing full well who she's talking about.

"You know, your family? Charlie, Cat, your ... ah ... ex."

She never refers to Fran by name, something which I find endearing, as if to use it would be to allow her some *ex post facto* status Cassie's unwilling to grant her.

"Not a lot."

"But do you miss them?"

"Sometimes. Oddly enough it's Cat I'd like to see the most. I don't think I ever really got the hang of Charlie ..."

"That's because our Charlie's hard to get a handle on. He's an enigma even to himself."

"I guess," I say somewhat sulkily because who wants the son whose grass you've scythed to be more enigmatic than you?

Then I say, out of the blue, "D'you remember that business on Lake Garda?"

"What business?" she counters warily.

"Charlie shoving his sister overboard. That business."

"Of course I do. What of it?"

"Did you ever ask him why he did it?"

Cassie looks at me thoughtfully. "I did, plus I told him that I'd told you I'd seen him doing it."

I'm seriously surprised, "Jesus! What did you do that for?"

"Dunno really. I guess I assumed you would have already had it out with him."

Guilty now, I say, "Never got around to it. Dumb but true. So, what was he up to?"

"Apparently it just came over him, but at the same time as he was doing it he regretted it. Hence the heroics. Come on, Ivor, let's talk about, no, do something else …"

In the morning the car's ready. With the temperature already soaring into the high thirties (with the humidity right up there) by ten o'clock, we decide that discretion's the better part of comfort and make a cross-country dash for the relative cool of the Pyrenees. We spend a week in a pretty mountain village on the French side of the border. Much to my surprise and I think to hers (apparently she was miles from being a jock in any of her former incarnations), Cassie takes to hiking with a vengeance and so every day we walk for hours beneath a cerulean sky through brown valleys and over the passes and cols used for centuries by pilgrims to and from Santiago de Compostela.

"Look!"

We've stopped for a picnic near a tiny whitewashed chapel set high on an upland meadow with a view all the way to the distant hazy shimmer of the Bay of Biscay. Directly above us an eagle circles in the sky, a snake swaying helplessly in its talons.

"Christ, let's hope he doesn't decide to drop his lunch on us."

Cassie, who's peeled off her tank top, nods and shading her eyes follows the great bird as it travels in wide loops away, down towards the valley and finally out of sight. Seeing her like that so tanned, so healthy, so young, I'm filled with gratitude that she should see anything in a fifty-something with glabrous shins and incipient varicose veins.

"I seem to remember reading that an eagle bearing a snake was some sort of bad omen."

"You're dead right. It's in *The Iliad*. The Trojans saw it as a sign that they could not defeat the Greeks."

Cassie laughs and says, "Come to think of it, all I read was only an old Classic Comic I found in the mouldy basement of another of our rented bungalows. But what does it mean for us?"

"Whatever we want."

"Then let it mean that we'll go on as we are forever and ever."

Bless her. We rarely talk about the future. I think neither of us is ready to ask some of the hard questions that lie out there in the no-man's-land of tomorrow. But there will be time for that, and meanwhile there is this perpetual self-regenerating present which is more than enough.

The wild beauty of much of the Basque coast is one of the best kept secrets in Europe. While suntan-lotion slathered hordes slog over greasy beaches to claim their allotment of the tepid, turd and condom infested Mediterranean, the marbled surf of the Bay of Biscay pounds in on rocky inlets with lush green fields rushing down to virtually deserted beaches. While resorts along the various Costas burst at the seams with beer-swilling oafs, the villages along the Cantabrian coast retain a spirit and dignity of their own even at the height of the summer season.

Years ago - the summer before I met Fran, to be precise - I spent a month camping along that coast with a brainy Swedish graduate student named Lila Langseth. We'd met at a Wordsworth seminar, screwed a few times in her bedsit on Trumpington Street and decided on the spur of the moment to go to Spain together. Lila was a large-boned, sleepy-eyed creature who shaved nothing and with whom I was pretty sure I was in love. Occasionally I've wondered what became of her. Doubtless she's a Professor of English Literature (Middleton was her man) at Uppsala or wherever, with a social-scientist husband, two point three children, a Saab 900i, and a lover who's one of her husband's colleagues.

Certainly, she gave me some much-needed pointers in female anatomy for which I've always been grateful.

As I know she will, Cassie immediately falls for the region, so for the first few weeks of August we explore the coast moving from one fishing village to the next, staying in *fondas*. The weather is hot without being ridiculously so, the sea warm without being soupy, the seafood cheap and plentiful, the wine strong and no less abundant. Always we are our own headlines, and somewhere in there I realise that I've stopped waiting for the other shoe to drop. I understand that Cassie's not about to sneak off in the night, she's not going to leave me with a Dear John letter and a hole as big as Montana in my heart because she's where and with whom she wants to be. I love and I am loved: a perfect sentence.

Around the middle of the month my publishers return the last two chapters of my book with the tart suggestion that they be comprehensively reworked. Although they're right (the chapters in question bear all the hallmarks of the work of a seriously distracted mind), I resent this incursion into our space. However Cassie urges me to get to work, so we settle into a gloomily furnished room in a farmhouse above the lively fishing village of Guetaria where I try to repair the damage, but my heart's not in it so daily progress is measured in paragraphs rather than pages.

September comes. Spaniards and foreigners alike depart leaving the village to be repossessed by its inhabitants. Then for a full week fierce storms batter the coast. While Cassie reads *The Alexandria Quartet* in bed, covered by mounds of blankets, I manage to produce a sustained bout of work which sees the book to a finish.

That evening after Cassie has read and approved (not by any means a given) my efforts, we head off for a celebration dinner in the village. We stop at two or three *mésons* on the cobbled street which leads to the port as much to get out of the weather as for a shot of the thick red country wine on offer. The bars are filled with stocky, broad-shouldered, blue-jowled Basques much given to breaking into wild riffs of plaintive song.

"Here's to Chester Dillon."

I grimace. I've had the book up to my back teeth and now care only about having healthy royalties regularly transferred to my bank account. I tell her it'll be some time before I can get up for writing anything more demanding than a postcard. She shrugs and says she can understand in a tone that suggests she can't, and then we're back to her suggestion that I try my hand at something more serious.

"I'm not interested. Or at least right now I'm not. Anyway someone once said - I think it may have been Kurt Vonnegut - that it's just as well for novelists to have something on their minds. Well, I've you on my mind big time, but that's about it."

"I like being on your mind. I just don't want you to get bored."

Bored? She must be mad. I haven't spent a bored second in her company since the day Charlie brought her home for our inspection. Oh, there have been other emotions, plenty of them, but ennui's been notably absent from the check list.

After dinner as we're hurrying along the quay it's evident that there's been some sort of incident out on the sea wall. Half a dozen *Guardia Civil* Land Rovers, some regular police cars, motorcycles and an ambulance, all with lights flashing ominously are clustered around the access to the jetty. Red and white striped plastic ribbons cordon off the area and there's a palpable whiff of danger in the air.

Given the weather there are a surprising number of people milling about, but no one seems to know exactly what has happened although the word *asesinato* is often repeated. After some shadowy movement around the back of the ambulance, it suddenly bursts into action like some freshly awakened vehicle from outer space. With lights flashing and sirens wailing, it hares off down the quay behind two motorcycles followed by a small cavalcade of official vehicles all emanating bad news.

Wet and chastened we slog back up the hill to our farmhouse. Somewhere out there someone will surely soon be mourning the loss of a loved one.

Make that loved ones. In the morning Miguel, a waiter in the village who lived in The Bronx for fifteen years, tells us that rogue ETA hatchet-men murdered two *Guardia Civil* out at the end of the sea wall.

"Dey was garrodded, an dis here's supposed ta be de twenty-first century. Fuckin' animals, know whadamean? *Si, si, vengo.*"

"Oh God, that does it."

"What does what?" I query although I can guess.

Cassie stares moodily into her espresso and then without looking up says, "Time to strike camp."

The sky's cleared, and the day has dawned bright and fresh. But she's right. The village only yesterday so friendly and familiar now, in spite of the welcome change in the weather, feels cold and foreign. Suddenly there's a bad taste to the place which nothing but leaving it can put to rights.

"Fine. Where shall we go?"

"Dunno. South, I guess," she whispers miserably and then adds in a wail, "Oh, Ivor why are people so ... so ... unbelievably cruel to each other?"

There's real anguish in her voice, and as was often the case with the children as they reeled from one of life's harsh lessons to the next, I wish I could shield her from a world in which men who read bedtime stories to their children also strangle other children's fathers with piano wire and lob grenades into crowded supermarkets the better to make political points. But of course there's nothing to say save that for every murdered baby there are a hundred acts of grace, for every headline screaming hate and atrocity there are a thousand kind words blooming on the lips of men and women who seek no reward for their utterance.

By noon we've packed the car, paid our bill and left. The weather turns hot again. We travel with no itinerary. Rooms in *fondas* merge and gel into a sort of composite room: ponderous waxed furniture, rough sheets, crucifix, mildewed mirror over cracked sink, sound of eggs being beaten for the family *tortilla* coming from gloomy interior wells. I've grown not to mind these stifling rooms, shared bathrooms and cheap restaurants which are all that our budget can run to. Cassie (who seems impervious to most physical discomforts) remarks that it's good that we, not our creature comforts nor even the places we visit, are the main event.

After two sweltering days in Madrid (even the saints and sinners in the paintings in the Prado look hot), we leave the capital and head west again and are soon captivated by Estramadura's muscular beauty. We move from ancient walled towns to crumbling villages that seem to have no obvious reason for their existences, and in between the skies are enormous and the sense of being poised at the edge of the world real.

As September blazes we swing south each experiencing a sense of living at the centre of a script written for us. It's as if we are the stars in a movie most people only ever get to rent at their local video store. No doubt my middle-class upbringing and later life must have something to do with the inordinate pleasure I get from acting like a superannuated hippie on speed.

One night after a dinner in a *cantina* perched high above the Straits of Gibraltar, we walk along the path which winds along the cliff tops. It is a night of luminous, beauty. Stars quiver in the amphitheatre of the sky. A full moon hangs low on the horizon casting a foundry-lick of light across the water. There is no wind and far below the ocean murmurs in foamy phosphorescence. Across the straits the lights of Tangier twinkle on the rim of the crouching bulk of the continent. Ships inch across the water like tiny models in a diorama.

"Pinch me."

I kiss her.

"Now *that* was a much better idea. And now?"

"And now what?"

"Now that we're fresh out of Spain, I was wondering what you had in mind?"

I suppose I'd always assumed that once we'd got this far we'd simply carry on, take the ferry to Morocco, a country neither of us has been to, and continue to play our roles in the improbable story we're living.

I point towards the distant shoreline and declaim mock theatrically, "Would you believe *into* Africa?"

Cassie laughs delightedly and mimicking Meryl Streep mimicking Isak Dinesen growls, "Vee had a farm."

The next day we drive into Algeciras and buy tickets for the ferry to Tangier, which leaves in the early evening. The weather's turned and the wind sweeps across the little town bending the tops of the palm trees and sending miniature twisters of leaves and rubbish skittering up the dusty streets. We manage to kill the morning drinking endless coffees and traipsing around the town which has little save its very ordinariness to recommend it. We draw lunch out as long as we can and then settle down in a café near the ferry terminal and share a week old *Sunday Times*.

"Wow! Get a load of this."

I've been reading a review of a biography of Joseph Goebbels and have just come across the truly astounding fact that as the war was rushing headlong to its apocalyptic conclusion, Hitler's crazed Reichsminister of Public Enlightenment and Propaganda managed to convince his even loonier boss to release some 180,000 troops from the real war on the Eastern Front and elsewhere in order to act as extras in a movie then being filmed about a nineteenth-century Prussian non-victory over Napoleon at a place called Kolberg on the Baltic. Vital supplies were diverted, a train-load of precious salt was sent to simulate snow, munitions factories were ordered to manufacture blanks, horses and turncoat Cossacks requisitioned, special colour film was produced, huge amounts of money spent.

"Hm ... you've got to be joking," Cassie muses thoughtfully.

"Apparently not although I agree it's hard to believe. Can you imagine being one of the lucky sods ordered to give up real fighting and piss off back to Germany for a spot of pretend fighting instead?"

Cassie appears not to have heard but after a long pause says, "I can, but can *you* see what a great idea for a book it is?"

"What sort of book?" I reply warily.

Suddenly animated she launches into a breathless monologue, "It's terrific ... let's see ... conscript Fritz freezing his balls off on the Eastern Front ... suddenly finds himself safe and sound on some cushy movie set hundreds of miles from the front playing an Uhlan or whatever in a pretty uniform ... fact and fiction intertwined ... Goebbels and real actors and Fritzy all together ... let's see ... what say he falls for an actress ... deserts ... survives the war ... maybe emigrates to the States and becomes a famous spin doctor ... Goebbels' vile legacy alive and kicking ... in the beginning was the deliberate lie because it works better than the truth ... which leads more or less directly to our sound-bite culture ... the book starts as Fritz ... now of course Frank ... vast and rich and riddled with cancer dying in Manhattan loft ranting to his daughter who's not really his ... more mirrors ... more deception ... how am I doing?"

"You're miles ahead of me, but I follow your drift." I say impressed by her improvisation.

Thus was the idea for my Big Serious Novel conceived (by someone else) on an October afternoon in a dreary Algeciras café with fly-spattered walls and, incredibly, a faded portrait of Franco on the wall behind the bar.

The ferry is crammed to its evil-smelling gunwales, mostly with Moroccans returning home after stints performing the menial tasks Europeans have for some considerable time declined to do for themselves. There's also a smattering of hard core lotus-eaters distinguishable by their native accessorising and the goat gazes of folks who've done so much dope all roads seem the same to them.

As we stand at the railing, the ferry pushes out of the bay. First the lights on the Spanish side and then those of Gibraltar recede and disappear altogether. The cloud cover is beginning to break up and now we and we can see dramatic stretches of sky through rents in the fabric.

We return to the bar where, snacking on beer and pistachios, we pore over maps and brochures of Morocco and try to ignore the motion of the boat as it wallows towards North Africa. We plan to head inland immediately (Cassie's had a thing about the High Atlas ever since reading a book on the local warlords as a teenager) before the colder weather comes.

In Tangier I find an English bookstore where I buy up all they've got on Nazi Germany and order a ton more. While Cassie's enthusiasm for her idea is infectious and of course I'll do anything to please her, I think the real reason I'm so attracted to it is the vast amount of research I'll have to do before I can even think of starting to write. I know no more than the next man about the Thousand Year Reich so if I'm to write a credible novel I've got my work cut out for me.

The Atlas mountains are all they're cracked up to be, and we spend a month wandering back and forth through them, visiting casbahs and delighting in (though not without sometimes being threatened by) the strange and austere beauty on offer all around us. We stay in simple hotels and for the most part eat local food.

TIMBUKTU - 58 JOURS

"Is that it?"

Cassie is, to put it mildly, disappointed by the Sahara into whose shaled and blasted badlands we are now staring from a promontory outside the oasis of Mhamid, *dernier centre administratif du Dra Moyen* according to our guidebook.

"What did you expect?"

"Would you believe some sand, maybe Beau Geste crawling out of mirage, a dune or two? About turn."

That night we limp into the town of Ouarzazate with Rigoletto exhibiting all the symptoms of a big end about to pack up. In the morning a one-eyed *garagiste* confirms my diagnosis and estimates that it will cost more to repair the car than the crate is worth. So we execute a drastic triage on the junk we've accumulated on our travels, send parcels of books and clothes *poste restante* to Tangier and, not without a pang, bid adieu to the fallen Rigoletto and take a bus to the coast.

CHAPTER FOURTEEN

Tangier.
Breathe the word and a raft of names of people mostly famous for their restlessness, their sexual proclivities and the elusive quality of their personae is conjured up: Barbara Hutton, Truman Capote, Paul Bowles, Tennessee Williams, William Burroughs, Allen Ginsberg, Jack Kerouac, Francis Bacon, Joe Orton ... the list stretches and the names are linked indissolubly to flight and exile and are redolent of the long slow decline of the Western world.

Tangier with its movie set air of artifice masking a complex subtext. The Medina tumbling seaward beneath the broad boulevards and leafy suburbs of the modern city grafted onto the pulsing heart of the old town. The Grand Socco now just a shadow of the great Arab market which used to exist there but nonetheless alive with snarling multi-coloured buses, dusty taxis, crowded cafés, urchins up to no good, merchants selling everything from *djellabahs* and embroidered slippers to kitchenware and objects of no perceivable value to the jaded European eye. The Medina and the Casbah still warrens of narrow alleys, sudden doorways, hole-in-the-wall shops, shadowed angles, busy cafés; places pervaded by the smell of spices, *kif*, sweat, tobacco, coal fires, rotting fruit, donkey dung, diesel fumes, mint tea, burning vegetable oil and hot nougat; still slashed with sudden riffs of Arab music, dimly heard flutes and bells, the quick flare of raucous disagreement, click of cards and markers, the call of the muezzin and the distant bray of traffic from the boulevards.

I don't think either of us would have stayed more than a few days in this ghost of a notorious bolt hole if we'd arrived during the seven or eight months of the year when by all accounts it is besieged by wave upon wave of tourists and the narrow lanes of the Medina are more Euro Disney than North Africa. However, arriving as we do in mid-November, we come upon a city leased back to its multiracial rainbow of inhabitants. Although obviously outsiders, we immediately feel at home in the Medina and to a lesser extent in the European section of town with its meretricious shops and air of not knowing exactly what it wants to be like.

After a few nights in an hotel with a view over the cascading white cubes and missile minarets of the Medina, the blue bay and the distant mauve and taupe presence of the Spanish coast, we set up house in a small furnished flat in a lane between the Petit Socco and the Grand Mosque. Tolerably clean, the apartment has a tiny bathroom, a sparsely equipped galley kitchen, a windowless bedroom and a living room which looks out over some rooftop gardens of varying ambition and sophistication. A moveable butane heater is all that stands between us and the *chérqui*, the raw wind which blows most of the time. The noises and smells of the Petit Socco are never far away although we soon adapt to them but not so readily to the doleful electronic bleat of the muezzin from the various mosques in the area.

"Your move."

It's six o'clock, and as has become our custom at that hour, we're playing backgammon at a window table in our favourite café in the Petit Socco. But tonight, Christmas Eve, I've not been concentrating (attentive or not, I mostly lose) and have been idly watching people scurrying across the rain-swept square and remembering that exactly a year ago we were in Abbeville. One year, twelve months, fifty-two weeks, three hundred and sixty-five days, some nine thousand hours (it somehow seems there should be more of those) spent exclusively in the company of this woman who even now I can barely look at without a hitch in my heart and a quickening of the pulse.

"I surrender."

"What's wrong?" she asks warily.

"Not much. I was just thinking how time not so much flies as goes supersonic when you're having fun. I sometimes wish everything would slow down."

Cassie closes the portable set with a snap and leaning across the little wooden table frames my face with her hands and says lightly, "But that's the whole point, silly. Slow the merry-go-round down and you notice the cracks, have time to get bored, speed it up and the ride is practically over before you can appreciate what's happened. Another of life's nifty paradoxes."

"Sounds like a lose-lose situation to me."

She shakes her head emphatically. "Not a bit of it, but the trick *is* to hang on for dear life and milk the ride for all it's worth."

I have a mental image of Cassie and me grimly clutching onto an old fashioned merry-go-round as it hurtles around and around in a deserted fairground.

I trace the line of her jaw with a finger and ask how she reckons we're handling our ride. She laughs and says "Oh, we're doing pretty well" and then in one of the sudden switches of tempo I've come to expect, she stands up abruptly and says, "Come on, let's treat ourselves to a Christmas Eve drink at the El Minzah."

So we leave the café and make our way past the abandoned Spanish cathedral, the dimly-lit covered market exhaling its

PATRICK STARNES

patina of odours, and through the deserted Grand Socco to the celebrated hotel where we have a drink at the bar. However, we're soon driven away by a drunken American who wishes (as do we) that he were back with his family in Coeur d'Alene.

The following day we exchange token (we've agreed to a 100 Dirham limit) presents, and after breakfast I'm buffeted and blown by the *chérqui* as I make my way to a phone booth next to the Poste Maroc building where after a number of false starts I get through to London.

"Château Buchan, Catherine speaking," Cat chirps.

I'm taken aback. For some reason it hasn't occurred to me that she might answer the phone. I was prepared for Fran, or even Charlie, but not Cat ... ah, Catherine, that is.

"Hello?"

Panic grips me. What the devil do I think I'm doing? Why on earth would any of them want to have anything to do with me? When Cassie suggested I give them a call it sounded like an okay idea, now it seems like an extremely poor one.

"Hell-o? Anybody home?"

"Hi, Cat, it's me."

The silence is thunderous. I wonder which of the four phones in the house she's using.

"Oh, hello. What d'you want?"

The anger squeezes down the line and oozes out of the receiver. I see my reflection in the door of the phone cabin and feel totally dislocated from it. Can that middle-aged guy in the suede jacket and crumpled chinos possibly be me?

"Just to say hello. Merry Christmas. You know."

"I don't think I do. Still, where ... ah ... are you?"

Obviously, her curiosity has got the better of her ire. She sounds different, but then it's been a year and she *should* sound and be different.

"Never mind", then add hopefully, "How are you?"

"What's it to you?"

I am of course getting no worse than I deserve, but it still hurts.

"A lot," I reply honestly.

"Oh, I'm okay for somebody's who's been turned into a studying machine that is. You still with whatsherface?"

"I am. How's your mother?"

Once again the silence deafens, and then I can hear Fran's voice in the background and ... of course it's Christmas Day and Kenneth and Muriel will be there. Cat must be in the kitchen. The ghosts of Christmases past obtrude.

"I guess she's okay too. Want to speak to her?"

"In a minute. And Charlie?"

"You've got a nerve."

"Please, Cat," I plead, unable to help myself.

"He's AWOL, has been for three months."

"AWOL?" I repeat stupidly.

"You heard. He's 'opped it, buggered off, scarpered, done a bunk. We think he must be living rough here in London, perhaps on and off with friends. He phones in from time to time, tells us not to worry. Ha! Good work, Dad, *félicitations*."

There's a roaring in my ears, and I feel sick to my stomach. Charlie living in Cardboard City or whatever that place in Waterloo Station is called. Or Lincoln's Inn Fields. Or under some stinking bridge. My son Charlie, Gold Medal winner Charlie, full scholarship to MIT Charlie living rough in the streets of London? And all because of me. All because I fell for his girl who fell for me.

"Cat?"

"Yes?"

"Has ... has Mum got the police onto it?"

"Negative. Rightly or wrongly she feels that if Charlie wants to run away from his own life, hide his head in London's sewers that's his business. The current theory is that he has to get it out of his system, whatever that might mean. But anyway, even assuming he can be found, no one can force him to come home."

Of course they can't, but they could bloody well find out where he is, keep an eye on him, try to talk some sense into his thick skull. But I've forfeited my right to do anything other than wonder about the son who I've never really understood anyway and who by my actions I've apparently driven into some inner circle of urban hell.

"Christ."

"Tell us about it. Here's Mum."

There's a brief hiatus during which I imagine Cat mouthing 'It's him' with her hand over the mouthpiece, maybe Fran rolling her eyeballs, the cork notice board behind her head aflutter with memos, snapshots, recipes. My home, never to be my home again. Talk about being out in the cold.

"Where are you?" Fran's tone is as impersonal as a shopping list but then why shouldn't it be?

"Morocco. Listen Fran, about Charlie, I know I don't have the right to ..."

"*You* listen to *me*. I'm fed to the teeth with Charlie Buchan's shenanigans, let alone his hyper-sensitive little soul. As you yourself once pointed out he's not the first person in the history of the world to have lost his girl although I admit the circumstances are ... ah ... unusual. Still, to be honest I was on the verge of kicking him out of the house when he did his runner."

"That bad?"

"Worse. Oh, don't worry about him, he'll be all right. In spite of his egocentricity, or perhaps because of it, he has a pretty well-developed sense of self-preservation. Where in Morocco?"

"Around and about. And you, how are you?"

"I survive. I've got to go now, we're late for church."

"Yes."

"Will you do me a favour?"

"Of course."

"Don't phone again ... ever."

A sucker punch if ever I walked into one. She hangs up, and I'm left holding the buzzing receiver and staring at a neatly penned item of graffiti: ARSE ARTISTS OF THE WORLD UNITE. Feeling old and tired and out of sorts, I leave the building. The wind is roaming down the boulevard Mohammed V, and low white clouds scud and tumble over the tops of the buildings for all the world like special effects in a disaster movie rather than natural phenomena.

I set off for the Medina with my mind in turmoil. Trust Charlie to go off the deep end, but this running off to live in Strand doorways is one tantrum too far. There's obviously nothing I can do about where the son I've abandoned chooses to live but knowing he's sleeping rough is one shitty Christmas present.

That afternoon we take a bus to Cap Spartel where we walk along the deserted beach with the surf pounding in beneath a sky which seems to go on forever. Click: Cassie, barefoot, jeans rolled up above her ankles, hair a stream in the wind, gulls swirling, sea behind. An image for all time.

"Your ex is right. Don't worry about Chuck, he can take care of himself with the best of them."

"I hope you're right. I've quite enough on my conscience as it is."

"That's bullshit and you know it."

"Do I?" I reply huffily.

"Well, you certainly should. You know the timing as well as I do, and you know that Charlie's always enjoyed pushing things to the limit. God knows that's why at least part of me always wanted out: he was too tiring, not to mention possessive."

"How possessive?"

But she's had enough, "Come on let's head back."

The New Year comes and goes, and we make vague plans to leave Tangier, seek better weather down south, but we never do much more than talk about it. The fact is that we're both infatuated with the city, a place that somehow seems to nourish our need to be both somewhere and nowhere at one and the same time. Perched on the furthermost tip of the African continent and yet by no stretch of the imagination African, within sight of Europe yet hardly European. The former International City with its diverse community, dodgy past, ongoing identity crisis and dreamlike sense of existing outside conventional time, accepts us unquestioningly as for centuries it has accepted saints and sinners alike. Compliant captives, hostages to each other's fortune, we ask nothing more than to be left to ourselves.

That, however, is not the way it works.

It's a windy evening in February. Cassie has gone to shop for dinner and I'm ploughing through a harrowing account of the experiences of Jewish children in Nazi Europe: *The baby was crying somewhere in the distance and I couldn't stop and look. We moved, and it smelled, a horrible stench. I knew that things in the fire were moving, that there were babies in the fire ...*

Sickened, I go to the window and gaze out over the twilit city and am moved by the quiet beauty of the scene so starkly contrasted to the horror of what I've been reading. I reflect, not for the first time in the recent past, that not a great deal of anything makes sense. Here and there things seem to add up, click into place, glimmer in the dark, but surely there cannot be more than the illusion of meaning in a world which can produce Ethnic Cleansing and the Moonlight Sonata, Joseph Mengele and Mother Teresa?

Then something impinges on my consciousness. A sound. A scratching and a faint knocking coming from the back of the studio. Mystified, I go to the front hall and realise that the noise is coming from outside. Warily I open the front door and am shocked to see Cassie propped groggily against the landing wall, her face covered in blood and her jacket and blouse ripped and soiled.

"Jesus, what on earth happened?"

But she's beyond words and collapses with a moan into my arms. I carry her to the bathroom where I soon discover that the blood is coming from a gash in her scalp that's not deep but being a head wound gushes copiously until I manage to staunch it with towels. She's shivering and her teeth are chattering uncontrollably, but apart from the cut she doesn't seem to be seriously hurt. I clean her up, get her out of her ripped blouse and into a bathrobe, and gradually she calms down enough to come to the kitchen where I ply her with coffee and Fundador and she tells me what happened.

After shopping for meat in the covered market, she set off down the hill towards her favourite vegetable stall. Just below the Petit Socco she began to sense that she was being followed but, being unwilling to succumb cravenly to the European in Sinful Casbah syndrome, had carried on even though there weren't many other people around and common sense should have told her to head back to the safety of the bright lights of the square.

"And then there he was right *in front* of me. As long as I live, I shall never forget the look in his eyes: pure, undiluted hatred fuelled by God alone knows what cocktail of dope and booze."

"Who ...?"

"Darius. Darius bloody Lascelles as high as K-2 on something or other and intent on making me pay for apparently having made a fool of him by leaving him ... he looked awful ... wild eyed, dishevelled, maniacal. He pushed me into a cul-de-sac - God, the smell of his breath was revolting ... started mouthing foul things at me … I struggled but he's very strong and at one point I must have hit my head on a door knocker or whatever because I think that's where the cut came from. Then he started to choke me … slowly … deliberately, and I could see he was getting a kick out of it, but just when I was beginning to think I'd had it, a group of men stopped at the end of the alley and demanded to know what was going on … Darius relaxed his grip and jokingly told them we were … lovers … ha, ha, ha … not to worry … ha, ha, ha … I managed to squirm free and I ran as fast as I could … he … he … called after me promising he wasn't finished with me yet and that he'd get me and … hold me, Ivor … hold me tight."

I do, and for a long time she shivers and shakes in my arms while I try to figure out what comes next. Clearly Lascelles is both deranged and dangerous and for all we know has found out where we live. Even if he hasn't the Medina is a fairly restricted area and surely a hard place for any *gringa,* let alone one of Cassie's presence, in which to hide. A few hours later after I've made us something to eat, we inch reluctantly toward the conclusion that as infuriating as it is to be run out of somewhere which suits us so well, we'll have to get out of town.

Cassie, who is still obviously in shock, shudders and intones, "Wouldn't you know it, wouldn't you just know that the sleazy fuck would come back to haunt me."

Unhelpfully all I can think of is the crude if depressingly accurate 'shit happens' mantra. That it should happen to us in the form of Cassie's brute of a husband is to me no more remarkable than the fact that he, drifter that he is, should fetch up in a place like Tangier long renowned for harbouring precisely his sort.

But Cassie doesn't see it that way. Profoundly unnerved by Lascelles's assault, in her over-wrought state she imagines fantastic connections, sees her husband's unwelcome appearance in our lives as an omen, a harbinger of some barely imaginable future grief. And she is very frightened. Nor can she be talked down. No arguments can convince her that the encounter with Lascelles was simply a highly unpleasant coincidence. Finally, I slip a couple of sleeping pills into her drink, and soon she's content to be led to the bedroom and put to bed.

After that I sit in the darkened living room taking in the late-night show for the last time. I have to admit to myself that Cassie's funk has got to me. Perhaps she's right, perhaps the events of the evening are the thin edge of a wedge called nemesis. Perhaps this is the pay-off for Charlie sleeping rough (while I sleep with his girl) wherever he's sleeping rough. Or Fran betrayed and abandoned? Cat left fatherless? As they say it's all in the head. Where else would it be? I've had too much crap brandy. Time for bed.

In the morning Cassie is brisk and business-like. "Sorry about that. Must have talked a load of rubbish. Nerves. Fine now. Come on let's blow this rat's nest."

We pack quickly and scurry down to the port - not without apprehensive glances over our shoulders - where we catch the hydroplane to Spain and all that follows.

CHAPTER FIFTEEN

On the rough and noisy crossing to Algeciras, I discover that Cassie has plans for us. Apparently we're headed for Barcelona, a city where I know she spent some six months after walking out on her husband and a place for which she's retained fond memories. Barcelona is fine by me, but then again I'd live in the Gorbals or Upper Volta if I knew she would be there with me.

We take a series of dilapidated local buses up the coast and arrive in the Catalan capital on a dull March afternoon. After the usual teething problems (this time greatly reduced because we are helped by those of the expat gang Cassie used to hang out with who are still around), we find a small flat on the fringes of the *Barri Gotic*. And so once again we settle into a routine which has mornings spent with me continuing my research for the Goebbels book (Cassie's really) which for her sake I've agreed to have a crack at. Cassie does the shopping, takes Spanish lessons and reads what seems to me at least two or three novels a week. Most afternoons are spent taking in the many delights and surprises of one of Europe's most stylish and quirky cities.

Cassie's friends are an interesting and generally likeable bunch of late-twenties whose bodies are seemingly capable of withstanding industrial levels of alcohol, drugs and sleep deprivation. There's Josh, a tall handsome painter from Texas with whom

I reckon Cassie (like a great many other women) has slept. There's Larry a gay Aberdonian junkie who plays the alto sax in various discos and clubs around the city. Rachel's a statuesque New Yorker who studies design by day and tends bar in a dive near the *Plaça Reial* by night. Frank's a Dubliner who works part time in a travel agency and pushes dope for pin money and to gain 'background' for the Barcelona low-life novel he's been writing forever. And Suzy's a Berliner who came as an *au pair* for a rich industrialist's kids a number of years ago and stayed on, flitting from job to job and compulsively bedding as many as she can of the surprising number of flamenco dancers there are in the city.

At first I'm worried that Cassie will want to pick up where she left off with her younger friends (perhaps, awful thought, that's why we're here?), but she swears that her clubbing nights are over and that she's content simply to keep in touch with her pals and let them do the candle burning.

"I'm just not interested in that stuff anymore, honest."

We're having morning coffee in the *fin de siècle* splendour of the Café de l'Opéra. Outside, tree-lined *Ramblas* is bathed in spring sunshine.

Knowing that I'm about to make a fool of myself but unable to stop, I say, "Perhaps you would be if ... well, you know ... keener if you didn't have yours truly around your neck."

She goes off like a fire alarm. "Stop it! Stop it right there! Understand for once and for all: *I've no interest in clubbing*. I'm interested in being with you, loving you, having you, being had by you, eating and drinking with you and tons of other with yous in the spaces between. Got it?"

Just then all six foot four of Josh appears towering over our table. After greeting us and sitting down, he drawls, "Could you guys tell me why you two are looking so mighty vexed on such a beautiful day?"

Cassie shrugs. "I was just checking to see if dumbo here can get it into his thick skull that I don't miss staying out until five every morning, pissed out of my mind and wondering what century I'm in."

The Texan laughs his big fake Texan laugh and booms, "To tell the truth I'm getting a tad sick of it all myself. Must be getting old."

Cassie shakes her head sceptically, "Go tell that to the marines."

"Honest. I woke up a few days ago in bed with this filly I'd never seen before who claimed I'd asked her to marry me and I thought to myself, 'Hey Josh old pal, maybe it's time to cash in the Beat Generation shtick and get a life.'"

Of course neither Josh nor any of the others have the slightest intention of changing their lifestyles one iota. The accelerator will remain firmly to the floor, and the wonder is that they've got the stamina to keep up such a punishing pace. But in the weeks and months that follow Cassie shows no signs of wanting to return to her wild ways although there is one abortive foray (instigated by me) into the hectic underworld of clubland (graffiti in the can: IF THE MUSIC'S TOO LOUD, YOU'RE TOO OLD). I'm too old. Neither of us is having any fun and we leave after fifteen minutes.

Spring gives way to summer and the city ruefully accepts its annual deluge of tourists. The hot bright days bleed seamlessly into each other and according to Larry, Cassie and I continue to exhibit all the symptoms of 'insufferable happiness'. Most nights we take an after-dinner stroll down the ever lively and entertaining *Ramblas*, often meeting various members of the gang for a staid drink to kick-start the night's activities for them and to herald its end, or thereabouts, for us. I join Cassie's Spanish class (she's a far better linguist than I am) and continue to devour books on the Third Reich.

The only fly in the ointment is the almost pathological aversion I develop to Josh, who is of course the member of the gang we see the most of and the only one in whom Cassie confides. Okay, so they shagged way back when. I can live with that. What I don't seem to be able to live with are his unguarded looks which all but undress her, the long Texan fingers lingering on her forearm the better to make a point, the youthful smirk as I clatter heavily to the pavement my gimpy knee having given out ("Here, you all just take my arm"), the smell of paint and turps in our flat when I return from a walk.

"What's got into you?"

"Not a thing," I lie.

"Come on, Ivor, you can't fool me, something's bugging you."

"Well, let's just say that it certainly seems you and Josh are hitting it off famously ..."

"So that's it. Jesus H. Christ, I've known the guy for a long time, we're what's called old friends, he's a good listener and ..."

"And a handy swordsman, I'll warrant," I say with scarcely credible vulgarity.

She slaps me hard. I see stars, my ears zing and I wish beyond wishing that I'd kept my big trap shut.

"If you won't or can't trust me, then we're through, done, toast, *finis*. D'you understand what I'm saying?"

The fear which spreads through me is total, and I climb down so fast I practically get the bends.

"I'm sorry, that was sleazy beyond belief and I do trust you, completely, I promise. Peace?"

She cocks her head and gives me a frowning once-over. But then she smiles and kissing me chirps "Sure, peace in our time" which, given the provenance of the quotation, doesn't totally reassure but will have to do.

Thus do we dodge our first live bullet. The second will prove more difficult to avoid.

PATRICK STARNES

One morning in late July I return to the flat after a mind-clearing walk to the top of Montjuic only to find a note on the kitchen table and no Cassie.

Ivor, my only love,

Panic not. I've gone (I've no idea where) but I'll be back soon. To be precise I'll be at the C de L'O at five p.m. the day after tomorrow. I just need some head space, time to do some thinking on my own. Don't worry it's not about US: in fact I feel more strongly about you and love you more than ever. I thank the God who I'm pretty sure I don't believe in for having seen to it that our paths crossed and that we have had - and hopefully will continue to have - such wonderful times together. You are a good and kind man, a great lay and I miss you already.

Tout à toi

C.

p.s. Sorry about this, as you know, letter writing was never my thing.

I'm unnerved by Cassie's absence. After all we haven't spent more than a few hours apart for more than eighteen months, and I feel unprotected almost naked without her.

What the hell does she need time to think *about*? If not us, what then? And so on and endlessly on.

The next forty-eight hours seem like the longest of my life. Unable to sit still for more than a few minutes at a time, I trail around the city like a stray dog. The heat is intense, and at night I lie on our bed pining for her as I would not have thought it possible for anyone to long for anyone. On the second night I have the first wet dream I've had since I was a teenager.

At four o'clock in the afternoon, like some funked-out matador, I shower and shave and dress (beige chinos, pistachio chemise Lacoste, Bass Weejuns; my God, won't I ever grow up?) and set off for the café with time and then some to spare.

Five o'clock and no Cassie. Well, she's always late but surely this is different. After ten minutes I'm in a state. I order another beer and try, without much success, to push the ugly, even despairing, thoughts which are swirling into view to the back of my mind. She's run off with Josh. (I know she hasn't because of course I've checked that one out). She's returned to the States. She's met another guy. She's been abducted by ETA or whatever the Catalan separatists are called. Drugs. Ah, yes, of course it's drugs …

"Trick or treat?"

Cool hands cover my eyes, firm breasts push into my shoulder blades, stomach and sharp hips nuzzle my buttocks. I don't understand how she's come upon me from behind because I've been keeping a casually sharp eye on the café's only entrance. Who cares? She's here now. She's in my arms with her smell all around me and her hair an event caught in a refracted sunbeam.

"Thank God, I was beginning to …"

"I'll just bet you were, oh ye of little faith. I think I'd like one of those too."

So we stand at the bar and drink beer and babble like lovers who've been parted for years rather than a scant forty-eight hours, and she tells me about the village where she found a room in a *fonda* and went for walks in the surrounding countryside and missed me.

"You didn't *have* to go."

"Oh, yes I did." She asserts.

"Why?"

"Because I needed time to think it through."

"Think what through?"

"The consequences of the fact that I'm pregnant," she replies evenly.

The hairs on the back of my neck stand on end, and my stomach goes into free fall. My mouth has fallen open, and I know I'm gawking at her like a village idiot but I'm unable to do anything about it. Pregnant? A kaleidoscope of vignettes from pregnancies and infancies past races through the theatre of my mind: Fran's debilitating morning sicknesses (particularly bad with Charlie), the late night dash through a blizzard to the Montreal General, colic, chicken pox, first sailor-lurches on the blue Chinese carpet in our living room, Charlie eyeing the newly arrived Catherine with deep suspicion, love for the two blond heads I see bobbing in the rear view mirror as we drive to the lake on mazy summer evenings ...

"Hello?"

I'm standing at the bar of the Café de l'Opéra and the woman I love has just told me she's with child, my child, our child, and I'm appalled to discover that I'm appalled.

"Sorry. I'm ... well ... I'm ... ah ... surprised. Are you sure?"

"Very. I take it you're not best pleased."

Careful, Keir, careful.

"Ah ... I'm not sure what I am other than ... well ... as I said, dead surprised."

"Well you look as though you've just been told you've got pancreatic cancer."

My breath is coming in panicky little gusts as I envisage the future, our future fatally compromised by the strain of the eternal triangle because I know, just know, that Cassie's decided to have this child. The man I see standing next to the tall redhead reflected in the mirror behind the bar is a stranger with a problem.

"Come on, let's get out of here," I suggest.

"Don't you want to know what I think about being pregnant?" she asks somewhat testily (and why not?) as I pay and we push out into the furnace of the afternoon.

"You want to have the baby, it's our love-child, right?"

"I want to have the baby because I love its father beyond imagining, and yes, if you want to put it that way, because it's the product of something which until it actually happened to me I thought only existed in books or at least only to other people."

"But don't you see that having this baby may very well destroy the love which produced it?"

Cassie looks at me with something not far short of pity and says levelly, "That's a risk I've got to take, but if you think about it it's the same risk all couples who are going to have a child take."

I back off. What's the point of my saying that we're not like other couples, that my being twice her age ... Christ almighty I've got it; she wants the child precisely *because* she's twenty-six to my fifty-two, precisely because she wants something of me (which bits of the curate's egg?) to survive long after I'm dead and our song is little more than an ancient melody occasionally evoked by her on long winter nights.

We move on in silence until we reach the Plaça Reial where we sit on a bench in the shade of towering palms amidst the non-stop activity characteristic of that magnet for everything from pimps, touts and pickpockets to pork-pie hatters from Iowa, Africans selling leather goods, tramps and flakes from everywhere.

I try to think if not necessarily clearly at least with some semblance of objectivity, but that's not the way it plays, and I'm beset with gloomy thoughts of an unwanted future domesticity in which I'm first gently edged, then pushed to the periphery of Cassie's galaxy by the demands of motherhood. I'm hardly proud of the selfishness with which I am reacting to what should be good news, but there it is, that's the way I feel.

I want her to myself.

"Oh, Ivor, don't be angry with me, please."

"I'm not angry with you, just confused."

"There's no need to be. It's very simple. I want this child as I've never wanted anything - you aside - in my life, but I swear I won't let it make a scrap of difference to us."

There speaks the twenty-six year old who's never woken already dumb tired to the sound of a baby bawling its lungs out for more sustenance, for the teat that already aches intolerably. There speaks a woman with only the vaguest notion of the sheer critical mass of attention required to keep a tiny representative of *Homo sapiens* clean, fed, warm and safe in an unfriendly world.

"If you're so sure you want this baby, why did you have to go off into the desert to make up your mind about it?"

"I just did. I only got the result from the pharmacy the morning I left. I won't pretend it wasn't a bit of a shock, but once I got to thinking there wasn't really any choice. By the way, I'm not against abortion, just *for* this baby."

"Of course."

"What's that supposed to mean?"

"Only that I would end up on the wrong side of that particular contradiction, wouldn't I?"

She shrugs impatiently and looks away, but not before I glimpse tears brimming in her eyes. Just then a cruelly malformed beggar mounted on a kind of customised skateboard stops in front of us, and by the time I've extracted some coins to give him, she's composed herself and the moment has passed.

"It's not a contradiction. If I was bearing anybody's child but yours I'd probably opt for an abortion ..."

"What makes it being mine, or half mine, so special?"

The green eyes brim again with tears and then looking down she whispers, "Just because. I'm afraid that'll have to do."

I can see she's close to losing it. I'm angry with myself for not being more sympathetic, for not sharing her joy and know it's time for me to do some thinking on my own. When I say so, she nods and says, "Of course."

I give her a distracted kiss and set off I know not where. I wander through the hot streets of the city with my mind in a state of insurrection. At one point I find myself with scores of other people in the surreal surroundings of Gaudi's Parc Guell, and up there amidst the manic contortions and exuberant whimsicalities of the site's bizarre structures it belatedly dawns on me that I'm not being offered an option. Cassie's going to have the baby, and I'm welcome to be a part of her (make that their) future, but that's it, that's the deal, take it or leave it.

Oh, I'll take it all right. I'll take it.

Then I convince myself that once the dust has settled and the first exhausting months have been weathered, a new order will emerge, one in which the baby will actually act as a bond rather than a divisive presence. Perhaps having a child will roll back at least some of the years for me and give us a focus outside the hothouse of our closed circuit system? In short, my love for Cassie is stronger than my disinclination to father another child and that, in the final analysis, seems to me to be a fine thing. *My* capacity for self-preservation has kicked in and is running on high octane fuel, so by the time I've tramped around the city for a couple more hours and am making my way wearily up the steep steps to our flat, I've arrived at a sort of truce with myself and an acceptance of a future very different from what it was a few hours ago.

Cassie's in the kitchen washing dishes. She hasn't heard me come in, and I stand for a moment in the doorway watching her as she somehow manages to invest one of life's most banal tasks with high style. She's humming *La Donna* è *Mobile* and sashaying from the sink to the draining board and back. Her hair's held in a messy top notch by a scarf. She's wearing a shocking pink tank top and white shorts.

"Cass …"

"Yipes! You scared the daylights out of me. Hey … you all right?"

"I'm fine. Just all walked and thunk out."

I go to her, and we kiss long and hard.

"Wow! You should bottle whatever it is you found out there."

"Would you believe acceptance?"

She leans back and holding me at arm's length smiles and says simply, "I'm glad".

Over her shoulder I can see the last rays of the setting sun caressing the ugly tower of the UGT building and swallows dog-fighting across the limpid sky, and it occurs to me that there are some things that do make sense.

Later after we've made love, we lie in the dark listening to the sounds of the city on a summer's night and waiting for the sap to rise again, for tonight is not a night like other nights. Indeed it's dawn before we're finally finished with each other and fall exhausted into a deep sleep from which we are rudely awakened at seven by Larry, Frank and Suzy fresh from a revel and in search of beer, gossip and breakfast.

In August we spend most days on the beach at Barceloneta either taking a picnic or eating *tapas* at the many bars in the area. For me it's a strange and poignant time as my heart tries to catch up with what my mind has come to terms with. I struggle to master the niggling resentment I can't stop myself feeling towards the tiny being growing inside Cassie, but I'm helped in this by the certain knowledge that I can't have one without the other and that life without her is not an option.

CHAPTER SIXTEEN

As the weeks click by I find that not only am I no longer jealous of what I too now see as our love-child, but I am actively glad for its presence inside its (we make no effort to determine the baby's gender) mother. Thus, in large part due to the logic imposed by the process of gestation, I'm nudged along the path to a serenity which only a few months ago I wouldn't have thought possible.

By September when the phalanxes of tourists have thinned out and most Catalans have returned to work, we set about looking for a more suitable flat. Neither of us doubts that Barcelona is where we want to live. The city has everything either of us could want (and then some) and we feel at home in it while agreeing that the *Barri Gotic* is hardly the place to bring up a child. So after tramping up numerous gloomy stairways and being terrified by many dodgy looking lifts, we finally find a bright two-bedroom fifth floor flat in the Extension district overlooking the famous Casa Thomas and sporting a spanking new Otis lift. The rent's more than we'd hoped to pay but the Chester Dillons are selling briskly, Cassie's nest egg provides us a small but steady drip of extra cash and anyway, as she says, what the hell. We sign the lease for November 1 occupancy and celebrate with dinner at Los Caracoles, a restaurant we sometimes go to in spite of its being firmly on the tourist trail.

"Here's to 28 Carrer de Massanet *quinto izquierda*."

We touch glasses. Cassie, who so far has had an easy pregnancy and looks great, says "And here's to us, all three of us" and another piece of the jigsaw slots into place.

After dinner we join the throng along *Ramblas* and stroll arm-in-arm, pausing here and there to take in various street shows, inspecting exotic birds in their cages and tropical fish in aquariums. I buy a ludicrous battery-run canary whose off-key singing delights Cassie. I have a beer (she's off the sauce for the duration) at an outdoor café and listen to the haunting sound of Andean Pan pipes played by short, cinnamon-coloured men with high-cheeked Indian faces and sad eyes speaking of a thousand indignities stoically borne.

Something in the plight of these poor displaced minstrels so far from their mountain homes obviously gets to Cassie because she twines her fingers through mine and says in a voice suddenly husky with emotion, "Oh, Ivor, we're so lucky, it's just not true."

"Don't I know it."

"Sometimes ... look there's Josh. Whoo-hoo, Josh, over here!"

The Texan sights us and forges his way through the crowd for all the world like a cow puncher cleaving through a herd of steers.

"Hello, you guys. Jeez, Cassie, you look terrific. Being in the family way sure does suit you."

Although of late we haven't seen much of the gang, they all reacted to the news of Cassie's pregnancy with touching enthusiasm and I think a certain measure of anxiety that, at least for some of them, it might herald the beginning of the end of the party. If Cassie who's the youngest of the group can go domestic, how far behind can they be?

Josh fills us in on their comings and goings - Larry's just found out he's got Aids; Frank's in some murky trouble with the police; Suzy's unearthed a fresh flamenco dancer. Josh adds nonchalantly that he's going to have a one-man show in Madrid in the New Year.

"A one-man show, wow! How marvellous for you Josh. Oh, I *am* glad." Cassie enthuses.

Jesus, it's just a piffling one-man show not a Nobel fucking Prize and what about poor Larry? But I keep my bad thoughts to myself and try to appear interested in their small talk (they're both big *Barça* fans, whereas I could care less) while watching a gold painted Roman centurion mime for change.

Later, after Josh has loped off to the first party of the evening, we head on home.

"You still don't like him, do you?"

"Like who?"

"Ivor!"

"Okay, okay. No I don't. I can't help it but I'm sorry if it shows. By the way was Josh the guy who turned up in London way back when, the guy who Char ... Charlie was so jealous of? "

"The same," she replies thoughtfully. "The jealously thing didn't last, and in fact they became quite good pals, did a lot of stuff together in London. Galleries, the RA, that sort of thing. I've never asked, but I'm pretty sure they've kept in touch. And, as far as you and Josh are concerned I doubt he even notices your dislike of him. Josh's not one of your great observers."

I then tell her that I have a vague recollection of their Hampstead breakfast talk about some cool American painter guy who was staying with Cassie not long after Charlie had met her.

She nods and says, "Yup, that'll have been Josh. Slept on the hide-a-bed for a couple of weeks, all six foot whatever of him. Listen my love, would it help if I told you I've never slept with the big lunk?"

We're standing in front of the Florida Sex Shop. Behind Cassie's head I can see a display window stuffed with an astonishing array of sexual props and paraphernalia.

"Are you serious?"

"I am. It just so happens he's not my type."

It does help, and I say so. Then I remember about Larry and the long cold road he has ahead and I wonder out loud what sort of God could have invented both the Aids virus and the food blender.

"A perverse one," Cassie answers wrinkling her nose the way she does.

After breakfast some weeks later Cassie does housework while I send off a raft of businessey e-mails, try and fail to figure out our finances. Around noon we leave together: she bound for her gynaecologist, I to our new flat where I've arranged to meet the owner so I can measure the windows for the curtains Cassie's going to make. It's a clear day with more than a hint of fall in the air and we stop for an *espresso* in a bar near the cathedral. Cassie's wearing jeans, a green blouse and a suede jacket and looks ... well, radiant.

"Tortilla okay for lunch?"

"Great."

"What time d'you think you'll be back?" She asks.

"Mmm ... better say two-thirty, three."

We're standing by the door of the bar. The bead curtain clicks in the wind, there's a pervasive smell of freshly ground coffee in the air.

"Fine. *Ciao*. Love you.'

We kiss, and she turns and hurries off her hair shining like a talisman amidst the darker heads around her as she threads her way along the crowded pavement and disappears around a corner.

I'm late. The measuring has taken much longer than I'd anticipated, and I've misjudged the walk from the Extension district. I clatter up the narrow stairs and let myself in.

"*Hola!* I'm famished."

Silence. The tiny kitchen is empty. I go into the living room.

"Cass ..."

She's fast asleep on the sofa with her head propped up by pillows and her joined hands curled over her stomach. I reflect that this is the first real sign of the effects of her pregnancy because in all the time we've been together I've never known her to take a mid-afternoon nap.

But.

Advancing into the room I see that her face is drained of colour and that there's a plum coloured mark the size of a pencil eraser behind in her right ear. Words fail, meaning eludes.

I *am* dread. It's as though my veins have been injected with novocaine. There's a roaring and a rushing sound in my ears, and in place of my stomach there's a well of nothingness. I sink to my knees and whisper her name and then, prising one cold hand from the other, I seek the pulse which I know will not be there. And isn't. In a numbed agony of loss I embrace her lifeless body, breathe in her familiar scent, will her to be alive, will this cruel and senseless dream to end and Cassie to be restored to me.

But there's no rewind button, no reprieve from the Gothic horror of this tale, which is not a tale. Cassie's dead and already cold. She's been shot by some lunatic, some hopped-up junkie, some two-bit burglar she'd surprised in the act, some vagrant ...

And then I see the pistol. I don't even need to turn it over to see the chip out of the butt and know that it's the Kaba Special, bought by my father on his way to Korea in 1953 and passed on to me at his death. I take refuge in a spiral of irrelevance and see the squat little pistol wrapped in its yellowed oilcloth and placed with its box of bullets under Dad's underwear and handkerchiefs. Forbidden to touch it on pain of dire consequences, Jamie and I often did as I'm sure Charlie and Cat did when I put it under *my* handkerchiefs in my bureau drawer where it was when Cassie and I left London.

My numbed mind slithers off meanings, glances off consequences as I retrieve the pistol from the side table at the end of the sofa, take note of the chip in the Bakelite butt and recoil at its evil heft.

A perverse God, she'd said only a few days ago. A perverse God invented Aids and the food blender … and … this horror of horrors. Tears surge from my eyes, and I am racked by wave after wave of sobs which seem to come from some vast artesian well of sorrow within me.

Time ceases to have meaning. Long after the swallows have finished their aerial acrobatics and the sky has thickened and then disappeared altogether, I kneel in the dark with my arms around the woman I loved, with the corpse of our child entombed within her, and the pain is beyond imagining.

I am riven by bouts of anguish so acute that at times I literally feel as though I shall simply expire, die like a dog there on the sisal matting of a rented flat in Barcelona's *Barri Gotic*. No such luck, my heart beats on unaware of the suffering its efforts sustain.

Somewhere in there I stagger to the bathroom and retch until it seems that my stomach will come spewing out. I return groggily to the scene of what is of course Charlie's grim settling of accounts if that is the correct expression for this abomination. This I know, have known since seeing the Kaba. But knowing and accepting are two very different things, and adrift as I am in a trackless ocean of loss my mind simply refuses to process the fact of the carnage my own flesh and blood has wreaked.

With the first feeble glimmerings of light slipping stealthily into the flat I make an effort to focus, to see my way beyond the wall of grief that is defining me. Confusedly I wonder how Charlie has found us, and then remember Cassie telling me just a few days ago that he and Josh had become good friends and I surmise that there must be some connection. But, who cares? Cassie's dead and the grim truth is that my son has tracked us down, has exacted a terrible vengeance for my sin of having loved his ... but I can go no further, am once more buried beneath a sorrow that assails like a physical force.

Then, just like that, I fall into a sleep that is more like a reproach than a reprieve. With truly startling perversity (what sick game can my subconscious be up to?), I dream Cassie and I are walking along the white beach at Cap Spartel stretching off to a distant marriage of sky and sea. I awake with a smile on my lips and a hand instinctively feeling for her warm presence.

But it all comes flooding back and wrapping my arms around my shoulders I rock back and forth and howl like the lost soul I am while all around the indifferent city stirs into life and the day dawns. Finally when I'm seemingly drained of all emotion I try to think clearly although the truth is that I already know what I shall do. Like many sinners I yearn for a punishment commensurate to the crime.

Around eight I shower, shave and change into clean clothes. Then I make my way through the narrow streets where the cleaners are hard at work and some bars and cafés are just beginning to open. I stop for a coffee in the *Plaça Reial*. It tastes like mud.

Ever since I've made up my mind a calm has descended on me not unlike that which came over me when I'd decided to take my own life way back towards the beginning of this movie. The house always wins, I know that and now it's payback time.

Ramblas is virtually deserted. A man in striped pyjamas throws open green shutters on the second floor of the Hotel Oriente. He's bald and has a thick walrus moustache and he stretches and yawns hugely. Next door the entrance to the ugly modern building housing the police station beckons in the strained morning light. The bleary eyed, blue-jowled policeman at the desk blinks disbelievingly as I place the Kaba on the counter and explain in my halting Spanish that I've killed my partner and am handing myself in.

Enough.

CHAPTER SEVENTEEN

The on-duty policeman at the *Ramblas* cop shop was way out of his depth although as it turned out his English was far better than my Spanish.

"I repeat. I've shot and killed the woman I've been living with. Her name is Cassandra Laporte. You will find her body at 4 Carrer Rull *segundo derecha*. This is the pistol I used, these are my keys."

The policeman who is probably only used to processing pick-pocketings, bag- snatchings and muggings clearly wishes he'd drawn a different straw, gulps and then making the not unreasonable assumption that since I'm handing myself in I'm unlikely to do a runner, says "Wait please." He dives into the office behind the desk leaving the loaded Kaba on the counter and me wondering why getting arrested is so difficult. However he soon reappears trailed by two sleepy colleagues with drawn automatics, and it seems appropriate for me to raise my hands, palms out, arms to shoulder height although I feel not a little ludicrous standing there surrendering like a baddie in a B-movie.

It turns out to be a very long morning.

After endless filling in of forms, I'm filed into a grim holding-cell littered with the night's scrapings: mostly drunks sleeping it off although there's an alarming man with two rows of gleaming stainless steel teeth who offers me a blow-job at a rock bottom price.

Next morning I'm moved to a single cell from which I'm dragged for endless interrogations by a succession of policemen both in and out of uniform. My story is as simple and old as unfaithfulness itself; I killed Ms Laporte in a paroxysm of jealous rage after she had told me she was having an affair with an unnamed younger man. It's an easy fiction to maintain as the only person who could credibly deny it (apart from Charlie who's doubtless on his way to Kathmandu or Bali) is dead. They'll be onto the gang in no time, but none of them knows what really happened do they? Anyway, why should the police doubt me? Like cops all over the world these folks want answers, want to be able to close the case. Well they have a body (two, to be precise), a suspect, a motive, a weapon and a confession. QED.

I for my part am the living dead. I want nothing, care about nothing. They can do what they will with me, and I say as much to whoever will listen, but it seems there are to be no short cuts on the road to the oblivion I crave, and I'm pestered remorselessly.

The weeks pass in a continuum of internal pain, a pain which I actually cherish because, by some convoluted psychological process I do not understand, Cassie still exists because of it. I am moved around the city, poked and probed and analysed and questioned, but it all could just as easily be happening to someone else. Somewhere in there (I make no effort to keep track of time) I'm visited a number of times by an official from the British Consulate who makes little attempt to hide his distaste for having to deal with someone as contemptible as me. And, indeed, why shouldn't he despise the *Monstruo* of Carrer Rull as one tabloid has dubbed me?

"I've had chats with some of the people you and ... ah ... Ms Laporte associated with."

"Yes?"

"Well, they all expressed considerable surprise at what transpired."

"Believe me, so did I. What's your point?"

"Just that none of them were aware your ... your friend was having an affair with someone else ... and she *was* pregnant with your child."

"First, she was not my friend. She was a lying, cheating slut. Second, since it was probably one of them, they would say that, wouldn't they? Third, she told me she was going to have an abortion. But the real point is: why should she have lied to me about having an affair, if she wasn't?"

"Point well taken. Listen, Mr Buchan, I've been talking with the lawyers here. Apparently there's an old law - an 1861 one to be exact - on the books, which permits British citizens to be tried in the U.K. for murder or manslaughter committed in Spain. Not to put too fine a point on it, our legal department thinks it would be best for you to exercise that option."

I try to explain to the man that it's a matter of cosmic indifference to me either by whom or at which venue I am tried.

"I just thought you might prefer your chances with British justice. And I rather gathered these people would be ... ah ... not unhappy for you to be extradited."

So that's it. Let the famously just British justice system deal with its own (by way of the colonies) bilge. Fine by me. Bangers and mash instead of *chorizo* and rice. The Beeb for RTVE. What do I care?

And then one blustery day in November, two officers from Scotland Yard escort me in conditions of ludicrously tight security (haven't they yet cottoned onto the fact that prison's where I want to be?) to Barcelona's shiny airport whence we fly to England and my date with British justice.

Flying over south west France gives me a bad turn. The copper to whom I'm handcuffed (what am I going to do, hurl myself through the bulkhead?) is clearly embarrassed by the tears I shed as I gaze down at the lovely brown-on-brown countryside through which Cassie and I had travelled more than a year ago.

Rain falls on London town (the lines of a Pound Canto run through my head like a mantra: *And sorrow, sorrow like rain/sorrow to go, and sorrow, sorrow returning*) as the police Rover winds through the familiar streets which, once long ago seemed to be there for a purpose, part of a recognisable pattern, but which I now gaze at through the car window like a visitor from Mars.

If the truth be told, I don't pay much attention to the proceedings of the next weeks and months. I'm kept in solitary confinement at the Paddington Green police complex. (My God, how many times have I driven past that building, how many times have I heard that such and such an IRA, or whatever, suspect was being held in that incongruously spic and span building?). I push poor Swanton, the young barrister appointed by the courts to defend me, to the limits of his considerable reserves of patience. As far as I'm concerned I've said all that needs to be said, and it's up to them to get on with it.

"It would be helpful if you could display some elements of remorse, however rudimentary or insincere," Swanton remarks uncomfortably.

"Helpful to whom?"

"To both of us. Do you really not care whether or not you spend the rest of your life behind bars?"

Jesus wept these high-priced wankers are a thick lot. No I don't care a toss. I have lost the only reason I had for caring about anything, but all *they* need to know is that I've killed someone, that society has every right to demand its pound of flesh and as much blood as it can extract. Swanton blinks, sighs, shakes his head and indicates to the guard that he wants to leave, and I am returned to the balm of solitary.

A PERFECT SENTENCE

After a brief hearing in the Bow Street Magistrate's Court at which I plead guilty to first degree murder, I'm remanded in custody until my trial which takes place at the Old Bailey two days before Christmas. The Prosecution can barely be bothered to break into a sweat for which I suppose they can't be blamed. Cold-blooded double murder. Cynical unconcern for what I have done. That I gave myself up and confessed in full the only mitigating circumstances in an otherwise particularly unsavoury case. Swanton goes the hot-blooded *crime passionnel* route, but his heart's not in it, and it shows. I gaze around the sparsely populated (after all its Christmastide and the trial's hardly fast-breaking news) courtroom, and I fancy I see Cat right at the back of the room, but I'm not wearing my specs and can't be sure. Dear Cat, she's been conditionally accepted by Merton which is nice for her as I've always thought it the prettiest college in Oxford. A few snowflakes float around the high Gothic windows of the court. Cassie is sitting in a splash of sunlight at Rivoire's in the Piazza della Signoria. Her hair ...

"I'm sorry, your Honour?"

"I was merely inquiring whether we were boring you, Mr Buchan?"

Bored? No, m'lud I'm not bored but I do want to get on with it, have a burning need to get to the paying part of this *commedia* which is so far from being one as to not be true.

Guilty as charged. Her Majesty's pleasure. Yes, yes, get on with it. Life imprisonment. Of course. A perfect sentence.

CHAPTER EIGHTEEN

Slammer sounds.
An announcement over the Tannoy in another wing booms tinnily in the night. A riff of reggae quicksilvers up and away. A screw's voice raised in sudden exasperation is followed by the plangent clang of a cell door. Yelp of a dreamer dreaming freedom, buzz from the nearby Westway, clatter of trays from the kitchen, susurrus of a radio.

Slammer sounds. They can give you the creeps sometimes, but you get used to them, like most things on the inside, or on the outside for that matter. Man the great adapter.

Take me. I am, according to Brian Spence the Senior Officer on my wing (E), an 'exemplary inmate'. Well, doubtless that's because unlike most cons I've no interest in getting out of here even though I'm a lifer. I'm in for the duration, my duration.

Being where you belong helps a lot. Having reached the endgame of my desire to be anywhere but where I am is a great comfort. Now, my cell, the exercise area, the workshops and, at a pinch, the gym are the furthermost outposts of my imperial desires.

Yes indeed, being where you should be and where, barring the demise of the England and Wales penal system, you will remain certainly takes the pressure off. Farewell to the stomach knotted with apprehension as to whether the traffic will be impossible on

A PERFECT SENTENCE

the way to or from the airport. *Sayonora* to sweaty palms as the plane lifts off the tarmac and you wonder whether you've finally drawn the straw which will have you hurtling not quite dead through icy darkness to plough into a distant ocean at whatever speed bodies plough into distant oceans, Ukrainian countrysides or wherever. Yes, goodbye to all that and hello to another day in rat infested HMP Wormwood Scrubs.

Lefty Kelly, a mild and miniature Liverpudlian in for topping his best mate in a crack-induced dispute over the ownership of a pack of Silk Cuts, pokes his head into my cell and asks if I fancy a game of table tennis. No, but thanks anyway. Lefty thinks I don't get enough exercise (I don't) and spend too much time with my nose stuck in a book or 'fookin' fiddling on my PC. Well, he's right about that too, but the habits of a lifetime die hard. I still elicit pleasure from both general reading and researching the Big Book which I am working on because a lifetime ago Cassie urged me to, and which if only for her sake, I shall write.

In learning about Goebbels' crazed film project for a book provisionally titled *Goebbels Gift*, I have to date read one hundred and twenty-two histries, biographies and autobiographies; perused countless other learned papers, monographs, journals, newspapers, and magazines and dredged up vast amounts of archival material. My notes on my reading alone fill seventeen notebooks; blueprints (charts of narrative flows, inter weavings of sub-plots, character analyses) take up a further five notebooks. While it's true that so far only the first sentence (*The morning that Private Fritz Schmidt got lucky, the temperature fell to -30 C, and the sky was as clear as a fanatic's conscience*) of the book has been written, it's early days yet and in any event I'm waiting for photocopies of *Die Filmwoche*, some documents from the *Bundesarchiv Koblenz*, and a letter from a charming former *soldat*

I've traced who claims to have been an extra in *Kolberg*, the title of Goebbels's cinematic wet dream.

The evening meal and association have come and gone. The former was no more or less inspired than any of its predecessors, while most of the latter I spent chatting about *Tintern Abbey* with Tom Parks, a burglar in for five who's reading for a degree in English at my old pal the Open University. A fight broke out over whether to watch *Eastenders* or *Mastermind*, but the screws got that one sorted in no time. Being a man of considerable physical cowardice I've rarely been in a fight, which is as it should be as even tiny Lefty Kelly, let alone some of the Neanderthals around here, would surely make short work of me. The last time I was in a fight was back home in Waspy little Knowlton PQ in the eighth grade when Vike Svenson, who was at least a foot taller and some fifty pounds heavier than me, knocked me out cold for calling him a Swedish scum bag. I can still remember the sepia-coloured explosion in my head as I went down for the count, and then some. Hardly a fight, come to think of it.

438. My cell. My pad, in conese, is on the fourth floor of the decidedly grim nineteenth-century wing of the Scrubs and is thirteen feet by six. Brick walls painted a curious sort of Afrika Korps khaki that could depress if one were so inclined which one is generally not. Narrow bed, cot really. Seat less toilet breathing a far, faint odour of loss and decay. Sink. Scuffed blue linoleum floor. Melamine table and bureau. Window with rusting cream-coloured bars from which I can see C wing with its natty new blue windows, the roof of the chapel, the tops of a row of trees just now beginning to leaf out, and some anonymous W12 roofs beyond that. A shelf currently groaning beneath all manner of books on the Third Reich, my CD player, some discs, my laptop and printer. Metal door complete with wank-flap which I don't use because I never wank.

Blue HMP clothes are kept in a cardboard box at the end of the bed. Oh, yes, a poster of Piero della Francesca's *Resurrection* in Sansepolcro sellotaped to the wall. Christ, stern and resigned and not a little bemused staring out over his slumbering guards contrasts vividly and I think wonderfully with the tits and twats that adorn most cons' walls.

The sweet cloying smell of my neighbour's (Dazz White, black as Bunker C and a big time pusher both out and in) spliff coils into my space. Talk about passive smoking. I should sue. Now is the blue time. I lie waiting for sleep to come, staring at the changing patterns of light on the ceiling of my cell and listening, not unhappily, to the dark song of my lost self.

Yesterday I had an unexpected visitor. Cat, who's now eighteen, paid a call (her first) on her jailbird Da, bless her. If the truth be known, I'm perfectly content not to have visitors (not that there are armies of candidates lining up for the privilege), but Cat's appearance proved to be a real tonic.

The open visitors' room is full to bursting. Everywhere cons in their blue prison gear sit at the neatly ordered rows of desks across from an unsurprising farrago of visitors from outer space. The noise in the room is deafening. It's hot, and baby and con smells clog the air. A few infants, doubtless intuiting their guilt as drug conduits, howl. Two gimlet-eyed officers sit at desks at either end of the room.

"Hi, Dad. Over here."

Cat, who I haven't seen for more than two years, is still wearing a modified version of the endless flapping layers of her tribe, but that apart she's obviously done a whole lot of growing up and looks wonderful. She's sitting at the table by a window near the door. I wave and make my way through the throng. We kiss across the wooden divide.

"'Lo Cat. Fancy meeting you here."

Cat has always been just the wrong side of pretty. In fact at the peak of her *fauve* period (now mercifully apparently history) when the ring appeared in her right nostril, the fake diamond winked in her bellybutton and her hair most closely resembled a looted bird nest, she was downright unattractive. But now, as I said, she looks terrific and my heart tightens and zooms off the flight deck of my chest at the sight of her.

"Sheer coincidence. I was in the area and thought I'd drop in. How ... how are you, Dad?"

I can smell the scent of the soap she uses. Lemon and sunlight. Her wide set forget-me-not blue eyes (a gift from her mother, mine are an unprepossessing grey) appraise with frank curiosity. "Can't complain. You?"

She wiggles her nose the same way she always used to and says, "The surgeon general, or whoever is in charge of these matters, should do something about A-Levels. Brutal."

"Blink and you'll be on the beach with Jeremy or Nigel or ...'

"Uh-uh. I'm off men at the moment."

Cat's never had much luck with her boyfriends, I suspect because she's a whole lot brighter than most of them.

Next to us Lenny Singer, a small time fraudster and car thief from Hackney, is speaking to someone who, from the look of him is probably his brother, with the fierce concentrated anger he brings to everything he does. "Tell the stupid fookin' cow oye ain't bleedin' payin' er a fookin' 'ayepny."

I wink at Cat, and she smiles the smile that got lost for a number of years in there when she was too busy being angry and existential to be amused by anything.

"We're an acquired taste, we men. Some never get the hang of us. How's your mother?"

Cat shrugs and fluffs her hair (now her natural dark brown, not the lurid hues of yesteryear) the way they do: palms out, fingers running up the back of her neck. "Okay ... I guess. She drove me over. Said to say hello. Hello."

I'm surprised. Fran, usually has better, or at least more socially constructive, more morally commendable things to do with a Saturday morning than drive her daughter halfway across London so that she can visit her villainous con of a father.

"She's waiting in the car?"

"Yep. Doing some paperwork. She had a dust-up with her current main squeeze last night."

"Who is?" I hear myself asking although in reality I don't give a tinker's curse with whom Fran is getting it on these days, or even if she is for that matter.

"A bit of a nerd from or near her office. A probation officer or some such. He wears woollen socks with his Birkies and has one of those somewhere-south-of-the-river accents that make you want to move to Ulan Bator."

Catherine Buchan can be pretty good value in any of her reincarnations.

"You tell that silly cunt I'd raver fookin' burn in 'ell than so much as look at her ugly fookin' puss again. An' no dosh, not a fookin' farvin." Lenny really has a way with words. Sometimes I position myself near him in association or in the exercise yard to be able to drink in the pure, savage poetry of his hatred.

"A probation officer who wears socks with his Birkenstocks?"

Cat shrugs. "Takes all sorts."

"Sleeveless nylon Mormonesque shirts?" I suggest.

She giggles. "Most probably. And by way of contrast, Y-fronts with hot lips stencilled on them."

Good old Cat. However, it seems I do give a tinker's curse about who Fran's seeing because I find myself absurdly irritated that my elegant, fastidious ex should be consorting with a man who wears woollen socks with his sandals. Slim, nervy neurosurgeons in Armani suits or tweedy, bearded astrophysicists I can just about get my mind around.

"Dad, what's it like, I mean really like being in here?"

I resist the urge to be flippant because I can see that Cat's been doing some thinking, that she really wants to get a sense as to what it feels like to be a lifer in one of HM's prisons. So I tell her that I can only speak for myself - although I do know that the vast majority of cons want out so badly they can taste it - but that now, after having been in for more than six months, I can honestly say that I don't dislike being inside, that, while I wouldn't say I'm exactly happy, I'm as content as I'll probably ever again be.

"What it comes down to is No Decisions," I finally say, realising as I do it's probably no less than the truth.

The blue eyes consider. Then she nods and says, "I can understand the attraction of that, but what about the violence, the degrading rules, the boredom?"

"No one has laid a finger on me. I mean, I haven't been gang raped or anything. The rules are no more ridiculous than those on the outside and I'm rarely bored. I'm learning how to make increasingly elaborate cabinets, I'm getting through a vast amount of research on Nazi Germany for a novel I'm planning, and I'm making some progress on the latest Chester Dillon confection. The food's passable and there are some interesting people in here ..."

I can see that Cat doesn't believe a word. Well, that's her problem.

"You mean if someone said, 'Listen up Buchan, there's been a terrible cock-up, we're awfully sorry and you're a free man' you'd tell them to shove it and please be sure to lock the cell on your way out?"

"I would," I say, and I would.

Cat closes her eyes. I can see that this must be incredibly difficult for her to process, but I'm touched at some fundamental level of my being that she has asked, that on a Saturday morning with A-Levels looming she's chosen to visit the Scrubs to try to find out what her Dad thinks about being a jailbird.

"Cat?"

"Yeah?"

"I'm ... well, I'm sorry about ... all this. I mean, you needed it like a hole in the head."

She shakes her head, extends a heavily be-ringed hand (last hangover from the bad old folkloric days) and touches mine.

"It doesn't matter, really it doesn't. No one gives me a hard time about it. Honest."

She's lying of course, but I'm absurdly grateful that she's bothered to fib. It's barely credible that having a convict, let alone a double murderer of a father, won't have had some considerable impact both on the way Cat views the world, and how it, in the shape of her posh Hampstead pals, sees her.

We talk about her exams (Spanish, French and Eng. Lit.), what she'll do in her gap year if, as expected, she does well enough to take the conditional place Merton has offered her. And then all of a sudden visitors' time is nearly over. All around us cons and their loved ones (where applicable) are going through the rituals of imminent separation. The harsh reality of what it means for most of them to be in prison can be read plainly in their eyes. Failure on a massive scale is in the air: theirs, the prison system's, society's, civilisation's, even God's if he's your cup of tea.

"Return the hello to your mother for me."

She nods. Her relationship with Fran is not an easy one. They have always fought like alley cats. Next to us, Lenny is winding up his brother's visit with a final vivid broadside of high-octane venom.

"Any news of Charlie?" I ask conscious of the tension in my voice.

She shrugs and answers, "He phoned from somewhere in darkest somewhere, India I think, the other day. I didn't speak to him, but Mum says he's okay. To be honest, I'm not sure I give a shit one way or the other."

That makes two of us.

Then almost diffidently Cat says, "You know, Dad, I woke up yesterday morning wanting to see you so badly it hurt. I guess that must mean that I miss you, which is sort of funny because for the longest time I was so mad at you it wasn't true."

I'm taken aback but experience a furtive warming sensation in the pit of my stomach. The last time I'd spoken to her (eighteen months ago), from a malodorous telephone booth in a Tangier Poste Maroc) she'd been plenty angry.

"I'm glad you came. Time to go."

"I'll be back."

"I'd like that. *Merde* for your exams."

At the door leading to the world she turns and waves. I lift my hand in an unintended parody of a papal blessing, and then she's gone.

I return to my pad and listen to a pundit explaining how Teresa May will handle the truly mind-boggling fuck-up the Brexit idiocy has created, followed by an interview with an American chef with an offshore accent so ludicrous as to defy belief talking about how best to 'chaup choives' (sideways one would imagine) and then it's time for the evening meal - roast pork, cauliflower, spuds, trifle - and evening segues into night.

That was yesterday. Now today, a Sunday without incident, is nearly over. I can hear Dazz prowling around his cell reading the bible out loud in a low rumble like the distant sound of weather in his native Jamaica. In spite of his drug dealing (because of it?) Dazz is a born-again Christian and when not totally out of his gourd takes the matter of his salvation with some seriousness.

Sleep finally comes and I dream of Cassie.

CHAPTER NINETEEN

Dazz is smoking up a storm next door. The thick, grainy odour of his spliff coils under the metal door of my cell and puts me in mind of the Patels' lethal curries. Oh my, how long ago and far away is all that now. And yet sometimes how near.

There was a nasty fight in association today. Most flare-ups are fairly tame, a split lip or shiner here, a broken tooth there, but this was the real McCoy with both contestants ending up in the infirmary, one with a serious concussion having been brained with a chair, the other with a nose shattered by a billiard cue. I doubt if I'll ever get used to these sudden eruptions of violence, and as ever this one left me sickened and shaky even though I cowered at the back of the hall and was separated from the real action by a seething buffer zone of over excited cons.

It's midsummer and Donald Trump has broken all known records for wilful mendacity let alone world historical foolishness, a curmudgeonly Scot has just won Wimbledon for the second time, and Syrians are still slaughtering each other in droves. Through my barred window I see a 747 lumbering up from Heathrow, and I imagine the crowded interior of the huge plane as another four hundred odd pilgrims settle down for the long flight to fun and games in some half-built Shangri-La. I miss all that not one whit. The PA system at the nearby Linford Christie Sports Stadium requests the 9-10 boys relay teams to go to their starting places and shortly thereafter the sound of youthful cheering is borne on a breeze also carrying a whiff of London Underground (above ground division), diesel fumes, freshly mowed grass and boiled cabbage from the kitchens.

One Siegfried Kracauer's portentously titled *From Caligari to Hitler, A Psychological History of German Film* lies open on my table, but right now I don't feel up to my never-ending research. Actually, I don't get too many down days, but they do occur from time to time and just have to be got through. Usually when the hump is upon me I throw myself into an orgy of carpentry, but after the fight the screws ordered a lock-down, so that's not an option.

As an exercise in self-avoidance I lie on my cot and try to segregate the different sounds drifting in through the open window: The PA system from the sports field signing off ("Well done all of you"), another jet rumble-roaring overhead, the muted thrum of traffic on the Westway, the hollow rattle of barred gates opening and closing, jangle of key chains, muffled footsteps along deserted corridors, tangled tresses of music and, once, the anguished cry of some poor soul for whom the bleak truth of his bungled life has returned with the long unravelling of the day.

But of course there's no keeping the past at bay for long and as the barred rectangle of my window changes from pale to royal blue and beyond and the details of my cell dissolve into nothingness around me, I'm beset by random images from the heady days when Cassie and I dared believe we were giving the gods a run for their money. Then, like the large damaged mammal I am, I cry myself to sleep and dream my brother Jamie (who I haven't dreamed of for years) and I are paddling a canoe across a crimson lake which narrows up ahead and rushes down ... I awake with a start. My pad is as hot as Hades. I'm bathed in sweat and have a painful crick in my neck from sleeping awkwardly. I have /pee and brush my teeth and return to my cot where I attempt to go back to sleep, but as is frequently the case these days I'm overdrawn on my sleep account and seem doomed to fretful wakefulness until it's officially morning at HMP Wormwood Scrubs.

The key grates in the lock and the door to my cell is eased open. I've fallen asleep after all and am surprised to see Deputy Governor Peter Oblonski standing in the doorway.

"Morning, Keir. Good sleep?"

"Passable. To what do I owe, etcetera, etcetera?"

Oblonksi, one of the better of what are actually a pretty good bunch of officers in a pretty crappy prison, leafs absently through Herr Doktor Kracauer's book on German film and finally says coyly, "A party's requested a visit with you this afternoon."

A party? What's he on about? Only Cat ever visits, and she's in Turkey with her latest boyfriend (so much for her having gone off men) and there's no one else in London, or anywhere else for that matter, who'd want to see me unless my in-laws are in town and have gone all wobbly around the edges.

"What party?"

"Your wife."

"I'm divorced."

Fran wants to see me? I'm not sure I need this in my life.

"Sorry, your ex. She says she wants to know whether you'll see her or not. Doesn't want to drive over here only to be told you're not receiving visitors. Can't say as I blame her."

I've not set eyes on Fran for more than two and a half years. Not surprisingly given the pain and suffering I inflicted on her, she has excised me from her life as neatly and completely as one would a malignant tumour. But now she wants to see me, wants to visit the Scrubs on what looks to be a scorcher of a July day. But only on condition that I actually consent to see her beforehand through the good offices of a senior prison officer to be on the safe side. Christ, how like Fran. Think of the unconscionable waste of her time if I the Achilles of Hammersmith and Fulham should chose to sulk in my goddamned cell.

"Well?"

"Oh, what the hell, why not? What's with the VIP treatment?"

Oblonski shrugs and says with a hint of what I take to be distaste for string pulling, "You know the form, someone knows someone who knows the Governor. Promise you'll see her?"

"Cross my heart and hope to die."

It *is* a scorcher. The visitors' room is crowded, the con pong factor right off the scale. I see Fran sitting at our allocated place. She looks exactly as I know she will look: cool in spite of the heat, trim in a pleated white skirt and blouse, beautiful in her unfussy way. Virtually unchanged. Fran to a T.

"Hello, Fran, you look great."

"You don't look too bad yourself," she says coldly.

"Nonsense, I look like everyone else in here, which is to say like the underside of a flounder. How're things?"

She shrugs and looks around her. Apparently this isn't going to be easy.

"When does Cat get her results?"

She looks at me directly, her tarn-blue eyes as arresting as ever. "The middle of August. She'll have done just fine. She worked like a …"

"Politically correct personage?" I venture knowing that she won't be amused.

Again, I am perused with distant interest as though it's just beginning to come back to her that I am the wiseacre with whom she shared a life for all those years.

The question has to be asked, so I ask it, "Any word of Charlie?"

She arranges her hands in a neat little construct on the Melamine table which is giving off the depressing odour of a surface which has been cleaned too often with a stale cloth.

"Not for some time now. I assume he's still at his ashram seeking Enlightenment or whatever claptrap it is people are after in such places."

I'm not surprised by the bitter tone. Cat has told me that all along her mother's taken a very dim view of Charlie's histrionics. Knowing what I do, it occurs to me that the silly little sod is going to need more than a spot of ganja-induced, hand held Enlightenment to help him live with himself. Or not.

"How're your parents?"

Aware that I couldn't care less how my ex-in-laws are, she ignores the question and fixing me with her Exocet gaze and lowering her voice until I have to strain forward to hear her, whispers, "I know about the gun."

"Gun? What gun?" I ask genuinely mystified.

"Pistol then. Yes of course it's a pistol not a gun, how stupid of me."

"What on earth are you talking about?"

"This. After you left I naturally cleared out all your things. I found that horrible pistol object your poor father left you in your top drawer. I hadn't a clue what to do with the damn thing so I wrapped it up and put it in a trunk in the attic with a lot of other junk ... it's no longer there."

Everything has gone quite still. I'm in a zone and thinking very, very slowly: if Fran's knows that the Kaba was there *after* I left, well, obviously that's why she's come today, but if she's known all along, then why hasn't she ...

"Keir?"

Next to us a small man with terminal acne is gazing fondly at the baby crawling around in his missus's lap. A fly buzzes around Fran's head.

"I hear you."

She rearranges her hands on the tabletop: tanned (where have she and the Birkenstock wonder been if indeed he's still in the frame?), sensibly manicured, nails unvarnished, a ring I've not seen before.

"Well?"

I try to think clearly but I'm like a drunk attempting to figure out some simple problem and making heavy weather of it.

"Well?" I parrot wishing the fences weren't coming up so damned fast.

"Oh, for goodness sake, Keir, I didn't come down with last night's rain."

You can say that again. Fran has never been anybody's patsy least of all mine.

"What are you getting at?"

Fran gives a curt shrug and says with icily, "I'm getting at the fact that Charlie, not you, must have killed your … ah … little friend and her unborn child."

"I see. Well, if that's what you think, why haven't you done something about it?"

She produces another impatient flick of her head and says, "Because I didn't put two and two together until long after your trial which I deliberately didn't follow. However, some time later Cat did read me an account which mentioned the pistol and its significance, and then I remembered and I went to the attic. Of course it wasn't there. So you see I know."

Doesn't she just. I try not to panic but I can feel what I can only describe as a terrible *fear of freedom* gripping me. What's her game though? What's she doing here?

"I repeat, why didn't you go to the police when you didn't find the pistol where you'd stashed it?"

For one of the few time since I've known Fran, something remarkably akin to a look of guile, almost shiftiness mars her fine features as, speaking directly to her hands, she murmurs, "I made a bad call. I figured that since you'd already ruined your family you deserved to be behind bars whether you were technically guilty or not. I think most mothers would have reckoned the same way I did: on the one hand there was Charlie with a brilliant future, a useful lifetime ahead of him, and on the other there was you with ... well you know all about you. Also, for whatever convoluted reason you yourself have chosen to keep quiet about the pistol, take Charlie's rap, isn't that the term ... so you see ..."

Sure I see. What I do not see is what Fran's doing here now. What awful misplaced spirit of truth can have wormed its way into her heart?

"Fran, you've got to understand one thing: I'm not in here *for* Charlie. I'm here because like you I believe this is where I have earned to be. Frankly I don't much care about our son after what he's done, and I think if we're both honest, the truth is that he's quite simply a nasty piece of goods, a bad 'un. Our fault? Who knows?"

Now almost inaudible, Fran says, "That's more or less the conclusion I'd reached although I'm more inclined to see him as sick and in need of help rather than plain bad. I was prepared to give him the benefit of the doubt although God knows I've had some sleepless nights about *that*, but only on the condition that he do a St Francis or a Lord Jim or whomever and try to atone for what he did, knowing of course that there can be no atoning for it."

"Ashram-hopping doesn't qualify?"

"Very funny. Coming back to face the music, most probably do some time, would be a start but that doesn't look like what's going to happen ... so ... Keir, I'm offering to try to see what's needed to get you out of this place ... talk to some people ..."

"As I told you, I am where I belong," I say meaning it.

Fran looks slowly up. Her eyes are misted with tears, and her chin is quivering.

"I guessed you'd say that, or something like it. And what am I supposed to do about Charlie?"

Ah, that one is simple. That's one about which I know a thing or two.

"Let him stew in it if he's capable of it, which I rather doubt. Listen Fran, one thing I've learned from this whole sorry mess is that there are laws and laws and that it's the ones you least expect, or plain hadn't heard about, that find you out. Anyway who knows maybe an ashram's where *he* belongs?"

She wipes her eyes with a knuckle. The baby next door begins to bawl, and the heat and smell in the room are overpowering.

"Are you sure, really sure, Keir? You always were such a stubborn cuss."

I say I have never been surer of anything in my life, and I haven't. She nods. I've a notion that she does understand. Sort of. In truth I'm not sure *I* fully understand, but I know beyond a shadow of a doubt that I'm doing what I must do, that I am where I should be.

I can see Fran has had enough. Well, why should she hang around? I'm of no more interest to her than the football pools or potholing. The audience is over.

"Is there anything you want ... anything ... else ... I can do for you?"

"No thanks, I'm fine."

"Then I think I'll be going. Goodbye."

"Bye Fran. Love to Cat when she gets back."

That evening after association I station myself by my window. The sun is setting and I can see the tops of trees beyond the prison walls shimmering in the wind like great bulging nets of sardines. The sky is a translucent blue, backlit with beaten gold, and way off to the west towering pink and white thunder heads mass like plotting barons in their plumed helmets. It will be raining in the

West Country, a swift summer's storm sweeping over the hills and fields, hosing down the land after the heat of the day. For some reason the thought of this fills me with a quiet joy, and I reflect that there is much to be said for living, as I largely do, in my imagination for there my decisions, or lack of them, can do no harm.

I lie on my cot in the dark listening to the myriad sounds of the night, waiting for sleep to come. But sleep eludes and instead I am joined by a host of memories from another time, a time when the world was green and I was a part of that other, so very different sentence.

Lightning Source UK Ltd.
Milton Keynes UK
UKHW01f1051150518
322625UK00001B/72/P